"YOU ARE DESTINED TO FIND THE UNICORN!"

"Surely any maiden will do."

The wizard towered over Alorie, reining in his anger even as he spoke. "Do you think a unicorn is some tame pony? Remember your stories, Alorie. The beast demands uncompromising goodness and valor if you would face him! The earth trembles beneath his hoofbeats, and his horn severs the very sky. He knows what the gods know. None of the Seven True Races can stand before him."

"And what makes you think I can?"

"Because it was granted to you . . . to me . . . if you are willing. If you pass the ordeals it will set before you, one day in the future, a unicorn will meet with you."

"That is what you foresaw for me?"

"Yes."

"And what if you are wrong?"

"I cannot be wrong, for the fate of all the Seven Races depends on your success!"

THE UNICORN DANCER

by R.A.V. Salsitz

A SIGNET BOOK

NEW AMERICAN LIBRARY

NAL BOOKS ARE AVAILABLE AT QUANTITY DISCOUNTS WHEN USED
TO PROMOTE PRODUCTS OR SERVICES. FOR INFORMATION PLEASE
WRITE TO PREMIUM MARKETING DIVISION, NEW AMERICAN LIBRARY,
1633 BROADWAY, NEW YORK, NEW YORK 10019.

SIGNET TRADEMARK REG. U.S. PAT. OFF. AND FOREIGN COUNTRIES
REGISTERED TRADEMARK—MARCA REGISTRADA
HECHO EN CHICAGO, U.S.A.

SIGNET, SIGNET CLASSIC, MENTOR, PLUME, MERIDIAN AND NAL BOOKS
are published by New American Library,
1633 Broadway, New York, New York 10019

First Printing, July, 1986

1 2 3 4 5 6 7 8 9

PRINTED IN THE UNITED STATES OF AMERICA

Chapter 1

THE RARE EARLY-SPRING breeze of a day in the Twomonth wound its way through the five-walled city of Sinobel and found a princess marking time in the Inner Circle, leaning wistfully on her elbows and looking out over the stone barriers. The wind teased her long oval face until it brought a curve to her full, heavy lips. She tossed her head back and drank in the scent of early spring, too early even for Sinobel.

The icy rains were gone for a span or two, and the snow melted back, and the trees reached upward eagerly. The sky was the pure azure blue that made her own eyes reflect a deep blue, just as its usual clouded gray skies made her eyes gray. Now her eyes clouded a little, as she leaned back over the last stone wall and looked downward. If she could but see the trouble . . .

She wasn't really a princess, but granddaughter of the High Counselor. She was waiting restlessly for her valet to tell her that her horse was ready. Alorie planned to go riding along the forest border, a pleasure usually left until true spring, but she couldn't wait. The snow had been heavy this year, unusually and unseasonably heavy. Though the customary warm winds of the Twomonth melted it back, the lower rings of Sinobel had flooded, and deep trenches had been dug for the run-off, and the normally secure city found itself as breached as if an enemy had done it.

The floods gone now, the city prepared itself for

festival, for a ceremony as rare as the deep snow—High
Counselor Sergius was abdicating his position in favor
of his son Nathen. The Inner Circle had been preparing
for weeks. Alorie had to get away. She'd been darning
linens and baking sweetmeats and braiding dried flowers into wreaths until her hands were blistered, and she
couldn't stand another minute of it.

A pebble ground as her valet approached from behind, and she swung around with an anticipatory smile.
It faded as she saw the Mutt with his eyes downcast,
tugging on his forelock nervously. "Ah'm sorry, milady, but no one is to leave the city."

"By whose order? Tell my father . . ." Alorie began
sharply, and then curbed her voice, for Tomas began to
whine softly in agitation. "Tell my father that I really
need to get out, just for the morning."

Tomas didn't raise his soulful brown eyes. "Not your
father, missy, but your grandfather."

Sergius, then. Alorie sighed, then said, "All right,
Tomas. I know you're busy. I'll just stand here for a
while then, and let the wind bring me news of the
forest."

The Mutt bowed and loped away, relieved of his
duties. Though he stood a man's height, walked upright, and wore a man's clothes, the creature looked
more like her own hunting dog, Marshall. It was said
the Mutts had once been dogs . . . generations ago. For
a moment, she felt bad for having spoken so sharply to
Tomas.

Having felt bad for Tomas's sake, she took a moment
to feel bad for herself—cooped up, alone, overlooked.
Then she took a moment to feel bad for her father, as
the burdens of High Counselor hovered over his already
sloped shoulders and furrowed brow. There were burdens she knew little of, but she had heard them hinted
about darkly in the kitchens.

Strange sightings in the forests. Kills mutilated and
then left—no wolf or wild dog would leave meat in
wintertime, but these were tainted carcasses even the

scavengers wouldn't touch. All of this told in hushed tones that quieted when she approached, the sentences left hanging in midair. Something was up—and no one knew it more keenly than Sergius, or else he would have waited until the full flower of spring to turn over his office. Something that couldn't wait for a younger, more vigorous man to take charge.

She loved her grandfather, but knew well the stern lashing of his voice, the piercing anger of his dark eyes, the hammering of his staff on the throne-room flooring when he was crossed. Even the people of Sinobel rejoiced that the mantle of leadership was being passed to Nathen on the morrow, despite prosperous years under Sergius.

An unexpected shuffle and click interrupted her thoughts. Alorie turned slowly. No one passed into the Inner Circle without intense scrutiny, for such was the security of the walled city, and she had no fears. Yet her mouth dropped open as she swung around.

A dusty cloak covered the old man from head to toe. His cloak was threadbare and darned, and covered with brambles and thistles of the old road, making the wearer look almost like a dried-wildflower arrangement. As he straightened and shook the cloak, the flora snapped into the wind and drifted off, leaving behind a sweet fragrance. He leaned heavily on his staff of peeled wood, its end blunted by much use.

If I were a wizard, Alorie thought, as she closed her lips firmly, I could read the mud and track on his boots and staff and know exactly where he's come from—and likely where he's going to.

The old man pushed back his hood and smiled. His skin was the rich warm brown of newly loamed soil, and creased with intelligence; his hazel eyes were clear and sparkling. It struck her that he wasn't nearly as old as he pretended, bent over his staff. Perhaps not even as old as her father. He nodded. "Good morrow, milady. I trust I haven't startled you."

She shook her head, and her long dark hair swung

about her shoulders. "No, you didn't. May I help you? Are you a guest? May I show you to the hall?"

He held up a hand and took a seat at the foot of the wall, on the archer's step. "I'll just rest here, if you don't mind." His heavy dark eyebrows, sprinkled with gray, went up. "It's likely to be stuffy inside, is it not? And the new spring is so fresh out here."

Alorie grinned, and sat down on the neighboring archer's step, and spread out the skirts of her dress.

The brown man drank deeply from a hard leather flask, corked it, and returned it to his satchel. "Shall I amuse the two of us for a while, milady, and ply my trade? I'll tell you a story."

A storyteller. The warmth of her amusement flooded through her, and the sharp wind died down a little. Alorie lifted her chin to look past him, to see if any of the Inner Circle's children were about to hear him also, but it appeared just the two of them braved the outside. She looked down to meet the storyteller's patient gaze as he waited for her attention.

"What would you like to hear?"

Alorie began to shrug, then changed her mind. "Do you know any tales of the unicorn?"

"The unicorn, milady?" The old man laughed sharply. "The unicorn is not for the likes of you! He shakes the earth with his hoofbeats, and breathes fire from his nostrils at the very scent of mortal man, and his horn pierces through any armor, even the soul."

She clasped her hands in delight, for it was obvious the storyteller knew a lot about unicorns. He put his hand up, pink palm creased with strong, deep lines, and silenced her. "I'll talk instead of the Twelve Races, and how they came to be. This is a story I intend to tell tomorrow, to remind Sinobel of how we came into being."

His voice wove about her, deep and rich and sonorous. "Of the Twelve Races, man numbers four: black, white, red, and yellow. From the mountains deep and forests high come the dwarves and elves. From the hand of man are the Mutts, and from the hand of the Despot, the battling reken and the nightstalking malisons, and the secret races number three.''

Alorie leaned back against the stone wall, thinking to find it warmed by the sun, but its chill bit through her thick vest and blouse. She shivered and hugged her elbows as the storyteller took her deeper. She hadn't heard the tale of the Twelve Races for a long, long time, as Sergius was unfond of it. The words told her familiar legends of how man split into his many colors. How the dwarves, from delving in the mines of the earth for so long, came to have black blood instead of red, and how the elves came to have green, because their souls were linked to the well-being of their forest. But she sat up in surprise as the man spoke of the Mutts.

''And from the hand of man came the Mutts, loyal as the dogs from which they were raised, made to stand in battle instead of man, to spare him from death. Here man failed, for though the Mutts are loyal as children, they can only follow us where we would lead them and stay as long as we can bolster their courage. Yet where is there failure in bringing forth a gentle, guileless creature such as that? Would that men had those flaws!''

The storyteller looked up and pinned her with his gaze, eyes dark and flashing and passionate. Alorie sat quiet, afraid to dispute that the Mutts had been created to be cannon fodder! Now that he had her fear, he began to weave with it, telling her of the Despot, and his spawn on the face of the earth. ''And he brought forth reken, sinewy and heartless, with tusks instead of teeth, claws instead of nails, to battle mankind. And from the depth of his dark soul, he brought out the malison, walkers of evil. Where they walk, the land scorches and cannot nurture life. What they touch sickens and dies. What they see is your soul and beyond.

''And after the handiwork of the Despot was made known to all, the Three Secret Races came into being, and made themselves known, but in subtle ways, always keeping their secret from the other nine races, and though they work throughout our lives, we know them not to this day.

"We are left only with our charge to watch the Barrowlands, and Sinobel is the eyes of that charge, as the High King waits, not to rise again until the Despot rises again."

The storyteller pounded his quarterstaff then and lurched to his feet. Alorie came up with him, her heart pounding, though she did not quite know why. Then she cleared her throat. "Do you . . . do you know where the Despot came from? Which of the Twelve Races was he?"

The hood came down, shading his face once more. "No one knows, though it's said he was human, once. 'Tis no doubt the Corruptor, his right hand for many centuries, was human, for all his dabbling with dark powers." He shushed her, adding, "It's better not to speak of such things now, and in the open."

She laughed then, his spell over her broken. He had spoken seriously of things long dead and sealed power-less and broken in the ground of the Barrowlands. Her voice slowed and caught in her throat as he stopped hobbling away and turned and looked over his shoulder at her.

"Forget me not, milady."

Alorie nodded. "I suggest you find a happier story for the children tomorrow." A door of the fortress at her side flew open in the wind and banged loudly. She jumped. When she settled her nerves and turned back to the storyteller, he'd gone.

The banquet hall filled with people of all shapes and offices and ages, pressing shoulder to shoulder, a few waiting good-naturedly until a seat at a table became vacant. Others pinched food morsels off their plates as they stood; still others danced and wagered and told lies to one another. A wave of children swept by Alorie. They tugged at her skirts, their voices high and delirious with the excitement of the day. She grinned as they disappeared in the crowd. Everyone of Sinobel was welcome in the Inner Circle, and some, she was sure, had even come twice.

An old woman caught at the sleeve of her dress, and Alorie halted.

"Is it true," the woman asked in a quavering voice, "that the High Counselor, bless his heart, will be granting boons today before he gives over the office to Lord Nathen?"

"I think so. At least," and she lowered her voice, "those are the rumors."

"And will he let my brother out of prison?"

Alorie tried not to flinch under the pinching grasp of the old woman. She looked into rheumy eyes. "Has he hurt anyone?"

"Never! He was just too slow paying his debts."

She gently undid the woman's fingers. "Then your chances are excellent, old mother. My grandfather would only hesitate to pardon a murderer on this day." As the woman gasped and clutched at her shawl in happiness, Alorie moved away from her through the dense crowd. Her benediction followed after: "Bless you, milady Alorie. Bless you and keep you safe!"

A chill touched Alorie on the back of her neck, and when she turned, the old woman couldn't be seen, as the dancing people bobbed in between them. Alorie frowned, for she was not long of sight at any rate, often failing to see clearly what others could.

Tomas caught up with her, dressed in his best, clothes passed down from Nathen and made over to fit his lean form. He grinned from ear to ear. "Your father sends his greetings, Lady Alorie."

She nodded. Tomas's happiness was catching. "Is he all ready then?"

"From head to toe. He said to give you this."

Tomas pressed a brass key into her hand, the key to Nathen's former chambers, now to become hers, as he moved into those of the High Counselor and Sergius retired to a wing newly built for himself. She fastened it into her bodice. Why hadn't he given it to her that morning when she brought him breakfast? Her smile faded as she remembered that quiet time, as he lay in bed in his nightshirt, and took the breakfast tray, and her hand, and asked her if she still missed her mother as much as he did.

Her eyes stung and her vision blurred for a moment.

"Are you all right, miss?"

"I'm fine, Tomas." She sighed. "I guess he won't just be my father anymore, will he?"

Tomas shook his head. "No'm. He's going to be awfully busy as the High Counselor."

"Well then." Alorie snagged a goblet of fine wine off a tray going past. She lifted it in the air. "To the High Counselor Nathen!"

A hundred voices echoed her toast, and then were lost in the general clamor. Tomas trotted away, following his nose to the banquet tables, and Alorie was left clutching the chilled, half-empty goblet.

Sunlight poured through the high slanted windows, telling the time, and she pressed to the fore of the crowd. Her grandfather would be granting boons soon, and she wanted to be one of the first to ask. Besides, she didn't want to miss a bit of the extraordinary ceremony which would follow.

As she gained the fore of the crowd, she caught the eye of the square, compact man sitting on the platform, next to an imperious old man with short, fine hair wreathing a balding head, his torso still covered with a mailshirt, open robes fallen to one side to reveal silvery links. Lord Nathen smiled gently over her grandfather's head, the corner of his mouth curving up just slightly. He looks solemn, she thought, and smiled back, wondering what would happen to her when he became High Counselor. Grandfather wanted her to make a marriage, but her father had resisted diplomatic efforts, thus far.

Sergius stamped his iron-footed staff on the platform. It rang above the sounds of merriment, and instantly the crowd fell quiet, respectful and waiting. Alorie held her breath.

"It is time, good people of Sinobel, to begin our ceremony. I, Sergius, bowing to the whims of time, feel that it is better to pass the office of High Counselor to my heir, rather than to hold it past the time when I can serve the High King and his people well."

"Hear, hear!" a man called out and was hushed.

Sergius looked down from the platform, and Alorie could see the profile, marked by the large, hawklike nose. His hand clenched and released the staff. "Before I go, as one last duty of office, I will grant ten boons. Think well, O ye people, what ye would have of me!"

Excitement crested the voices, and the noise rose until Alorie could hardly think. She was crushed between shoulders, and had to shift through the press until she was in front once more.

The staff belled out, and the voices died down. Sergius called out, "Who will ask me first?"

"I, my lord father," called out Nathen strongly, before any other could break the silence. This was proper, but cries of disappointment broke the air.

Alorie held her smile, for she knew what her father intended to do, as did her grandfather, for it had been discussed the night before.

"I ask that you open the prisons, and free all who have committed no crime against the body of another."

"Done!" The staff rang like a loud bell. It fell into the quietude of the banquet hall a moment before the crowd realized what had been said and agreed to, then a woman cried, "My husband is freed!"

Then another and another took up the call, as the people understood. Alorie looked for the old woman who had captured her sleeve earlier, but didn't see her.

The crowd fell into another hush as Sergius commanded, "Who else would ask a boon of me?"

She opened her mouth, for it had likewise been decided that she would ask for Tomas's freedom, a diplomatic way of giving the new High Counselor a man-at-arms rather than retaining the Mutt, and Sergius looked her way, cutting her out of the crowd, but another voice rang out instead.

"I do, your lordships!"

The storyteller strode to the open courtyard in front of the platform and went to one knee. When he rose, he threw off his cloak. The crowd gasped, and Alorie blinked. He wore the black and silver of a Rover, and she wondered how she could have missed that—and knew then how he had been able to speak so familiarly of the Twelve Races, and the Despot and Corruptor.

The Rovers had been the personal guard of the Corruptor while he was still a human king, a company of men so skilled in warfare that no others dared to face them. When their king had turned corrupt, they rebelled against him, and it was only with their aid that the other kingdoms had brought the Corruptor down. As their reward, the guard had been disbanded and allowed to live, though forbidden to keep homes or swear allegiance to any but the land. They were dubbed Rovers, and so they had remained for these last three hundred years. Yet Rovers kept their guardianship, though men did not trust them . . . and wherever a Rover appeared, there was sure to be trouble. A Rover's appearance today was not a good omen.

Sergius frowned and leaned out of his chair, his eyes blazing into those of the Rover. "What business have you in my court today, Rover? Speak, and give me your name."

"I am called Brock, lordship, and I've come to ask something of you, and to give something in return." The dark man smiled grimly, leaning on his own staff, and kicked aside the cloak on the stone flooring, lest it tangle his feet. He wore his bow across his back, his sword on his left hip for an easy pull, and his dagger strapped to his right wrist. He looked today as Alorie had glimpsed earlier, older but still younger than her own father, marked by years of travel and hard weather, yet sinewy and agile. He would be as quick on his feet as an elf, she thought.

"Speak then," Sergius answered him grudgingly.

"I ask for the Lady Alorie."

A gasp ran through the banquet hall, and Alorie felt a cold hand squeeze her throat and let go, as she tried to breathe. Her father got halfway to his feet before Sergius pushed him down in his chair and stood himself, rage flushing his countenance. "What is the meaning of this? No Rover can take a noble in marriage. The Lady Alorie is beyond your reach."

Brock laughed, a soft gusting sound, and turned to look at her. Alorie noted that he knew exactly where, in all the hundreds in that room, she stood. He faced back to the High Counselor. "I don't ask her hand in marriage, Lord Sergius."

Another gasp raced through the crowd.

"Then what are you asking? What sacrilege is this?"

"Not sacrilege at all, for the girl is the one person who can face the future I have seen. She alone is the hope of the Seven True Races."

Sergius stamped. "Faugh! Superstitious old fool! What would a Rover know of being true? You were born of a traitorous company that shared dark power with its master! You were condemned to wander for that. Had I been High Counselor then, I would have had your heads ringing my walls!"

Brock said nothing, nor did he bow his head, as most men did who faced Sergius eye to eye.

The High Counselor looked about the room. "I refuse to grant his boon!" The staff rang, ending the interview, but Brock didn't heed it. He stepped forward.

"Then I still have to confer upon you, and upon Lord Nathen, my gift."

"What gift can be of any worth from a Rover, you who can't even keep your word?"

Brock remained undaunted by the furious voice of Sergius. He waited until the room quieted, and when he spoke, his voice was low and deadly. "My gift is a warning. Look to your own vows, men of Sinobel, for your guardianship was to be over the Barrowlands, to be the eyes of the Seven True Races over those who were vanquished . . . and in that trust, you have failed miserably. You have looked after yourselves well enough and prospered, but we Rovers have found no Watchers at the Barrowlands. When was the last time you sent out to the barrows, Sergius . . . and when was the last time you heeded what was found there? Look to your own now and fear what your laxity may set free!''

"Enough!'' Sergius bellowed. "Take that man, give him a lashing, and throw him out! His lies are a plague upon these proceedings!''

Guards seized the Rover and dragged him from the hall, his heels scoring the floor, but Brock's face wore a calm expression. As he passed Alorie, their eyes met. It was as if he sent her a message. Compelled, she dipped among the crowd, picked up his cloak, and followed behind as the guards dragged him from the hall into the courtyard.

No one followed her in curiosity, an odd thing in itself, and no odder than the two guards, who hesitated over Brock as they drew their short sticks from their belts to beat him as they'd been ordered.

"Mason! Cleave! Don't hit him, please.'' Alorie gripped the man's cloak tightly, feeling somehow that she had been responsible for the whole scene.

The guards turned and frowned at her. "Get back inside, milady. You'll miss your father's inauguration!''

"That'll wait a moment yet. There are more boons to grant.'' Alorie passed the cloak to the Rover, who took it with a grateful nod. She stared at the men until they, shamefaced, put away their clubs. "If anyone asks, I shall tell them you thrashed him soundly, as grandfather ordered.''

They bowed awkwardly and backed away, drawn by the sudden wave of merriment breaking from the hall, like the sound of a new keg being broken open.

She smiled. "Go on. I'm all right, really.''

Brock said nothing until the two had left.

"Why did you say what you did? Did you really see me in the future?"

The dark man turned and pointed across the stone wall. His finger limned the forest, its borders lush and heavy, cutting off all view of the horizon, save for mountains so far away they could barely be seen. "There was a time," Brock told her, "when the Barrowlands could be seen from here. It was meant to be so—this fortress was a watchtower. Far away enough to keep its garrison and population safe, yet close enough to be the eyes of the rest of the kingdoms. In the north lie the ruins of the High King's castle, fallen Cornuth . . . and dread things crawl its foundations still. Your grandfather has forgotten all that."

"No," Alorie contradicted him. "You're wrong! My grandfather is an honorable man. He has kept the office, as have all my ancestors, when many others have named themselves kings. He's kept our trust. No . . . or he wouldn't have passed the office to my father now, so soon. I think he knows he has weakened."

Brock stared at her, his eyes dark silent wells of thought. He answered, "Then he has waited too long, Alorie. But there's enough time for you. Come with me tonight."

"Me?" She backed up, sensing for the first time just how dangerous this Rover could be. "Our guards would hunt you down. Go! Leave now before I change my mind, and have them beat you after all!"

Brock straightened, stepped toward her, and looked down at her, "I know your mind better than you, it seems, milady." He backed off and gave an ironic bow. "Thank you for your company."

He tied the cloak on, and a light flashed in her eyes, reflected off a ring on his finger. When she'd blinked back her sight, he'd gone again.

Chapter 2

"If SHE WERE my daughter, I'd have her flanked by two valued guards and a chaperon," a man said, in a rolling tenor voice, as Alorie entered the hall. His words carrying to her, she shut the massive doors and took a deep breath. The room had emptied of most common folk. They had gone to dance in the streets and welcome the newly pardoned prisoners.

"Your highness," replied her father, but he was interrupted smoothly.

"Lord, please. Though my people crowned my father king, I follow the traditions of the Seven True Races, and call myself lord, as the High King decreed before his downfall. What difference does it make, eh, as long as we and they know who rules?" The man laughed heartily, but the sound turned her head, for it wasn't a fool's laugh.

As she looked, she saw her father standing off the platform. A tall, broad-shouldered man stood next to him, dressed all in dark blues, flattering to his weather-tanned face and silvery blond hair. His eyes, though, were a little too small as he turned and smiled, noting that Nathen watched someone approach.

"My daughter Alorie," said Nathen, waving with a goblet. "Lord Aquitane, of Quickentree."

"Your lordship," she responded, casting her glance down and curtsying deeply.

Aquitane put a hand out and helped her rise, saying,

"See what I mean, Nathen? This one's too precious to lose." The tall man looked down at her, and she felt her heart skip a beat in fear.

"What were you doing out there?" her father asked unsteadily, awkwardly trying to change the subject.

"When . . . when they were done with the Rover, I gave him back his cloak. I picked it up when they took him out. I couldn't bear to see it staining the floor, as he tried to stain our honor."

Aquitane continued to appraise her. "Well spoken," he said, his voice like a caress meant for her and her alone. He looked up, met Nathen's eyes, and changed tone. "Those Rovers have forgotten their place. I had to rout them out of the corners of my own lands last autumn."

"What had they done?"

His eyes didn't leave her father's, but he answered her smoothly, "Squatting. I caught them building homes in the high forest. They were swift enough in their explanations; these weren't homes, but havens, they told me—but I routed them anyway, and burned the places down. It was only by chance we even discovered them, but the harsh weather had sent my hunters a little farther to set their trapping lines."

"And?"

Aquitane smiled at Nathen. "And they brought back some superb furs . . . creatures thickening their pelts for the snow. I'll have some sent, with your leave, High Counselor, for yourself and your daughter."

High Counselor? Flustered, Alorie realized she'd missed the ceremony. Just how long had she stood in the Twomonth sun, blinking? "Father! I'm sorry . . ."

He waved his hand. "It's all right, Alorie. It's just as well. Your grandfather canceled the remaining boons in a temper . . . poor Tomas practically crawled out after him. By your leave, Lord Aquitane," and as the huge, silvery-blond man smiled down at her, her father took her arm and escorted her away.

As he signaled for another goblet of snow-chilled

wine, she waved it away, saying, "I'm going to the kitchen for some tea."

"Not well?"

"No, it's just—just—everything, I guess."

He wore the austere black cap of his office, and Alorie was ashamed for not having seen it the moment she came in, although her eyes were still a little dazzled, and his dark brunette hair, so like hers, camouflaged it. He looked over the top of her head as though waiting for something, then dropped his gaze back to her and smiled. "What did you think of him?"

"The Rover?"

"No, no. Lord Aquitane."

She paused, catching a hint of the importance of his question. "He's quite tall, and wears his power easily. Isn't he near your age?"

"Meaning that you think he's too old for you?" Her father smiled broadly, his eyes fairly sparkling at her. "The sun has weathered him. Aquitane's a vigorous man, but only ten years above your age. Old enough to be experienced and settled, but young enough to be a good husband."

"Maybe." She wet her lips and looked about for a distraction.

Nathen reached out and grasped her wrist, a gesture she recognized as like the way he soothed down his hawks after a good hunt. "The time is coming, Alorie, when we'll have to talk about such things."

"I know." She bowed her head, and felt the silver net binding her dark hair slip a little. She tugged it back into place, wondering what a queen could do if her coronet or crown fell sideways. The thought made her giggle, and her father echoed her humor and remarked, "You're still shy, my white dove, aren't you? Good! Stay that way. Young men have the tongue of the devil, you know!"

Alorie's face went hot and prickly, but she was saved by the imperious ringing of the ironshod staff throughout the hall. Nathen released her as he said, "Your grandfather's decided to rejoin the festivities. Run along now and get your tea while I go placate him for a while.''

She brushed a kiss along his cheekbone and escaped to the kitchens.

It was a dubious escape, what with the daylong banquet to feed thousands, and servants weaving their way in and out with trays, but the main kitchen she sought was only the command station of the five kitchens that worked to feed the throng. Hot food was being carted all the way up from the Fourth Ring.

The warmth and comforting smell of fresh bread hit her as she ducked in and wove her way through the immense room, servants and Mutts alike mopping their brows as they refilled trays from shelf after shelf of stores. The cook's broad form at the other end was flanked by a man she recognized as one of Sinobel's best huntsmen, and by one of the undercooks, a thin, plain woman with appealing dark eyes, whose arm encircled the waist of the huntsman.

They were talking in low tones and did not notice as she drew close.

''. . . lucky your pots are full, after what I found out there.''

The plain woman shuddered. ''Did you tell Sergius?''

''You know that I did. He drove me out of the hall with his staff, yelling that I told stories to frighten children. I tell you, Jana . . . nothing like it. Snow melted all around the snare . . . scorched, more like it . . . and the rabbits blooded. The bones and fur shredded all over the clearing. The game is fleeing, Twomonth thaw or not. After feeding this rabble, we'll be on short rations until midsummer. And he wants me to go back, spend a week or two camping out, to see what I can see. It's not what I can see that bothers me—it's what I can't see!''

''And what is it that you can't see, but my grandfather wants you to look for?'' Alorie broke in softly.

The huntsman spun around, startled, his face going

gray under his normal yellow pallor, his slanted dark eyes narrowing even further. "By the shades, you have an even quieter step than I do! Forget what you've heard, milady, or the High Counselor will pull my tongue out by the roots."

The cook put her beefy arm around Alorie's shoulders and gave her a half-hug. "Leave her alone, Shan. She's come to Bertha for some comforting, I can tell. Did they give you a hard time of it, dovey?"

Jana and the huntsman glided away, as Bertha took her into the smaller kitchen, where the cook usually handled dinners for the family. A pot of herbed tea already steamed on the wooden block table, which was nicked and sliced from years of work. Alorie smiled to herself, knowing that she'd been outmaneuvered. Bertha poured two bowls of tea and laced them liberally with honey and brandy.

"I knew it would come to this," the ample woman said as she sank down onto a bench, thrust her legs out in front of her, and eyed her swollen ankles. "They're talking marriage alliances out there, are they not? An' your father should be ashamed of himself for not talking to you in privy, first." She glanced at the bowls as Alorie hesitated. "I'm sorry about the crockery, little one, but the good stuff's all been used up."

"No, it's not that. Did you hear about the Rover?"

The cook's face, already bright pink, turned pinker. Wisps of gray-streaked hair escaped her net, and she tucked them back. "Bold as brass, he was, asking for you—and not even for your hand in marriage, mind you, but asking for you as if you were a trussed pig!"

"Not quite like that." Alorie stared into her tea, then took a cautious sip. The cook watched her as she sat back and flexed her shoulders. "He said I was the last hope of the Seven True Races, or something like that."

The cook signed herself against sorcery and sucked in her lower lip. "No!"

"Bertha, you came from the south to work here, when I was just a baby. You know Grandfather doesn't allow the old stories to be told very much. Is it . . . is it true that Sinobel is a watchtower, that we're supposed to look over the Barrowlands?''

Bertha's thick fingers signed herself again, and she shook her head, chins bouncing. ''Your grandfather, may he retire in peace, has worked hard to carry out his office, and look what honor is given him—smeared in public! The Barrowlands are a place of the dead, and dead they'll stay, mark my words. Now, you finish your tea and don't worry your head about it.'' The cook tilted her face, listening. ''Hist! The dancing's started. Now you get your pretty little fanny out there and dance enough for the two of us!''

Gulping down the rest of her hot tea, Alorie felt the glow light her throat and spread a comforting warmth throughout the rest of her, as though the cool breeze of Twomonth had chilled her without her knowing, and the tea combatted it. She blew the cook a kiss and left, eager to play a role in her favorite part of the festivities.

If what Shan had hinted at darkly was true, that all of Sinobel would be on rations following the inauguration, not many would worry about it. Every citizen of the walled city who visited the banquet hall or one of the three outdoor dining halls had eaten and drunk his weight, she was ready to wager. Then danced and gamed and joked and eaten some more.

Head spinning, she retired at the moon's peaking in the night sky. She walked unsteadily to her rooms after first politely but firmly refusing Lord Aquitane's help. Upstairs, she leaned against her door to steady her, and there was a clink. The noise reminded her of her father's key, laced to her bodice, and that she would have to pack and change quarters as soon as possible. He had already moved, and the great chamber now lay bare, stripped of everything but the bed in which Alorie had been born and, probably, conceived.

She closed and latched the door behind her. Her father's door was hewn of solid oak, and carved, with great drop bars that could be let down into place—it was one of the hidden sanctuaries of the Inner Circle. Only the rooms of the High Counselor, and her grandfather's new wing, were more secure. She leaned against her door and listened . . . and slow, sure bootsteps followed her and stopped outside the door, and the latch wiggled. Then, as she held her breath, Lord Aquitane moved away and returned downstairs.

Or at least she was ready to swear it was the great blond lord of Quickentree, for a big man's steps creaked the landing outside. She couldn't know without opening the door, and that she had no intention of doing. He was too ready to try his hand without an invitation from her.

Music from below welled up. It took her in its embrace, and she danced across the flooring. Then, with a tiny gasp of dizzy surprise, she collapsed in a heap on her bed, unused to the strange magic of strong drink.

She awoke, head pounding, to pitch darkness and lay there, startled, for she had the habit of lighting a small lamp before she slept. Darkness that she couldn't see in frightened her. Now she lay quietly, too ill to be frightened, and waited for her head to stop throbbing. Her hand dropped over the edge of the bed.

A great, cold nose thrust into it, and Alorie smiled as Marshall nudged her into wakefulness. The big, tawny dog shook his head, bouncing her hand off his muzzle. She'd neglected him shamefully, and now the dog was telling her, in his own emphatic way, that she needed to take him to the courtyard garden, where he could relieve himself.

As she lit a taper and stood up, she discovered her party dress was crumpled and a few buttons had popped from the tight bodice while she slept. Quickly, she undid all the ties, laces, and buttons and let the dress drop to the floor, yards and yards of material, which she kicked aside. She pulled on soft leather hunting trousers and a thick, finely spun woolen shirt, kicked off her dancing shoes, and tugged on her riding boots.

The hall was silent as she pulled her door open and Marshall surged past her impatiently. A chorus of snoring could be heard drifting up the massive staircase. She went after her dog with a short, soft whistle, and he stopped for her to join him. Together they went to the balcony, and she unlatched the window door to the courtyard.

Marshall jumped over the threshold, knocking her aside in eagerness. His great body was almost as big as a small pony. Alorie followed him out into the night, and the coldness of winter hit her. The brief, springlike spell of the Twomonth was leaving, and winter would be back again, until real spring. She shivered, her teeth chattering, as she went in search of her dog.

The chill crept over Sinobel, opening winter back up like a raw wound. She leaned over the balcony, squinting into the night, and grew aware that no lights burned in the windows below . . . not a taper or a lantern. Orange glows paced the circles beyond as guards walking the walls carried their torches, but other than that, nothing lit up the night. Everyone must be drunk or in a stupor, she thought. A chill made her hug herself and call softly for her dog.

Marshall responded with a low whine, echoed by a second whine, not born of his throat, yet full of pain and bewilderment.

Alorie froze. She turned from the wall, peering into the night shadows. "Marshall?"

The dog whined louder, and his nails ticked on the stone as he trotted back to her. Her hand brushed against his shoulder—and came up sticky. She held it close to her eyes and saw the dark stain. She sniffed. Blood! She leaned over quickly to search her dog's fur, and found no wound on him.

Yet something had whined in pain. Something bled in the balcony courtyard garden. Alorie turned to go back to her rooms, frightened. Marshall leaned on her legs, pushing her in the other direction. He had not growled or given an alarm. Trusting him, she pushed into the night and let the dog lead her on.

She stumbled as she rounded the corner near a parapet, and went to her knees, as a shadow darker than the night grabbed at her and whined low again in pain.

"Mistress!" the being gasped. "Ah'm coming to warn you . . . run . . . run . . . all dead below, or dying. . . ."

She knew the hands and voice well, and shifted to see his pain-twisted face. "Tomas?" She didn't recognize the blood-smeared face, but she clasped his hands tighter in response to his agony. "What—what happened?"

"Through the flood trenches. No one below sober . . . or awake . . . my wife and pups, dead . . . I got away to warn you, and Master Nathen. . . ." The Mutt stopped, and took a low, whining breath that whistled through his ravaged chest. "Reken soldiers, mistress . . . and humans, renegades. Run!"

"But the torches—"

"Not ours," he panted. His hands were like ice. She stroked his head, his hair like the soft pelt of a dog, and Tomas clung to her gratefully. Then he pushed her away. "Go!" His voice rang with fearful purpose.

"Thank you, Tomas," she whispered. "I promise you I'll be safe." She twisted in the darkness and ran across the garden, as a mournful howl began and cut off in midcry. The noise sent another shudder through her as she climbed through the window door and back into the house. She must give the alarm in the great hall—soldiers invading Sinobel and the Inner Circle!

As Alorie reached the staircase, Marshall threw himself in front of her and blocked the steps with his huge body. She looked down to the feasting hall below.

The moon cast a pale light from the high windows on dark, twisted figures moving below without lantern or candle. Marshall growled.

"Father!" Alorie screamed as the rank scent of reken foot soldiers reached her.

"Alarm! To arms, Sinobel, to arms!" A guard staggered, lighting the great hall sconces. He froze in astonishment as reken rose from behind bodies. Longknives flashed, swords rang, and the dance floor wiggled with the dead or dying.

Below, drunks reeled to their feet, reached for ornamental daggers, and struggled feebly with shadows that fought viciously and silently. Their death cries brought others to their feet. A torch flared, then another. Alorie backed away from the landing, her next scream caught in her throat. She'd never seen a live reken before, but knew from the tales of their long-armed, death-dealing forms. They gnashed their tusks as they rushed the hall.

Sergius came alive, from a chair in the corner of the room. He threw off his silken robes, and his mailshirt dazzled in the torchlight as he pulled a sword and held his quarterstaff like a shield. "Come get me, then," he cried. "If you can!"

From behind the wave of reken strode a tall, brawny figure, dressed in blue, but now wearing a mailcoat himself, his sword shining in his hands. Lord Aquitane laughed at the drunk old man facing him with countenance purple with fury. He looked up at Alorie's gasp and smiled. He pointed at her with his sword. "Save the girl for me!" he called, his voice carrying over the noise of the carnage. Reken soldiers twisted about to eye her, beady eyes glittering, and they grunted in acknowledgment of his orders.

Sergius twisted also to see her. His expression flashed in defiance. "Run, girl!" he called. "Last of our house . . . run!"

She froze, to see the front of his clothes splashed with blood as the body of her father fell at Sergius's feet, the black cap of the office of High Counselor rolling away, to be trampled under reken feet.

Even as he called, Aquitane swung his blade again, and cleaved him nearly in two. The old man crumpled to his side, his blood mingling with that of his son. He gestured to the landing, to her, as Aquitane turned with a triumphant laugh—but Alorie was gone.

She grabbed her training sword off her bedroom wall

and frantically kicked over her party dress, searching the bodice. She found the key and ripped it from the laces.

Marshall blocked the stairs as she came out of her door. The great hall below now rippled and bellowed with noise, and the stairs thundered. She didn't wait to see more, but ran down the long corridor as fast as she could, gasping in fear, her eyes blurred so that she could barely see, her face hot and wet. She came up against the door of her father's chambers with a sob. Her hands fumbled to hold the key fast. The lock clicked neatly as the key turned.

She tried to whistle for Marshall, but she couldn't make a sound through quavering lips. She heard growls and the hunting dog's fury as he held the stairs for her. Alorie screamed, "Marshall!"

The dog came running down the corridor, his tawny body splattered with black blood and red, and skidded into the room. She slammed the door shut, locked it, and dropped the two heavy crossbars into place.

Heart thudding, she stood in the nearly empty room. Not a window graced it. She looked overhead. Yes— with enough persistence, Aquitane and his murderers could come through there, even if the door held. There was no safety here. Tomas had already told her of the river of blood washing through the lower circles. There already might be no one left alive in Sinobel but her— and the murderers.

She went to the far side of the room and ran her hand over the intricate paneling of her mother's bed. There was a faint click, and a wardrobe door, hidden inside that headboard, opened. She pulled Marshall inside, along with the linen he'd bloodied, determined to leave no sign where they had gone. They cowered in the wardrobe as thunder boomed, and she knew they were trying to batter down the door.

Without light, she scrabbled against the inside of the wardrobe door and found an old lantern. A dusty bag containing flint and iron hung next to it. She wrapped the precious items in the linen and continued searching the wardrobe. Marshall whined, their bodies packed and entwined together. She shushed him, broke a nail, and then, triumphantly, found the second lever.

The back of the wardrobe swung open, dumping them into a dank, empty passageway. Alorie snapped the panel shut behind them and stood listening. No close sounds reached her, although the entire fortress of the Inner Circle reverberated with the sound of battle and dying. The complete darkness of the tunnel swallowed her whole—yet she sensed something in the room she'd just left, as the thundering splintered the door and the reken stampeded in . . . and something else. It searched not only the stone wall between her and it, but probed at her mind, her panic, as though it could see her clearly. She froze and fought a desire to go back, to show herself, to give up. Aquitane? No! Not that . . . something else!

Marshall butted her thigh, breaking her trance. The wave of evil patting its way after her broke, and Alorie shook herself and ran, wanting to escape before the invaders found the panel doorway.

Hugging her bundle and carrying her sword, she lurched down the secret passageway, too much in shock to cringe at the webs that swept her face, or the slime that twisted her footfalls this way and that over the rock. Marshall trotted along beside her, his hackles raised.

Someone cried. Someone cried a low melody of curses and vows against Lord Aquitane of Quickentree, and sorrow for the murdered Sergius and Nathen. Alorie stopped in amazement. She pressed her fist to her mouth . . . for it was she making the noise.

Hands shaking as she leaned against the ancient stones, she took out the lantern and knelt to balance it. The flint and iron were old, and the air was damp. Finally, she managed to light the wick, and the slightly rancid-smelling oil flared up. Blue-white light filled the passageway.

Marshall's ears went up. A slash ran along his lean rib cage, matting his fur, but otherwise, most of the blood covering him seemed to have come from his opponents.

As she stood, shadows flared up, given life and form by the lantern. Her fear closed her throat, and Alorie stood, fighting for the breath and will to go on. What if reken awaited her at the other end? What if Lord Aquitane knew of the secret egress? And what if the other thing which hunted her succeeded in finding her again?

She swallowed the panic. "What if," she muttered to herself, "I only live a day longer than anyone else!"

Marshall whined and pushed his head up under her hand. She clucked to comfort him and started off down the passage.

Alorie had traversed it only twice before in her life. The first time she barely remembered, for she had been carried most of the way by her mother. The second was implanted more vividly in her mind, because her mother had just died, and she had run away to be alone, hiding in the panel of her mother's familiar bed, and tumbled into the passageway before she remembered it was there. She'd had no choice but to take it all the way down through the mountain to the outside, alone, in the dark, grieving.

But she'd made it, and her father had found her outside the walled city, and hugged her and explained to her what she had done.

She stumbled now, half in shock, half in panic, bumping into the walls and bends of the convoluted passage, despite the lantern's aura, only the occasional touch of Marshall's body against hers keeping her balanced on the fine edge of sanity. When she was young, the journey had taken her the whole of a day . . . now it seemed to take a lifetime.

The lantern illuminated the rusted grating ahead of her. It twisted out of the tunnel mouth, the rocks that held it cracked and broken. Alorie lurched to a halt.

"Oh God," she said softly. The echo of her voice

startled her. She jumped, and then took a deliberate breath to quiet her pounding heart.

Marshall dipped his head and sniffed, then dug at the rock pile. The grating moved ever so slightly.

Alorie dropped to her knees. She set the lantern to one side and began to dig herself.

Three torn nails and ten raw fingers later, she rocked back on her heels. She wiped her forehead with the back of her hand. It smeared the sweat into a grimy streak.

"It's no use."

Marshall lay on his side, digging frantically. A rock began to shift, dirt cascading down. Alorie plunged the sword in all the way to the hilt, to stop the slide, and Marshall pulled himself out. He sneezed.

Alorie hesitated, then pulled upward and forward on the sword, trying to lever the rock aside. The metal groaned as the rock moved, and then the sword snapped, throwing her back. When the dust cleared, there was a space under the grating wide enough for her to crawl through.

Marshall was already free when she pulled herself out and raised her head to see a grayness to the night sky. "We made it!" she whispered jubilantly.

She staggered to her feet and the tunnel collapsed with a roar, burying her lantern and broken sword. She coughed and reeled back.

A hand reached out of nowhere, caught her by the shoulder, and spun her around. A damp cloth muffled her scream of fear, as a dark hooded face loomed up in front of her.

Chapter 3

As the girl reeled back, he took the cloth off her nose and mouth. He only wanted to calm her, not put her under so that he'd have to carry her. He tossed the herb-scented cloth away. She sagged on his arm, her eyes wide.

"Bring her back as innocent as you find her," Brock had warned him, and innocent described her perfectly . . . that, and frightened almost more than she could bear. A round softness blurred her limbs and features, the softness of a child approaching adulthood. It was a softness and fairness that none of the Rover women he knew had. A season in the wilderness would make her lean and nut-brown and scratched, and fleet as a deer, Rowan thought.

As she blinked, he whispered, "I'm Brock. Remember me?"

The Lady Alorie nodded. She brushed her hand over the head of the great dog pressing against her legs, quieting his growl.

Rowan brought his hood up swiftly. He thanked his luck that the dawning was reluctant and she couldn't see his features better, or the disguise he wore as the dark-skinned Rover would easily be pierced. "Come quickly and be quiet about it."

She took his hand, warm and gentle fingers in his own cool and dry ones, and let him lead her away from the collapsed tunnel.

Luck rode with him that night. He'd come too late to help Sinobel as the wallkeepers fell, their throats grinning into the darkness, too late to be trapped inside as everyone else was. He'd come on the heels of the stinking reken and recognized their foulness almost immediately, though he'd not been prepared to find them there. Old Brock would have his ears full when Rowan caught up with him. He'd been told it would be an easy job to breach the walls and take the girl from the Inner Circle. He'd not been told he would have to weave his way through a massacre to do it!

Once he knew that he couldn't make his way into Sinobel, he'd begun searching for the escape passages at the foot of the mountain, on the far side, just ahead of scouting troops of grumbling reken who searched as he did. They had begun to stab frantically at the shrubbery after a signal came down from the mountaintop, and Rowan knew then that someone they wanted badly had escaped their slaughter. Sergius, perhaps, or the new High Counselor. With luck, he could find a tunnel and get in to bring the girl out, for Brock had told him he'd put a charm on Lady Alorie to ensure her safety until the Rovers had her. Rowan didn't need telling that, once again, Brock had cheated fate.

Now that he had her, the charm was broken, and it was up to him to get them out.

Rowan settled into a loping stride, and the girl panted after him, paced by her dog. Both ran quietly, but he knew from listening to her breathe that the reken, dogged trackers that they were, would be tough to shake. She was in no condition to run all the way to the havens. Once in the forest, he'd have the advantage, but there was the open belt of grasslands to cross first. They ringed Sinobel, making any passage to and from clear to sentries from above.

They rounded the curve and came to a halt. Rowan dropped her hand and went for his sword, as a handful of reken faced them.

They hesitated. The half-light made it difficult to see

faces clearly, and their own brown leather faces wrinkled as they sniffed the air. Rowan had caught onto one of Brock's tricks: the dark man was the same color of skin as they, and Rowan wore that skin color as a disguise. He barked one of the few words he knew of guttural reken speech. While they paused, he charged them. The dog flew by his side, white teeth flashing.

He cut two of them down, and the dog worried at a third, blood splattering the grass. The remaining two pulled their weapons and made to come at him, spitting him between them, then stopped in their tracks. They parted to let something approach from behind them, something out of the gray mists, something dark and feral.

The dog whined and crawled back to his mistress. Rowan staggered back himself. He gripped his sword tighter, trying to see what it was that approached.

Reason bolted. The being floated above the ground a handspan or two, enveloped in a cloak of nothingness that was neither black nor white. It towered above him. As he backed up, he felt something part his hair under the hood, pierce his scalp, crack through the very bones of his skull, and sift through his mind.

Alorie moaned. She clutched at him. "Brock! Run!" She twisted around and lurched from the shadow of the creature.

It was then Rowan knew what he faced . . . what he had never thought to face in his lifetime. A malison. He fumbled at his belt, ripped off a bag of herbs and spices that Brock always made him wear, and threw it at the being. The bag spumed out its contents at the malison.

Gasping with pain, Rowan pitched after the girl and caught her up by the elbow, and the two of them ran for the forests, heedless of being caught by sharp-eyed sentries.

The dog sprinted past them, his hackles raised, leading the way to the forest border. They leaped into thick, crackling branches, regardless of the pain and prickles, hearing the branches swish into place behind them, cutting off the pursuers, if only for a moment.

Alorie staggered to a halt and gasped for breath. She touched her throat. "What—what was that?"

He shook his head. "Not now. Later." He grasped her hand again and pulled her after him, fear driving him on. Brock would hang him by his heels. He'd thrown the whole bag in a bloody panic, when a pinch would have done the same. Now he had nothing to defend against the malison when they followed. And they would.

He found his stride, ears pricked for noises behind them other than the girl, who struggled to keep up, and her dog. They would have to shake their pursuers, then confuse the trail. And somewhere, somehow, he would have to find a mount for Lady Alorie to ride. He looked over his shoulder at her. She gasped through open mouth as she ran, but she seemed to have found a second wind, or perhaps it was the inner strength the House of Sergius was famous for.

The soft carpeting of leaves, needles, and moss muffled their footfalls as they raced. Behind them, Rowan caught the tinny note of a reken horn. The hunt for them was being called to hand. They had no time. He flicked a look over his shoulder. The girl followed him gamely, her dog bounding by her side. Crimson slashed her otherwise pale cheeks. She wore no cloak, and here, in the cool underside of the deep forest, patches of snow still glistened.

He knew the reken. They trailed not only by track, but by body heat. He palmed the hilt of his sword. Damn Brock! Why couldn't the mage have foreseen the massacre?

A steep bank plunged ahead of him, and he skidded to a halt, throwing his arm in front of the girl. Her feet slid out from under her, and he pulled her to him tightly, while she gasped and trembled. The dog went over, rolled once or twice, and stopped at the edge of a stream that cut sharply into the ground, its edges still iced.

Rowan was aware, for one brief moment, of her warmth and softness before she pulled away and stood, eyes wide, looking down.

The sound of swiftly moving water drew his attention. "What is that?"

She swallowed. "The Frostflower. I—I'm not sure. It could just be a run-off stream."

The Frostflower ran from the steep mountain peaks that separated the Barrowlands from the ranges of the dwarves. Rowan knew its lower regions well—a wide, white-watered river that went far before it calmed, its waters always chill from the snow that gave it birth. If this was the Frostflower . . .

"Will your dog heel you, even if we go into that?" He nodded at the gray-blue water.

She shivered. "I'm not sure."

"He has to. If not, the reken will scent him as surely as they would have scented us. If he doesn't . . ." Rowan left the last unsaid, but loosened his sword in his sheath.

The Lady Alorie's lips tightened. "We can only try," she answered, and without another word, she ran down the bank and plunged chest-deep into the river. "Marshall, come!" she sputtered, her teeth already chattering.

His plumy tail thumped the riverbank as he got to his feet and looked at her, a dog grin across his tawny muzzle.

"Come!"

The dog lowered his head and followed his mistress into the water. Rowan scampered down after them and joined her, clenching his own teeth against the stabbing, numbing cold of the water. None of them could take much of this.

She followed in his wake, saying nothing as the spray flew up as he breasted the water. Finally, in a low voice, she chattered, "Is this necessary?"

"They'll lose the scent, and the body heat. That's how the reken trail, if there's no sign. At this point, it's our only hope."

She looked up at the vast canopy of green branches overhead. Sun and gray clouds glinted through. A damp lock of sable hair trailed across her chin, and she absently removed it. Already he could see purple marks of fatigue under her stormy eyes.

"If this is the Frostflower," she said painfully through her teeth, "it'll soon be too deep to wade."

"Then we'll be in luck," Rowan answered. Marshall stroked past him, unable to wade or swim entirely, and the dog showered him in jeweled droplets.

The wind through the forest and the roar of the stream covered any sound of pursuit, but he knew the reken would follow unerringly to the riverbank. Then the hunt would split, upstream and down. Soon they would have no advantage at all. But the Rover caught the signs of the river widening, its cut into the earth getting deeper and sharper, and he found it harder to keep his balance as the current pushed at his back.

Alorie cried out as she slipped, and her feet went out from under her. The stream caught her and whirled her past. Rowan snagged her as she fought to regain her balance. Marshall gave up the river and dragged himself onto shore and stood, head down, quaking.

"Marshall, come!" Alorie pleaded.

Rowan stopped her. "No, it's all right now. In fact, if you can stand a little more cold, I think we just saved our skins."

She looked at him oddly. He guided her to the shoreline beside the dog and left her there while he scouted the riverbank, looking for a fallen tree.

The forest was a healthy one, solid and verdant. Rowan pivoted in dismay, looking for what he sought. There was no time to chop down a tree! Then, on the other bank, he spotted what they needed.

Alorie watched in astonishment as he leaped down the bank, forded the river, and emerged on the other side. With several grunts, he shouldered the heavy tree off the rocky shore and slid it into the water.

"Your ferry, milady," he said, and bowed.

She shivered. "Back into the water?"

"We have little choice on that. But the current is strong, and if you can pole at the front end while I take the rear, we'll be moving fast."

"Until white water."

"Or until the reken catch us."

His words fell solemnly. She hesitated a moment longer, then bent and picked up a limb from the forest floor. As she passed her dog, she pulled at his damp fur. "Come, Marshall."

She strode into the river and mounted the front of the log much as she would a horse. Rowan noted that the thickness of the log was like a pony's, and she held tightly with her knees as she would to a mount's girth. The dog paddled out to her, and she pulled him in front of her, wedging his body into a fork of small branches.

Rowan pushed the log into the current and jumped on it as soon as he saw the girl was secure. It bobbed under his additional weight, but it refused to sink. The icy water surged up to his crotch, and he took it with a sharp gasp. Gripping with his knees, he put all the strength of his shoulders into poling, and the river current swept them away.

Moments later, he wondered if they might not have been better at the mercy of the reken than the mercy of the Frostflower. The river bucked and plunged underneath them, sucking at the buoyancy of the log. The girl tried to keep the blunted end of the tree clear, but her slender strength wasn't enough as the river widened.

A fine spray covered them both from head to toe. Marshall whined, his voice keening above the roar of the current.

"Keep it clear!" Rowan shouted at Alorie's bent form, unsure if she could hear him or not.

Her pale face turned to eye him over her shoulder. "I can't control it!" she shouted back, and he nodded grimly.

They were on a hell ride through white water. The bark turned slippery between his knees. His face grew numb as the spray sheeted him, and the log tried to roll under him.

"Keep it straight!"

Alorie nodded, her long dark hair pasted to her back. Staff in her hands, she righted their vehicle, until the branch suddenly dipped into the water, dragging her down, and the water tore it from her hands. Marshall snapped at her, catching her sleeve in his jaws as she cried once, and she frantically grappled herself back onto the log.

She looked back, once, at Rowan.

Then the log was caught by a whirlpool, spinning wildly, throwing him sideways. Rowan threw his arms out and caught at a limb. The river pulled him down, and he gasped as the icy water filled his mouth and his nostrils. Twice, he came up choking, as the Frostflower dragged him down.

Just as suddenly, the rapids calmed, and Rowan threw his numb leg up to climb back on, panting. The log righted itself as its passage threw little circles of current onto the pool, and a ray of sunlight broke through the forest roof.

The calm wouldn't last, Rowan noted, as he spied the narrowing gorge ahead, and the roaring grew close.

"Hold on tight," he commanded.

Alorie shuddered. "I can't feel anything! I'm too c-cold."

"Just a little farther. We're almost out of the borderlands now. We're two days ahead of them, on foot. We'll need that lead."

The girl hugged herself and crouched low over the dog's back, to wrap her arms about the tree fork that secured him. She ducked her head just as a spume of white water washed over her, and with a gasp, the rapids took them all.

Rowan forgot everything but hanging on. The world slewed past his watery sight. He knew only that he breathed, somewhat, and his heart pounded, as the chute carried them far, far beyond the walls of Sinobel. They'd be safe, if only they lived.

Alorie wrapped her arms about her knees, her white teeth clenched in the dusk, as Marshall stretched out on the moss in front of her. She took in a deep breath of the smoky air as though to warm her lungs as well. "Can't you build it any higher?"

Rowan basked in the fire's heat as he fed it slowly, and shook his head. "A fire trail is easily spotted. I wouldn't risk this, but the river's too cold. We can't sleep wet tonight. Tomorrow, you'll travel with no dinner and no fire. Tonight, luxury, milady." He lifted his chin to look up and smile at her, and saw the terror written across her face.

He'd swept the hood and cloak from his shoulders, and as he faced her he knew she'd guessed the truth about him. Indeed, he was a little surprised she hadn't guessed it earlier, but surviving the day's travel had been of utmost concern to them both.

"You're not Brock!"

With his hood off, his dark auburn hair drying in the breeze, he'd lost all pretense to his disguise, and the river had paled his color as well. He grinned at her.

As if accusing him of murder, she added, "You're as white as I am!"

"Not quite, milady. But yes, I'm white and no longer Brock . . . but he sent me."

"How—why—"

"Would you have come with me, a stranger out of the dawn, otherwise?"

She looked down at her hands and clenched them

tight, then stretched them toward the fire. "No," she answered slowly. "I don't think I would have."

"That's why Brock disguised me." Rowan fed the last dry branch into the flames. "Though he didn't warn me what I might find when I entered Sinobel."

"What do I call you?" she asked.

"Rowan." He stood up and checked his cloak, drying on a framework of green twigs. The intense heat from the fire would soon have it warm enough to swing over her shoulders. He opened another of the small bags tied to his belt, and with the aid of a river-soaked rag in his pack, scrubbed what was left of the nut dye from his face and the backs of his hands, taking care that the cleft scar in his chin was scored clean as well. When he finished, the rag was dark, and the flesh he could see looked more like himself. "There."

But if he expected approval from her, he got none. Instead, her eyes were clouded gray with thought as she watched the fire and gently chafed her dog's sides. Without looking at him again, she asked, "What was it . . . that thing that followed the reken?"

"The tall, shrouded being?"

She shuddered. "Yes."

"Something I never thought to see in my lifetime, though Brock has warned me of them often enough. It's called a malison."

"From the Despot?"

"So it is said."

Her face turned now toward him. "Brock was right, then, when he accused Grandfather of betraying the Seven True Races. The Despot is free!"

"Oh, no, milady. Not even the Corruptor—though that one stirs and tosses restlessly in the barrows, or at least he did last time I was through. But Sergius the Third, may he rest in peace, will bear some of the blame for that."

"Then you're a Rover, too."

He bowed. "At your service."

Alorie ducked her head again and was quiet, and she

did not even stir when he took the nearly dried cloak off its frame and tucked it about her shoulders. He saw then that she had fallen asleep sitting up. He sat down next to her, to bolster her tired frame, and tried not to think of the day they had faced together.

He awoke, stiff and cold, in a misty dawn, and a short, squat figure sat across from them, watching them with silver eyes as opaque as the moon.

Chapter 4

"BROCK THOUGHT YOU might be wantin' some four-footed transportation," the dwarf grunted dryly. He warmed his damp boots in the ashes of the fire.

"How did you find us?"

" 'Twarn't hard. Saw the campfire last night, though I didn't expect to run into you this far south. You made good time," the other answered, and his silvery eyes gleamed. Under the royal-blue wool of his hooded cloak, bright yellow hair curled tightly to his head and hugged the curve of a big, square jaw.

Rowan sat up so as not to disturb the girl, and leaned forward, extending his hand to the dwarf's, and clasped it tight. "Well met, Pinch."

Like his head, the dwarf's hand was nearly as large as that of the man. Pinch answered the squeeze with a firm grip of his own and dropped the shake with a pleased grunt.

The opaque eyes flicked to the still form of Alorie. "You can open your eyes now, girl," the dwarf rumbled. "There's no more need to be a-feigning sleep."

The girl rose, shrugging her cloak off and blushing faintly. Her hair billowed about her shoulders like a dark cloud, and she bent her head as she combed it back with her fingers, hiding her face from the dwarf.

Pinch pulled his feet from the ashes and tucked his legs under him as he searched a furry vest for a pouch.

Rowan's surprise ran through him and filtered away as the dwarf pointed a thumb at him.

"You'd best learn to check on your sleepin' companions, boy. She's been awake since I came over the ridge, and lay here a-watchin' me with one eye, figuring out what to do. The dog, too."

Alorie cleared her throat. "I'm sorry, good dwarf—"

"Stow it, milady," Pinch interrupted. "You did as you needed to do. I'm not a trustful-looking person. Dwarves and men have been a-squabbling for centuries, though some of us have better sense." He measured a bit of leaf from his pouch and tucked it between his cheek and his gum. "The reken will have lost your trail, since you came down the Frostflower, but I heard the drums last night, and new troops will be out a-lookin' for us. Amenities can wait until we've made the Haven."

Steaming ponies stamped in the clearing. " 'Course," Pinch added, "not all amenities. I brought a breakfast with me." He pulled a bulging saddlepack from its resting place in the small of his back. Both Rowan and Alorie sat up alertly, and Marshall gave a whuffle and crawled forward to investigate the offering.

"Why do they call you Pinch?" Alorie asked, as the dwarf checked the length of her stirrups and made sure she was astride her mount properly. The soft furred covering over the saddle cradled her, and she hugged it gratefully. She had thought she'd never be warm again. An extra fur covered her shoulders, with a leather thong tight at her throat to secure it. Its rusty warmth tickled her throat. Pinch spat, and looked up at her in amusement.

"Well, it could be because of my leaf. But then again, probably not. More likely it's because some of us races grow tall like weeds, and others of us are pinched to the ground." He slapped her booted ankle. "You sit a pony well, milady."

"Thank you." She watched as the dwarf consulted with Rowan. Her legs ached so much she had barely been able to hobble across the clearing to mount, and her shoulders felt as though she'd been stretched on a rack. Whenever she met a hot bath again, she was willing to bet the insides of her arms and thighs would be bruised purple—but she was alive! In pain, but alive, much more than any other citizen of Sinobel could claim this morning.

Alorie wrapped the reins tightly about one tender hand. She wouldn't give in to the luxury of grieving. Not yet, not for many mornings, not until they reached what the dwarf and the Rover called the haven. Would it be like the squatters' buildings Lord Aquitane boasted he had leveled? The thought of the man fastened in her throat, a cold lump that made it difficult to breathe or swallow. The Rovers thought too much of themselves and their prophecies. Sinobel fell not to a centuries-old evil, but to the petty politics of a man her grandfather and father had trusted, had even considered a marriage pact with. She thrust her grief aside and concentrated her hatred on Aquitane of Quickentree, even as Rowan mounted his pony and Pinch gave one last spit to the side.

As surely as she was born to the House of Sergius, her grandfather's last warning to her to run was not meant to save the skin of one girlchild, one Alorie, but a plea for revenge from the last drop of Sergius blood, whoever it was that held it. And that plea she would answer, if it was the last thing she ever did.

The days on ponyback melted into a blur of feverish pain and speed that Alorie would never, save for a moment or two, remember clearly after. Fever balled in her chest and she ached with every movement, awake or asleep, and took little note of their forest passage.

There was the heart-stopping moment when they crossed a pack of reken, each group coming upon the other with astonishment. Rowan threw his cloak aside, stood in his saddle, drew his dagger and sword, and leaped among them with a war cry. He cut three down in a whirlwind of motion before the reken even knew what to do. Pinch and Marshall brought two more down, and the sixth scampered off into the woods. A grim-faced Rowan raced after it, and there was more blood on his sword when he returned. Alorie had scarcely had time to blink.

Rowan came up to her still-dancing pony where she had curbed it on the path and brushed the back of his hand along her cheek. "It's all right, milady," he said, then frowned. "Pinch! She's burning up."

The dwarf couldn't reach her until he was astride his pony again. His grizzled hand mopped her brow. "Indeed, she is that. Well, the havens aren't far off. I reckon she'll have to do. I have a brew I can give her t'night."

And she would always remember the moment, in a brightly lit clearing, when the two reined in and got down, to look at a scoring in the grass, and a sapling that had been all but stripped of bark as though a blade had been taken to it.

Pinch rubbed the slotted tracks. He looked up at Rowan, the sun reflecting from his opaque eyes. "Deer, maybe."

"And they sliced the bark off like that? Not hardly, dwarf." The Rover walked about the meadow. He came circling back. "If I didn't know better, I'd say a unicorn had been through here. The tracks . . . the tree sliced up . . . it's possible their horns velvet the way the deer's do, and this one had an itch."

"Some itch." The squat being returned and gathered up his pony's reins. "The edges on that horn fair splintered the sapling." He shuddered. "Wouldn't want to meet one of those alone, on foot, fair and righteous dwarf that I am or not."

Rowan laughed. "And what would a unicorn do with you, Pinch?"

"Exactly," the dwarf grumbled. "Gie me a leg up, weedling."

Alorie stirred, feeling a break in the malaise that

seemed to wrap all about her. "Was that—" she croaked, then cleared her throat. "Was that really from a unicorn?"

Rowan took her hand. "Maybe. I don't know for sure . . . I haven't seen much of their sign. Brock would know. Brock says they're one of the Three Secret Races—"

"Harumph," interrupted Pinch. He scratched his blond, curly chin. "That's for Brock to say, isn't it?"

And that was the last clear thing she remembered, until the wilderness and day gave way to night. Their tired ponies stumbled onto a muddy track, and lanterns smoldered at a gatepost as Rowan stood in his leathers, calling out, "Hello the haven!" With a shout the night filled with people whose warm hands pulled her down and carried her gently to a steaming pool of water in a rock-lined cave, bathing and drying her, and then carrying her off to bed.

Alorie woke to the soft glow of candlelight, and blinked as its reflection echoed off a ceiling of onyx, and she patted down the coverlet from her sleep huddle. The tightness was gone from her chest. No sooner did her eyes flutter open than Rowan knelt by the bed and offered her a cooling sip of water.

She took it gingerly and slid back inside her coverlet, ashamed and embarrassed that he was in her bedchamber. Something of that must have flickered across her face.

He turned and yelled toward the tapestry doorway, "Medra! She's awake!"

He rocked back on his heels, adding, "You've been asleep for two days. We've had a watch on you, but the fever broke yesterday, and I'd say the steam pool has driven the ague out of you."

The tapestry moved aside, and a tall woman with a long, bony face moved in. She frowned. "Rowan! Who left you in here alone?"

He shrugged. "Calinthia was tired. I let her go."

The woman bent over Alorie, and her dry hand touched

her face and forehead critically before she gave a half-smile. "I would say she is well enough that you can leave your devoted watch."

Rowan stood, gathering his cloak about him. Alorie nearly laughed, for it was clear the woman scolded him much as any mother would, and Rowan looked a little abashed. His gaze tangled with hers, and he grinned suddenly, as though they might have shared thoughts. He ducked his head and brushed through the tapestry.

Medra faced her again. Her grizzled hair was cropped short and feathered about her angular face. She wore a rough shirt and trousers, and a long apron over them. Her many pockets were filled with things—bags, cooking utensils, flasks, and a slim dagger. She pulled a flask out, uncorked it, and helped Alorie sit up. "A sip of this three times a day for a few more days yet. The sooner you can get up and walk, the sooner you will heal."

"I know." Alorie stretched, gasped in pain, and yet could not resist the urge to stretch once more, though it pulled every aching muscle in her body. Her shadow danced on the cave walls and ceiling.

"I'll help you to the women's chamber," the woman said, "where you can relieve yourself and bathe. I'll bring you fresh clothes."

"One moment," said a voice from the dark corner of the grotto, and Medra whirled.

Alorie moved, too, less swiftly, but with his name on her lips. "Brock!"

The dark man stood up and stepped forward, though the candlelight barely illuminated his face.

"How long have you been there?" Medra demanded.

"Since before Calinthia. Long enough to ward the Lady Alorie, even in her fever and dreams, and to know that our bold Rowan means her no harm. Leave us, woman, for a moment."

The healing woman inclined her head. She looked back over her shoulder and smiled, adding, "I will see you in the chambers."

Alorie knew now that she was dressed in a long, if plain, nightshirt, and she swung her feet out of the bed to place them on the stone-and-dirt floor, and found it, to her surprise, vaguely warm. She pulled her coverlet about her. "Thank you," she said finally, "for saving my life." He merely stood, watching her, and she felt uneasy.

"I had nothing to do with that," Brock answered. He looked younger than she remembered. Now he resembled a vigorous, lean man in the prime of his years.

"You sent Rowan."

"To guide you out only. That he saved your life, and his, was entirely his own doing, though if I had known the danger, I don't think I would have sent anyone else. You have my condolences, Lady Alorie, in your hour of grief."

Alorie looked away quickly, biting her lip on her reply.

Brock moved, stopped himself, and stood taller. "I ask only that you keep your own counsel while you're here, milady. Talk to me first, if you have questions or doubts, and say little of who you are, and nothing of what I tell you."

Surprised, she faced him again. "But these are Rovers, too . . . aren't we in the havens?"

"Yes. This is one of the havens, called Stonedeep. But I will ask you to keep in mind the old saying 'The enemy of my enemy is not necessarily my friend.' " With that, and the crunch of his boots on the flooring, the man left as Alorie stared after him in astonishment.

Rowan caught an underbreath from Medra as she strode past him, muttering, "Brock," and so he waited in the passageway and captured the Rover as he left the sickroom.

Brock waved aside his exclamation, took him by the wrist, saying, "Not here," and led him out of the caves into the box canyon. A late-afternoon breeze moved through the grove of trees restlessly, and the gates leading into Stonedeep were already shut.

Rowan found his mouth creased in a tight line of irritation and forced himself to relax, as the man found a seat under a tree and beckoned him to sit down also.

"I've been looking for you."

Brock smiled. "Have you now? I thought the welfare of the girl foremost on your mind."

"That, too. Do you have any idea of what you sent me into?"

"Now I do."

"Now." Rowan encircled the hilt of his sword in irony. "Two thousand reken, and a malison or two."

The other straightened, and his eyes narrowed. "Malison?"

"Yes! And you'll be pleased to know your little mixture works quite well. I don't know if it was destroyed, but it stopped in its tracks."

Brock rubbed his bare chin. His fingernails made a tiny rasping in the beard stubble. "Malison." He looked skyward and said casually, "Were they directing the reken or observing?"

"How should I know? Do you think I had time to trail one and observe it?" Rowan stopped, as the other looked at him, and the gaze was sharp enough to pin him to the tree he sat against. The Rover did not look away until Rowan shrugged, saying, "It seemed to be in the background, until the reken caught us, then it moved out. I'd say it had been looking expressly for her."

"Then it's a good thing I sent you in. Lord Aquitane doesn't know what he deals with."

"Or he knows, and doesn't care."

"Yes. One makes him a fool, and the other ruthless." Brock stretched his legs out and crossed them at the ankles. "Did you follow them into Sinobel?"

"No, I was too late. The reken had already gotten in without a fight and slaughtered everyone they found on the lower levels. I came back out and decided to take a secret way in and was searching for it. I don't know how she got herself out, into one of the escape passages. I found her at the base of the mountain—I heard her digging out of the tunnel mouth, and waited for her. She keeps her balance well," Rowan added thoughtfully. "No hysterics or tears, despite all she'd gone through."

"She is the last of the House of Sergius." Brock's words fell with import and double meaning. Rowan did not respond. The dark man folded his arms over his chest and added, "And as long as she lives, the office of High Counselor is not fallen, Sinobel lives yet, unlike Cornuth, and the High King is still waited upon."

"I'll send the word out, then," Rowan said finally. "The other reaches have to know that."

"Not yet," Brock answered. "Not quite yet."

After a bath in the hot spring that bubbled into the women's chambers, Alorie felt more human. Medra left more than clean clothes—she left two slices of warm bread, some cheese, and a redfruit which crunched deliciously despite its winter storing. She dressed in a blouse of light blue, and a full skirt of darker blue, and her boots had been cleaned and oiled so that the leather was supple once more. The understockings she pulled on were not so fine as she was used to, but she was grateful for them anyway.

She paused, pulling on the second boot. Nothing would be so fine as she was used to anymore. The first thing she would do would be to ask that she not be called "Lady" any longer.

The second would be to send word to the other reaches of Aquitane's treachery.

A nail broke as her foot slipped into the boot, and Alorie looked at it sharply, then tore it off the rest of the way. Her words of ill humor were interrupted by a scrabbling upon the cave floor, and an eager yelp, as Medra shouted, "Get out of here!"

A tawny body leaped through the curtains, throwing

itself into Alorie's arms. Marshall wiggled like the
puppy he hadn't been in years and eagerly cleaned her
already scrubbed face with his rough tongue.

The healing woman followed him in, scowling. "The
beast belongs outside," Medra said. "But he's been
pining for days. When he heard your voice, I couldn't
hold him!"

Alorie grinned and pulled the dog out of the chambers with her. "Is there an outside? I'll take him."

"Through the lit corridor then. He'll be safe enough
outside, as the gates are already shut."

Marshall bumped against her legs as he frolicked and
led her out of the caves into the late dusk. She took a
deep breath of fresh air, out of the moist and hot
dampness of the haven, and looked up. A great stony
horseshoe of a mountain encircled her, boxing in a tiny
finger of canyon which stored sheep, horses, pigs, gar-
dens, a grove of trees, and a brook. Indeed, the haven
was meant for sheltering. Alorie spied a number of
children under the watchful eye of their mothers, but
only a few men.

Dinner that night was held on tables set out under the
stars. A wild boar had been pitted early that day, and
now it was dug up, its meat hot and juicy from a day of
cooking buried with fire and hot stones. Alorie braced
herself for an evening of ale and storytelling, of the fall
of Sinobel and her rescue, and the journey leading to
the haven, but she was introduced only as Alorie, and
no one asked why she had come, or from where. Did
Brock fear that she might be held for ransom instead of
treated as a guest? Or did he not wish that Sinobel's
disgrace be told?

She sat in puzzlement and worried over her dinner,
picking out choice morsels for Marshall, who guarded
her back. She caught Brock watching her, his face in
eternal shadow and his expression unfathomable. The
man, she realized, was not only a Rover, but also a
mage of some sort, a wizard perhaps, and even more
difficult to understand.

Stonedeep, she discovered in the days that followed, was not a home so much as it was a way station. Rovers passed in and out of it for respite, supplies, healing, or advice and then went on. Only Medra and a core of women stayed, for the haven was also a nursery for the children. Once those children reached an age, they also took up the homeless, ranging life of their elders, boys and girls both. They had been forsworn and denied homes and allegiance, and they took that seriously. Few stayed long enough to question Alorie's presence. Those that stayed lived in the wall of caves that climbed up the mountainside, a network of rope ladders turning the Rovers more into spiders than people.

She took long runs outside the gates with Marshall, limbering her body, and purged her mind of thought, while waiting for Brock to find the time to speak with her, as he'd promised he'd do. A handful of days passed before the dark man sought her out. They took a lunch to a grove outside the gates, where they could be alone. Most of the men had left the haven, and the day had quieted.

Stonedeep lay far south and east of Sinobel, as nearly as Alorie could tell, and though the winter returned, only its edge remained. Brock took off his short cloak and spread it on the ground for them to sit, as Alorie spread out honeycakes and mead and dried beef sticks.

The Rover appraised her quietly, then said, "You've been patient with me, as I asked."

"I've been cautious. You left me wondering if I live with friends or enemies." Alorie picked up a still-warm honeycake and nibbled it, savoring the treat.

"I know the House of Sergius well. While you've been here, you've been observing and listening, and learning. What have you learned?"

Alorie licked a finger and thought. "I think you wrong your fellow Rovers to suspect them."

Brock smiled, and relaxed then, as he crossed his legs under him and reached for a honeycake himself.

"Good! I wanted you to see for yourself. If I had told you, would you have believed me?"

She tilted her head and grinned. "Maybe. Then again, perhaps not. As Grandfather would say, actions speak louder than words. The Rovers are concerned with the land and the animals, and their own meager survival. If you plot, I haven't overheard it!"

"That's where you're wrong, Alorie. We do plot. We plot for a time when we can swear allegiance to the High King again, and be given lands of our own, to build upon and hold, and pass to our children. We hope for a time when our roving is done and all men can trust us and we them."

"Will that time ever come?"

His eyes of smoke and greenwood looked deeply into hers, and she saw sorrow in them. "When it does, milady, it will come hand in hand with great danger. What we hope for will not happen without great evil being loosed to walk again, and strife for all of us."

"So you hope, and fear that what you hope for will happen."

"Yes."

Alorie wiped her hands of crumbs. She took a long draft of mead to brace herself for what she knew she had to ask, and Brock was waiting for her when she lowered the wooden goblet. "Tell me what I have to do with all of this—and how near is your dream to my time?"

"I'm not yet sure, but the signs tell me that the evil contained in the Barrowlands is very restless. I'm not just a Rover—"

"You're a wizard," Alorie finished for him and laughed at his surprise. "Did you think I wouldn't guess?"

"Not many do."

"Not many have stood bedazzled in the sun by you and your ring. Not many have been cloaked by your protection while all others were slaughtered around them.

Not many have been touched by a malison and lived to talk about it." Alorie shook her head.

"Don't credit me with more than I deserve," Brock warned. "I have read a sign or two, that's all."

"Concerning me, and now I want to know what you know."

The brown man looked away, from the shadows of the grove to the sunlight playing on new grass. "I looked into a place where I'm not often allowed to see . . . but my questions weren't answered, and what I saw makes me even more desperate to know. Only you, Alorie, can find those answers for me."

"You saw me?"

"Yes."

Her hand shook as she held out the goblet and Brock refilled it with mead. "What was I doing?"

"That I could not tell you, only that I knew you, both as Alorie and as the last of the House of Sergius."

"Then you knew Sinobel would fall."

"One day, yes. Alorie, what do you know of the Three Secret Races?"

She licked the sweet foam of mead from her upper lip and smiled, thinking of Rowan. "Only that Rowan says you think the unicorns are one."

That brought a frown to Brock's face. "Rowan talks too much."

"Sometimes. Others, he's just as short of words as you are!"

He waved away her laughter. "Then listen to me now, for this is your answer. You must come with me to seek the unicorns out. There are questions only you can ask."

"Surely any maiden will do."

He thrust himself upward and stood, every muscle taut, as he towered over her. He reined in anger even as he spoke. "Do you think a unicorn is some tame pony, a little white beast that trots through forest glens looking for a virgin to bow down to? Remember your stories, Alorie. The beast demands uncompromising goodness and valor if you would face him! The earth trembles beneath his hoofbeats, and his horn severs the very sky from the horizon. None of the Seven True Races can stand to him . . . to what he demands of us. He knows what the gods know.''

"And what makes you think I can?''

"Because it was granted to you . . . to me . . . if you are willing. If you pass the ordeals set before you, one day in the future, a unicorn will meet with you.''

Alorie stood up carefully, bracing herself on the trunk of a tree. Mead raced through her like wildfire, and her pulse drummed. "And that is what you saw for me?''

"Yes.''

"And what if you are wrong?''

A muscle jumped along his jawline. "I cannot be wrong.''

"What about my father and grandfather? What about Lord Aquitane's treachery? What are you going to do about that?''

"There's no room for revenge, Alorie. The unicorn has promised trials of earth, air, fire, and water to prove you. You will be forged anew and tempered and pounded like new metal in the flames. All that you are now will be refined. You must be the best of all of us, so that we can be given the knowledge we need to stand against what stirs, turns, seeks to be free again—for he is undoubtedly the worst of us, and he will rise again, Alorie. I have seen it!''

His words pierced her. She put her hand to her forehead, feeling very giddy all of a sudden. "I—'' she stammered, and paused.

He reached out and gripped her by the elbows, his fingers bands of steel about her. "You can't fail us!''

She looked into his hazel eyes. She could never fulfill what he required of her, but if it was her only way to strike back at Aquitane, she would take it! She nodded. "I'll try then, Brock.'' She only hoped he couldn't read what was buried in her heart, for she knew his quest was doomed before it started. Once outside of Stonedeep, she would gather men wherever she could, until she had an army built. That army would tear Aquitane limb from limb and scatter his ashes over the face of the earth.

Brock left for a few days, and Medra took advantage of Alorie and Marshall by sending them hunting to fill up an always empty larder. The woman of Stonedeep would have been dismayed to know how far afield they went, and Brock would have been furious.

Still, Alorie chafed at being inside the caves, and though she enjoyed a short time caring for the babies, she was restless. She took every opportunity to stretch her legs beyond the gate. Frost still brittled the ground in the early morning, and a cold wind often chased her back at night inside the safety of the gates.

She jogged through the grasses, ducking under the wind-spread branches and into a dark grove, as clouds filtered out the sunlight. A chill lightly touched the back of her neck. She thought of reken, still hunting her, and then shook herself.

Marshall's lean body disappeared inside a thicket as she ran to catch up with him. Plunging through the shrubbery, she emerged in a meadow cupped in shadow and quiet. Even the birds sounded dim and far off. She found herself holding her breath as she lowered her bow.

The dog was nowhere to be seen.

She whistled sharply for him. A branch trembled above her. Uneasily Alorie paced the boundary of the glen, unwilling to leave without the dog, and unhappy with herself for being there at all. She'd wandered too far from the haven.

A twig cracked sharply. She jumped, then tried to quiet her pounding heart. "Marshall! I'm going without you!"

Her voice fell, muffled, into the silent meadow. Then a thrashing came from the far side as something broke through the brush and trees. She laughed at herself, knowing that the dog was coming back to her.

It was no dog that emerged and stood in the dappled shadows to watch her.

Alorie caught her breath. The bow dropped from her hands. The beast arched his neck, and the glint of his horn pierced the darkness of the shade, and he eyed her.

What a fool Brock was to think they would have to go far to seek the unicorn, and pass trials to face him—here he was, seeking her out! She stepped out into the meadow, grasses tangling about her booted ankles, the sky dimming from clouds as sunlight fled. A coolness passed over her and she forgot all else as she moved to meet him.

"Oh, you beauty," she said softly, and the unicorn snorted and tossed his head. In the bower where he stood he had no color, as the night sky isn't black, but is dark without light, and he pawed the ground.

In a single fluid movement he reared into a gallop and charged her, and the glen thundered with the beat of his hooves, and the air rang with the roar of his breathing. The deadly horn lowered at her, and Alorie froze in place.

The unicorn would have pierced her through, but she threw herself aside at the last second. The beast bellowed past her, as she rolled on the ground and felt it tremble under his weight. She shook in every limb as she got to her feet again. Her skirt tore as she stood on the hem.

The unicorn circled and charged again. His ebony hooves churned the ground. His eyes smoldered. Mane and forelock billowed with the grace and energy of his thrust. The feathered legs drove after her, as Alorie cried out and dodged again, and the beast pivoted, his four-hand length of horn seeking her like a lance.

Alorie tripped and rolled under his hooves. She gasped as the unicorn leaped over her. His gallop carried him beyond range, where he reared in fury and came after her yet again.

Power and hatred filled his lines, as his haunches bunched under him and launched him after her. Malevolence roiled from his body, a palpable aura that scorched her as it touched her. She screamed in panic. The black beast drove after her, and Alorie ran for her life, sobbing, across the meadow.

She looked over her shoulder, to see the horn tip just shy of her eyes, glowing in darkness, and she ducked. Fire stabbed across her back. With a scream, she threw herself to the ground and rolled, her blouse ripping. The black beast thundered past as she lay shuddering in pain.

A voice cracked the air. Marshall let out a belling, his body racing across the torn sod. The unicorn answered with a trumpet of fury and challenge, and then leaped into the shadows, with the dog at his heels.

Alorie sat up, holding the shreds of her blouse about her torso. "Marshall! Come back!"

Brock reached her and pulled her to her feet. "Alorie! Are you all right?"

She reached a hand over her shoulder to touch her back, expecting to find it sticky with blood, but a fiery welt met her touch. "Yes, I think so."

"What was it that attacked you?"

Her gaze met his. "Didn't you see it?"

"I want to know what you saw."

"A unicorn. A black unicorn."

His jaw tightened. "Are you sure?"

Her eyes filled with hot tears of fear. "Never more sure of anything. And you want me to go seeking that! It was evil, Brock. It reeked of hatred and . . . and death."

He shook his head and held her tightly, muffling her against his cloaked body. "No, Alorie . . . not that! It can't be. There never has been a unicorn like that."

Chapter 5

BEFORE THE GATES of Stonedeep closed that night, a handful of Rovers from the far corners of the countryside straggled in, greeting one another with hearty blows and loud voices. Their arrival must have been anticipated by Medra. She caught hold of Alorie as soon as Brock brought her in, sympathized over the torn blouse and skirt—"Brock, how could you let her get caught in a brier patch like that?"—and promptly set her to work setting up tables in the grove.

Another pig had been roasted in the firepit, and it was brought up. Its rind was thrown to the dogs, which snatched up the crackling morsels and raced back to the shadows, to lie and contently chew.

A tall, gray-haired Rover with deeply etched eyes of sky blue brought in another with him, a warlord from the south. He straggled through the gates, his destrier muddied and footsore, and slapped his gauntlets together before swinging down and appraising the haven.

The warlord pulled off his half-helm, his snow-white hair laid slickly against his wide and furrowed brow, his dark eyes snapping hawk-intent over the grounds. He grinned. "So this is the place that I sought, with so many traps and misdirections laid out to ensnare me. If not for you, Corey, I would yet be looking!"

The Rover Corey pressed the horses' leathers into the outstretched hand of an eager boy and gave a short laugh, empty of humor. "So has it always been, milord. Rovers are not landed, as you know. Consider this a nursery, a creche, the nest in which we raise our young until they are old enough to learn to love the endless road.'' His sharp gaze caught sight of Alorie listening to them. He frowned slightly, said nothing, and turned away, as the great wooden gates were pulled shut.

Alorie dipped her shoulder and returned to setting the table, knowing that the warlord could be no other than Rathincourt, the snow-haired lion, of the southern reaches of Sobor. White-haired since early youth, the man was in the prime of his years, a soldier of skill and intelligence that her father had once known and liked well. Rathincourt, she thought, and rolled the man's name about her busy mind, wondering if he could become her liegeman and if he could stand up to Aquitane. Even as she set the last trencher, a hail came from beyond the gates, a thin, weary cry. A broad-shouldered but slender frame squeezed through the opening on foot and stopped just inside, as the gates boomed shut and the crossbar dropped.

Alorie frowned as she tried to see who filled out that travel-stained cloak, then recognized Rowan's easy stance. She found herself smiling.

''Those who wonder at the difficulties of knowing a woman's mind have only to see one frowning and smiling at the same time.''

She found Brock at her elbow, where he stood whisper-quiet. She hadn't even known he was there. She brushed her hair from her face and tucked it behind her ear. ''I can't see as far as others, so I frowned, but then I recognized Rowan's presence, and so I smiled.''

''Another mystery of life that I can claim to know,'' Brock said. His smoke and greenwood eyes warmed as he teased her and took her elbow. His voice quieted, meant for her ears alone as he drew her aside. ''We'll be speaking of many things tonight, milady. I ask that you remember my cautions. Rovers from far and near are met tonight in Stonedeep.''

She felt a tremble run through her body, thinking of the dark unicorn, and of the deaths of her family. "Will they talk of Sinobel?"

"Perhaps. Yes, I think I'll listen to see what others know, and then reveal what I know. You are safe nowhere if you aren't safe here," the man said, and released her. He strode away quickly to seize Rowan's hand, and their voices rang out as though no one had a care in the world.

A wisp of cloud eddied across the late-afternoon sky. Alorie shivered, and found her hands clenched at her side. The moment she waited for was drawing near— and yet she was afraid to face it. It was as though the massacre she'd lived through was only a nightmare until others discovered it as well.

She felt the tension all throughout the dinner. The Rovers, hands and faces washed, but still dressed in their hard-worn clothes, sat down eagerly to the feast, while the children played a little while before reluctantly going to the second table. Medra ruled both tables with an iron hand.

She held up her palm, and the work-worn creases of her skin gleamed pinkly in the dusk and lanternlight. "Eat and drink well, first," she said. "And then we'll take news of the road."

What Alorie had heard before as a blessing she now took more as a command, and before Medra's stern voice faded away, the men fell to making short work of the roast boar and puddings and vegetables set before them.

Alorie sat among the women. She ate little, unable to think of the meal or even taste it. A short, chunky woman, mother of five of the youngsters who romped at the children's table, sat between her and Rowan.

The trenchers were scraped clean and thrown into a barrel at the tables' end, as no one wanted to be in the kitchen scrubbing when there were tales to be told. Of the Rovers Brock had mentioned, Alorie counted ten new to Stonedeep since she'd been there: sky-eyed

Corey, who had brought in Lord Rathincourt, slant-eyed and twig-slender Tien, another dark-skinned Rover called Longknife, and a brawny man with huge braids of burnished gold whose name she didn't catch. And then there was Ashcroft, who looked to be Rowan's elder brother, for he had the same easy carriage and grace, and the hair of deep, dark chestnut. He and Rowan gibed back and forth at each other. There was a lean woman with beautiful black hair, who smiled and introduced herself as Nerona; another woman, who might have been beautiful once but now had skin like old leather and fuzzy gray hair, named Dalla; and a third, called Tansy, a laugh-creased happy young woman who loved her life of rootlessness, despite the two children who had run to her and hugged her tightly when she first entered the gates.

Dinner disappeared and the Rovers grew quiet. The children burst away from the tables and raced across the new grasses, trampling the first signs of spring under their eager feet, while the adults watched them leave.

It was Corey who solemnly lifted his hand from the table and said, "I've brought a stranger, a guest, into our midst. He is man well known to you, who has pledged to keep our secrets, that our haven may exist yet awhile longer."

Lord Rathincourt gave a rueful grin. His snow-white hair had dried to a fluff about his once handsome face, and he wiped his mouth on his sleeve. "I have little choice," he said, laughing. "The man had me blind-folded for half the distance."

"Nonetheless," Brock answered, "your pledge is well received. Welcome, Lord Rathincourt. What brings you through a late winter to our gates?"

The lord frowned. He rubbed the bridge of his prominent nose before saying, "Not good news, I'm afraid. Lord Aquitane has sent out runners to all the lands and holdings . . . he was turned back from Sinobel because of heavy flooding and was unable to attend the inauguration of Nathen Sergius as High Counselor."

"This was news enough to make you seek us?"

"No . . . but it was plainly Sinobel's misfortune. If Aquitane had been there with his troops, it's possible that the city might yet stand."

A gasp ran through the assemblage. Alorie said nothing as Brock caught her eye with his own piercing gaze. She shuddered, remembering the Inner Circle when he had first silenced her that way.

"Sinobel fallen?"

"Yes . . . every last man, woman, and child. Even the Mutts and livestock were slaughtered and the fields outside burned. The orchards were still iced over, but that is all that remains of Sinobel. Aquitane says the stench of reken still hung in the air when he finally made his way to the outer walls to give his congratulations and ask for the hand of the Lady Alorie, Nathen's daughter. He says that although the betrothal was never formalized, it was intended in the last missive Sergius sent him. As such, he's asking the other houses and lands to recognize him as the heir of the House of Sergius, since he alone survives."

Alorie sucked in her breath and bolted to her feet, heedless of Brock's warnings. Heads along the length of the table turned to look at her, and color blazed in her face, fiery spots as though the news had slapped her. "Aquitane lies."

Rathincourt's dark eyes measured her. "The news is bad," the lord said to her quietly, "but should you take it so personally? Aquitane has faults, yes, but he's been a good lord, and a good soldier. Sinobel could do worse . . . yes, worse indeed, for if it lies empty and fallow, what stands between us and the Barrowlands?" He pushed his goblet away forcefully. "Worse, if Aquitane doesn't take up the reins, we are faced with the beginning of petty squabbles and quarrelings. The House of Sergius was ever our mediator and judge, and there is no one now who stands between an ambitious man and the prize he covets."

Dalla interrupted to say, "It's already happening in

the east. Small raiding parties are setting neighbor against neighbor. Any man with a strong arm and a good horse can be king, or so they seem to think."

Brock pushed himself to his feet, and murmurings ceased as his deep voice rolled out. "Then perhaps it is time, Lord Rathincourt, that I set your mind at ease. You can't carry this tale yet, for I have a journey to make first. The young woman you addressed is the Lady Alorie, late of Sinobel, and the last of the House of Sergius. She speaks ill of Aquitane because she saw him lead the reken in the massacre, and swing the blade himself that killed her grandfather, Sergius the Third."

"What?" Rathincourt's fair skin blanched, and his eyes blazed.

"They do the dirty work he doesn't dare," Alorie said bitterly. "And what is more, my hand was no more pledged to Aquitane than to a reken! He lies through his teeth."

"And yet," Rathincourt murmured, as he drew his goblet back and stared pensively into the depths of the watered wine, "I would almost rather the House of Sergius fallen . . . for then the prophecies dare not be true." He looked up quickly, aware that he had spoken out loud. "I beg your pardon, Lady Alorie."

She sat down. "I thought you lived by the sword, not the oracle."

"Indeed, but I would wager every Rover here who can walk can share my interpretation of the verse, for it restores them to favor once more, by the side of a new High King—even though they must face the Corruptor to gain it."

A deep silence had fallen on the rest of the table, and Alorie didn't need to ask if what Rathincourt said was true. She saw it written, though veiled, on the face of every Rover. As long as she lived, or an heir to the House of Sergius lived, they might yet gain lands and office again! No wonder Brock had brought her alive out of Sinobel! And no wonder Rathincourt spoke as he did, for facing the Corruptor once more was something none of the Seven True Races would relish. "Is this prophecy well known?"

Corey ran his high-veined hands through his hair. "In some lands and throughout all the races, milady, yes."

She felt her hopes crumble inside her. The fall of the House of Sergius would not, then, be such a disastrous thing . . . even if Aquitane's treachery be known. The people would rather be complacent, thinking themselves safe. "Foretold or not, if the Corruptor breaks his bindings, no one is safe," she said.

Brock seated himself then. He answered in his compelling voice, "No fact ever stated is more sure than that, Alorie. Regardless of the nightmares of kings, the Corruptor lies restlessly, ever testing for his freedom." He cast his gaze downward to the rough-hewn table in front of him.

"The old foe is no more restless than ambitious men," stated Rathincourt. "I fear this will be a bad spring for planting, unless it's of bodies, and a worse summer for harvesting, unless it's for kingdoms. More than small raiding parties are arming, and even if we keep our counsel and let Aquitane declare himself, we will have civil war."

"Is Sobor giving us a warning?"

The lord had the grace to blush at Rowan's question, and he shook his head. "My lands are enough for me," he returned. "But I can't speak for others."

"We already know Quickentree's intents. Before we send word of Lady Alorie's rescue, I suggest we do some scouting. Rathincourt, you risked much to come to us now. You've left your own lands without leadership, should Aquitane's greedy eyes look to you. For that, the Rovers and the last of the House of Sergius owe you."

The snow-white head bowed at Brock's words. "The telling of how the Lady Alorie was saved will be payment enough. I saw Rowan blush and figure he must have had a part in it, and if that's true, then a hair-raising, swashbuckling tale it must be. Will you gift me with it?''

Brock laughed heartily as Rowan blushed even more. Alorie tried to shake the cold feeling inside her, without success. She looked up and forced a smile. "If you gentlemen will excuse me, then, I will take my leave of you . . . giving Rowan the freedom to tell the story fully."

Laughter rippled up and down the table, but Brock frowned. "We cannot tell the beginning without you."

Stricken, she looked to the Rover mage. His dark skin appeared even more shadowed. The starlight breaking out overhead streaked his brown curls with gray she hadn't noticed before. His countenance was stern, and she knew she would have to tell of the night as she remembered it. Silently, Medra got to her feet and refilled Alorie's goblet of watered wine, as though to give her fresh courage. In a halting voice, she spoke of meeting the Rover disguised as storyteller, the banqueting and dancing, and then the tragedy. A hot mist rose in her eyes, but she refused to let it cascade downward, refused to let it wash away her voice, though her words knotted painfully in her throat. When she had finished, Rathincourt broke the silence.

He lifted his goblet. "To the Lady Alorie. May we all act so courageously when our time comes."

As the goblets were lifted to her, she stood up and climbed over the bench, stumbling away in the dark toward the safety of Stonekeep. This time, no one followed her and made her relive the experience. Marshall met her at the caves, and when she had found her sleeping niche, he wrapped his wiry body about her close, comforting her as her tears dampened his fur.

She did not see the lean shadow which followed her, braced his back outside her niche, wrapped his arms about himself, and rested watchfully.

Chapter 6

ALORIE SAT HER mount with forbearance as Rowan adjusted the stirrup length to her legs. Gray edges of dawn curled about the sky she could see through the box canyon's walls. It comforted her little, for she felt the chill of a light spring rain threatening.

"Where is it Brock says we're going?"

The young Rover grinned up at her. His warm hand stayed curled about her slim ankle a moment longer than necessary as he answered, "The mage keeps his own counsel. I would think this has more to do with his business than with Rover business, but I know little more than you do. He mentioned a journey when Rathincourt was here, and has been laying in stores for it since, pinching a bag here and there from Medra."

The sturdy pony stamped. It was the same beast that Pinch had brought for her. The thought of the dwarf made her shift in the saddle. She hadn't seen Pinch since she'd come to Stonedeep. As Rowan gave the last leather a pull and tucked the end away, she shoved both boots impatiently into the stirrups. "And where is Brock, anyway?"

"So he can answer his own questions?" Rowan laughed and took up the reins of his own mount. "He's outside the gates, waiting with that overgrown beast you call a dog."

The Rover mage did wait outside for them. His cloak was wrapped tightly about him, his hood about his neck, dark brown hair curled to the morning sun. Marshall bounded through the meadow and returned to Alorie's sharp whistle. Dew sparkled his flanks like diamonds. Her pony threw up its head suspiciously and snorted as the dog barked a welcome to his mistress.

The gates of Stonedeep rumbled shut behind them. Alorie twisted in her saddle, surprised, for they were never closed except at sundown.

Brock wrapped the reins about his hand and kneed his pony along the paths. "Stonedeep takes extra precautions now that true races are warring with one another. Aquitane has many spies. He may have learned that a haven is holding you."

"Is that why I'm coming with you?"

"One of the reasons. I've been summoned to a rendezvous. Rowan would always be my first choice on such a road. You I bring along because I think you safest with us."

She shivered as she passed under a long hanging branch. It misted a light spray over her, chilling in spite of her furred cloak. Rowan flashed her a grin then, reminding her that he had told her Brock would spare few explanations to them.

"Where are we going?"

Her voice sounded thin and frail on the early-morning air. She tucked her chin in embarrassment, hoping that Brock hadn't really heard her, but he must have, for he reined back to talk with her.

She met his eyes, for her grandfather had always taught her to look into a man's face when talking with him. His age seemed more defined. She read him now as a man well into his prime, hardened and sleek, like the hawk or falcon that skims the skies, though age may make the wingbeats a bit more deliberate. He smiled. The warmth spread into his hazel eyes and lightened his whole face, so that for a moment she caught a flash of what he must have been like when he was younger. That startled her, and it must have shown in her face, for Brock smiled wider. "We go to answer some of your ever-present questions," he said softly.

She dared to laugh back. "How else am I going to learn? It appears that my grandfather and father told me very little about the real world."

"Don't blame their intentions. From what I know of Sergius, he put aside much that he had been taught for a reason. The city of the High Counselors had feared to prosper for many decades, knowing that it might be inevitable to lose it all at the hand of the Corruptor and his master."

"But if grandfather failed in his duty . . . ."

". . . and succeeded in another, to rule his people wisely and fairly as possible, who's to say that we are right and he was wrong? Throughout his lifetime, Sinobel was a good place to live. He refused to deal with prophecies and fears that may never come to pass. He lived for the day, instead."

"But you—" She stopped, confused.

Brock's lean form swayed with the easy gait of his surefooted pony. "Part of my life is to deal with the nebulous things, the threads of what might have been and what may yet come. I suspect what others fear. I dare to live on hope alone, a far more risky thing than to live by the earth or the sword, and yet, if a farmer lived the way I do, we'd all starve!"

Rowan twisted in his saddle. "Lower your voices or we'll do worse than starve." He threw his cloak free of his bow and drew it from his back.

Brock's expression immediately sombered. "What is it?"

"Something paces us on a parallel track." He slowed his pony, threw his leg over the saddle, and landed on his feet beside it. Brock grabbed up the loose reins as Rowan faded silently into the woods beside the path.

The three ponies kept trotting along the path, but Alorie noticed now that their ears flicked unsteadily as though they heard, or sensed, something she could not. She stiffened in the saddle. Reken?

A bird winged swiftly overhead, frightened from its perch. Alorie ducked and watched it go by. Enemies so close to Stonedeep? They had hardly traveled farther than she had gone on foot when she encountered the unicorn. A chill touched the back of her neck.

Clouds bunched overhead, tinged with threatening black, and the air seemed heavy and damp. Suddenly, she noticed that she hadn't seen Marshall, not for quite a while, and it wasn't normal for the dog to range so far afield without returning to her side now and then. She pursed her lips to whistle, then stopped. If an enemy paced them, she would be a fool to signal.

Brush crackled and broke suddenly, and Marshall's furred body emerged, his crimson tongue lolling between open jaws. Rowan came out behind him silently and vaulted into his pony's saddle. Brock flicked back the reins.

He shook his head. "I found nothing . . . nothing but shadows. Yet I would swear something is out there."

Marshall's hackles stood up stiffly as he trotted steadfastly by Alorie's side. The dog, too, acted as though something followed them through the woods, something that had defied the Rover's ability to find it, but encircled them nonetheless.

The two men looked at one another, and Rowan frowned, but said nothing as he forged back into the lead. Brock pulled his hood up and shrouded his face from her sight as he followed after. They left her behind.

Marshall looked back, and Alorie turned to look back too, slowing the pony. Out of the shadow from where they had come, she thought she saw something move . . . something hard and dark . . . and it disappeared as quickly as she had glimpsed it.

Marshall's ears pricked forward, and he bared his fangs. Before she could cry out, the dog launched himself after the thing, growls rising with every leap.

"Marshall! Come back!" She set heels to the pony's flanks. It surged after the dog, its head down, mane whipping in her face as she leaned forward. The pony couldn't match the great dog's stride. Though it pounded in his wake, Marshall drew away until he reached the spot in the forest where the evil thing had disappeared. With a snarl, he threw himself into the thick woods after it.

The pony plunged to a stop. She grasped wildly at the saddle and its mane to keep herself from pitching over its head, as it stood in the track and shuddered. A rank smell, a greasy, foul stench, hung over the forest. She stroked the pony's neck as Rowan's mount plowed to a stop beside her. The Rover nocked an arrow to the bowstring.

"What is it?"

"I saw something cross the road behind us. Marshall went after it." Even as she spoke, the dog belled in excitement.

Brock joined them. He jerked his black-gloved hand. "Go after him, before he raises the whole forest after us!"

Rowan whipped his mount, and with a strangled nicker, it leaped into the dense forest. Impulsively, Alorie kneed her pony after, even as Brock shouted and reached for her, his gloved hand missing her arm. She heard a muffled curse at her back as the branches thrashed about her.

Marshall's belling call pitched into a high keening. She knew from his voice that he had trapped his prey, though the dog's voice held an edge of fear. She saw Rowan straighten in his saddle, drop the reins, and raise the bow, as Marshall reached a crescendo. He drew back and released the shaft. A sharp yelp bit through the muffled silence of the forest, and Marshall grew still. Rowan lowered the bow and kicked his reluctant mount after their prey.

Alorie found the Rover kneeling beside a bundle of cloak and shadow, as Marshall cautiously sniffed its outer boundaries, then went and rolled in the dirt as though the rankness of the scent could be scrubbed away. Rowan, using the bow's tip, had lifted away the cowl and was examining the body. He looked up sharply.

"Don't look, milady!"

His warning came too late, as the sight gripped her, and she froze in her saddle. Brock passed her and dismounted by Rowan's side.

"Wh—what is it?" she gasped.

"A messenger, no doubt, by the looks of the courier bags," Brock said, as he flipped aside the cloak, but that wasn't the question Alorie had meant to ask.

"It's a Mutt," Rowan said.

She shook her head in denial, trying to swallow the bile threatening to explode from her throat. "No, never—no Mutt ever looked, or smelled, like that!"

The beast that lay sprawled on its side, manlike and yet un-man, was dark-pelted. Its face was a travesty, sharp muzzle and weasel eyes which gleamed with a feral hatred even in its death. The ears stood up, pointed, and the brow was narrowed across, the fur a thick, coarse blackness. Fangs gleamed whitely from bared gums. One hand, grasped about the arrow shaft, was webbed and taloned.

Using the tip of his belt dagger, Brock dragged the courier bags out from under the fallen beast. One of the booted feet jerked. Alorie stifled a shriek with her fist, then realized the creature was dead though its body still twitched.

All three ponies bunched together, the two riderless ones crowding her, pressing hotly on her legs, the whites of their eyes showing as they scented death in the forest. Alorie reached out and gathered in their reins.

Brock made as if to slit the thong tying the bag shut, but Rowan waved his hand palm down over it.

"Watch it," he warned. "It may be protected."

Brock looked up in amusement. "Dare you tell me my job?"

Rowan blushed and sat back on his heels. Brock

indicated the insignia stamped into the leather. "No spell here. This is a military dispatch."

"From whom to whom?"

"That we shall know shortly." The silver dagger sliced neatly through the black leather, and a bundle of parchment slid into Brock's hands. He looked at the wax seal closely and his lips thinned into a line of anger before he tore the packet open, destroying the seal forever as it crumbled to the ground.

"Is it Aquitane?" Alorie asked.

"No." Brock shook his head. Tiny lines of concentration etched across his brow. "There is a traitor in our midst."

Rowan had finished replacing the cloak over the body, and this jerked his attention back to the mage. "What do you mean?"

"This is a response to news that we protect Alorie."

"Only Rathincourt—"

"No. No, he's been gone only a few days, scarcely time enough to alert anyone, let alone dispatch a messenger and receive a response. No, someone had to have sent out the news a fortnight ago when Alorie first arrived. How they learned who she was, I don't know. Worse, the writer here has anticipated my action and our current destination is blocked. A trap has been set and is waiting for me to spring it." He folded the parchment over and stood up, facing Alorie.

"This message contains, among other instructions, orders for your head to be delivered to the writer."

She smiled thinly, though her heart pounded oddly in her chest. "Then it's a good thing Marshall decided to go hunting."

"Yes. But there may be other couriers spreading the word to other unholy allies. Alorie, I was taking you with me to a counsel of my peers, so that they might meet you and advise us, and be aware of the unicorn you have seen, and other happenings. Now that avenue is cut off to me. Rowan, I want you to return to Stonedeep, on foot—we're close enough, and that will be faster for you. I want you to send out missives for me. I'll inscribe them on this blank parchment here. Use the birds—no other way is fast enough. Then I want you to bring Corey and Rathincourt, if you can reach him, to a rendezvous with us. Also send word to Kithrand and Dane.''

Alorie shivered as the names of warlords were called, for she had known of them at her grandfather's court.

''Where will you be going?''

''North. North and west. Bring them to meet us at the Barrowlands.''

Rowan's jaw tightened, and he faced the mage squarely. ''Not there. Take her anywhere but there,'' he protested.

''I have no choice. I must see the barrows and the bindings . . . now, before it is too late. The hunt is on for Alorie. Aquitane and others seek her death, and they're on our heels. She is safe nowhere if she is not safe with me.''

Her hands clenched on the reins, and tiny droplets of blood welled out from where her nails pierced her skin, unknowing. She would go anywhere but there, but it seemed she had no choice as Brock finished, ''I must know if the Corruptor is still laid down. There is no other explanation for the atrocity that lies here. Somehow, he is still at work.''

Chapter 7

Rowan ARGUED WITH Brock as they built a cairn to cover the body of the foul messenger. Their voices vibrated with tension, and Alorie could not miss the look Rowan gave her over his shoulder. She ducked her head in embarrassment, frightened and guilty to be the object of such passion between two men who could not be closer if they were father and son, and knowing that her presence drove a wedge between them.

As the last moss-covered stone dropped into position over the body, Rowan straightened and dusted his hands on his breeches. "It's done, then," he said, and sadness edged his tone.

Alorie felt the sadness was not meant for the dead creature. He did not look directly at her as he came to his pony's side, unlashed the packs, and balanced them over his broad shoulders. Then he looked up, and with a twist of his wrist, a silvery dagger slid into his palm.

He offered it to her. Tiny crescents cut the finely wrought metal, and sparklets of gems decorated runic writing on the handle. She hesitated, knowing it to be of elven work, and rare, for the elves hadn't run a forge in many, many years.

"Please take it. It's small enough to be a lady's dirk, and I—I think it's special. I think it could help you against even the Corruptor's evil."

Brock had come up behind him and watched solemnly over the Rover's shoulder. No expression passed his face as Alorie looked to him, then took the elegant weapon. Rowan smiled grimly and unfastened the wrist sheath to accompany it.

As he laced the sheath about her warm wrist, his touch quickened her flesh. She was keenly aware of his fingers, lean and hard yet gentle at the same time, and their gaze met a second before he dropped his hands away. He cleared his throat.

"A twist of the wrist, thus, activates the spring, and the dagger will glide into your palm. Be careful, or you'll find yourself with a fistful of reins and a weapon."

"I will. Thank you, Rowan."

"I'll be joining you at the barrows quickly enough. To know that you're there will give me wings." He pivoted and clasped the shoulder of the mage. "Remember your promise to me, Brock," and with that, he shifted into an easy lope. His worn and stained Rover's clothing blended quickly into the green, rust, and brown of the woods, and she lost sight of him altogether too quickly.

She pointed after him. "Marshall, follow! Stay with him."

The tawny dog hesitated a second, looking up at her with his large brown eyes, then leaped into the underbrush on Rowan's trail.

Brock watched the hunting dog go. With movements that spoke of weariness and sorrow, he pulled his pony over and mounted it. He looked up, as though aware Alorie watched him.

"What did you promise him?" she asked.

He shrugged his cloak about himself tightly. "I promised to protect you with every scrap of knowledge I possess, to sacrifice everything I must, short of my own life, to bring you back alive from the Barrowlands."

She swallowed tightly. "That was quite a promise."

The mage looked at her. For a moment, she felt herself drawn into the endless depths of those smoke-and-greenwood eyes, lost to herself, enveloped in mysteries she could not understand. "You will never know," he answered softly, and reined his pony around on the track.

A guttural howl broke in the air, and they froze, listening to it.

Brock said quietly, "Reken . . . hunting reken." After a moment longer, he urged the pony forward. "They're after Rowan. Don't worry—he'll decoy them deliberately before losing them. Quickly, now, stay with me!"

She kneed her pony into a lope after the Rover, as the mage led her north, toward the Barrowlands. She had a fleeting moment in which to think she was chilled, tired, and hungry, and lost it as the yelps of the reken spurred her on.

That moment dictated every waking thought for the next four days, until the ponies stumbled to a halt as Brock slowed them down to make camp. Alorie fell rather than slid to the ground. She looked up, her thoughts twirling as the foamed pony put its muzzle to her in equine surprise, not moving a hoof though she lay collapsed between its feet.

She literally crawled out from under it, and, shaking, pulled herself to her feet as she grasped the stirrup. Brock either didn't notice her or didn't care, as he dismounted his own pony and tied the third to a bush. He strode to the center of the small clearing, where he knelt and examined the remains of a fire. From the ashes he withdrew a small pebble, a rock that had been glossed by the fire but not destroyed.

He stripped his gloves off his hands to examine the pebble minutely. His staff, as always, hung belted by his side as though it were a sword, a twin to the real sword on his left hip. His black-and-silver garments were mud-crusted, like hers.

She staggered over and sat down on the ground, only slightly more gracefully than she had earlier collapsed. His eyebrow arched, and he bowed.

"Forgive me, Alorie. I've driven us hard these past few days."

She reclined on an elbow, holding her head up on a wrist that wobbled. "You're forgiven, if we can just have a fire tonight."

He held the pebble up between thumb and forefinger and gave a rare smile. "This is a Rover sign. We're in clear territory . . . this more than anything dictates that we can risk a fire tonight. And . . ." He looked overhead. "I think the weather will keep dry, this once."

The weather had been all too anxious to do the opposite in past days, though the mud hadn't slowed them down, and the rain did well to wash away their tracks. "You called the rain," she said. "But I think you overdid it a little." Her wobbling wrist gave way. She rolled over onto her stomach and let her chin rest on the backs of her hands as she peered up at him.

Brock had kicked the nest of kindling wood and logs into the firepit, and knelt down preparing to strike his flint. He paused and looked at her in surprise. "I called the rain?"

"Didn't you? I thought it was to cover us. You are a mage."

He gave a short laugh, one that bubbled out and refused to quit then, until a tear glistened at the corner of his eye. "I cursed every cloud that passed us! Did you think I was calling for more?"

"Well . . ."

He took a deep breath then. "I'm as impotent at sorcery as you are," he said finally, regretfully.

Alorie looked through her eyelashes at him. "You warded me that night at Sinobel."

"I merely asked the gods to bring you through, as befits your fate to be the last of the House of Sergius. And All-Mother, bless Her heart, heard me, as She always listens to even the most lowly of Her children."

Alorie sat bolt upright. Weariness loosened its stranglehold on her limbs, though she still ached. "But even Rowan said—"

"Want a charm for your warts? That I can do. A poultice for fever . . . a blessing for luck . . . at a snap of my fingers, milady." Brock's voice imitated the street hawking of a peddler. "A rainstorm? Fiery elements? Demons summoned and contained? Alas . . . not I. Not anymore."

She pointed at him. "You bedazzled me in the Inner Circle. That, I know."

"Herbs and powders. You inhaled them . . . in a pinch, I was gone, and you stayed asleep for a moment longer. How do you think I got past the gates? A Rover in disguise? I'd have been thrown out at the lower circles without my powders. Ah, girl, don't look at me so. I have much knowledge, and knowledge *is* power, though of a different kind. And I have promises in the future that my sorcery will be returned to me, when I need it most." He struck flint and iron and coaxed the spark to new life among the old ashes. "Like this fire, I'll be rekindled one day . . . and soon, from the looks of it. Then you will see what I can do, Alorie."

"Is that why you had to see the counsel?"

He looked askance at her, even as he fed the flames carefully. Then he smiled. "You see and hear more than most, don't you? I'll have to remember that. Yes, one of the reasons. I have to persuade them to release my powers to me sooner than they deemed, for if they wait, it may be too late. It was a fitting punishment to me to take my powers away—I was young and foolish and squandered them—but now it will punish all of the Seven True Races to deny me longer. *That* they will have to be accountable for, if what I suspect is true."

"The Corruptor is growing powerful?"

"Yes." He spread his pink palms over the growing fire, and its glow lit up his wearied face. "The Mutt courier I might have expected. But the unicorn . . . if what you saw was true, then the Corruptor reaches into the Three Secret Races, and there may be no way to stop him."

"I did see it."

"And I believe you, though I don't want to."

She smiled then, though the fire's warmth was coaxing her to sleepiness, and her eyes felt heavy. "I thought you lived on hope, Brock."

He looked sharply at her, then smiled widely. "Thank you for reminding me. Now go ahead and rest. I need the time to hunt."

Alorie needed no further persuasion and nestled her tired body into the unyielding ground. Thinking that she would never be able to sleep in a soft bed again, she drifted off with the scent of woodsmoke in her nostrils.

Brock straightened in his saddle. His pony snorted in the gray mist of morning, up to its hooves in a downy layer of ash and pale green moss as they crested a ridge. Alorie squinted at what he pointed to.

There was no mistaking it, though she couldn't see clear outlines. The Barrowlands lay ahead. To the south and east lay the heavy forest that bordered the barrows and Sinobel . . . and she could see the pale finger of the highest tower overlooking them. Beyond the barrows, stone mountains pushed impatient spires from cracked and slanted tables of granite. A single pass cut through them . . . the Eye of Cornuth, fallen city of the High King, who gave his life and powers so that evil might be stopped here.

Ridges of earth broke the waste. Binding the Despot and the Corruptor here was like salting the land, so that nothing green might ever grow again, though their ponies trampled small gray plants that opened violet eyes to the sky. Alorie found that she had been holding her breath, and took a sudden, gusty breath.

Standards stood yet, medallions hanging from them, twirling in the sun and the wind, their surfaces engraved with the sorcery that kept the barrows closed and quiet. If she were close enough, she could read those banners and medallions.

The pony moved forward to her unspoken desire, and

Brock leaned over sharply to catch the reins near the headstall.

"Not yet," he said. "We'll wait for Kithrand, Dane, Rathincourt, and the others."

"If Rowan got through."

"I must trust that he did . . . and that the others will, also. These are minor barrows to the fore. The ones that I must look at are deeper, close to the Eye of Cornuth." He moved, imperceptibly. She wondered if he shuddered also.

She had no time to wonder anything more, as the barking howls of reken sounded.

Brock cursed. "By the horn! I'm still a fool to be sitting up here on top of the ridge. Down, Alorie. Down with me!" He kicked his pony into a frantic slide back down into the woods.

She followed and tethered her mount hastily, as he returned to the crest, where he lay cautiously and looked out over the scene.

The reken hunted, but not them. She saw a force of men beating their wearied horses, swords bared as they fled the thick boundaries of the forest. She could not see the markings well enough to recognize who they might be, though she thought she recognized Rathincourt's frame hunched over a lathered horse to the fore.

Brock said grimly, "I still know a trick or two. Stay here . . . and keep your head down!"

"What are you going to do?"

He pointed. "In the last stand, there were trenches dug down there and filled with pitch to be fired. It's still there. We Rovers have used it from time to time to coax a reluctant fire on damp days . . . and I think a well-placed arrow might set a line of flame between our men and the reken."

She let go of his sleeve, and he melted away into the barren landscape. She rubbed her hands together, as the very fauna that bedded her tickled her with its unhealthy softness.

The reken broke out of the forest. Some ran on four

legs, like animals, most on two, with the swiftness and grace of ferrets. They gave voice with barking howls of approval as they saw their prey faltering in front of them. One of the riders leaned over and slit open the throat of a staggering packhorse. The animal went down without a sound, crimson wound fountaining into the soil.

The reken slowed and milled about the warm, twitching body. Alorie gagged as they dipped their hands into the blood and sipped it, before charging after their quarry once more.

But that pause, brief as it was, was enough. She heard the bow sing, saw the orange arch of the arrow through the sky. It struck the ground, quivering, in front of the reken troop. They slowed again, looking behind and to their flanks, uncertain. Suddenly the furrowed ground in front of them burst into flames. The flames reached higher and magically spread far along the border of the forest, a curtain of heat the reken recoiled from with howls of pain and bewilderment. They hopped up and down as the flames drove them from Alorie's view, and their prey escaped.

Brock appeared below her, and crawled up cautiously, with a boyish grin on his face. "That gave them the old hot foot, I think," he said. "Though whoever had sense enough to sacrifice the horse helped his own cause quite a bit."

The horsemen turned on the plain and circled briefly, as the trenches full of pitch kept burning intensely, clear to the northern wall of rock. No reken would break through that day. They conferred with one another, then headed unerringly toward the crest upon which Alorie and Brock rested.

Brock nodded then, as though satisfied. He stood up. His faded black cloak unfurled about him, his appearance on the horizon as sudden as a storm cloud.

It might have been a council of war, Alorie thought, as she looked about at the wearied men. They wrapped begrimed hands about tin mugs of watered wine, their helms resting by their sides, but their swords ready at hand. Rathincourt she knew well. She recognized the bald brow of Lord Dane, framed by wild red hair; he was from the far eastern slopes, on the seacoast. Lord Kithrand she had heard of, and watched now as inconspicuously as she could, for he was of the elves, and elves had been little welcomed at Sinobel.

The lord was lithe and slender, and shorter than the other men. His white-blond hair hung to his shoulders bound with a single strand of braided blue gems that matched the flash of his eyes. Were his ears pointed? She couldn't tell, to her disappointment, for the veils of hair concealed them, but there was no doubt that the lord was exceedingly light and graceful of movement, and as pale of skin as she had ever seen anyone. He wore clothes of ash and pale green, and his boots were of suede rather than coarse-grained leather. Feathery hairs that seemed as sensitive as his eyes adorned his brow. They arched in wry amusement as he spotted her wrist sheath. He made a remark in quick, lilting elvish to Rowan, who blushed and answered back, but didn't bother to explain to Alorie what they talked about.

Marshall pressed hard upon her booted ankles, and she slipped him another strip of the hare they had roasted and patted his too-lean flanks. He and Rowan had run nearly forty leagues without rest, and the dog's pads were inflamed and sore; he licked at them after devouring the meat. Yet Alorie knew that the Rover hadn't ill-used the dog. Reken had driven them nearly the entire way, and it was only by luck that the lords had all met, each nearly the sole survivor of the force he'd started out with, and by banding together, gained the Barrowlands.

Rathincourt swept a broad hand through his snowy head of hair. "We've supped enough, Brock. Let's have a look at that barrow you're worried about." His words fell as casually as though he talked about a lamed horse or broken cartwheel.

The redheaded Lord Dane, with a broken nose that belied his prowess with his fists, his long, tangled hair braided and pinned back with cloak pins, grunted and got to his feet. He ranged the most massive of all the men there, twice nearly the bulk of Kithrand. Great white scars ran across his knuckles and wrists. He held a hand out to Rowan and set him neatly on his feet. "I've wasted enough time, Brock. Aquitane makes ready to lay siege to my lands. Amends aside to the Lady Alorie . . . I've got me own people to wurry about."

Something flashed in Brock's eyes as he stood and helped her to her feet, but he did not counter the warlord's rough statements. "We'll go down on foot then, for the horses are nearly broken."

The handful of men that had survived their lords' encounters with reken sat about dejectedly, bruised and wearied. Alorie looked down at Marshall. "Guard," she said flatly.

Kithrand's brow antennae danced in hidden amusement. "The dog minds well," he said ironically, though Marshall looked too spent to be going anywhere.

Alorie shot a look at him, then realized he but teased her, and looked away. No doubt elves lived long enough to find humor in most things mortal men did, even war, she thought.

Once over the crest, she found the walking laborious. The ash drifted nearly to her knees, and more than once Rowan righted a misstep, until she found herself leaning heavily on him. A heaviness of spirit as well as body penetrated her senses. She marveled that the lathered horses had carried their riders across the furrowed land at all. She gathered herself and pulled away from Rowan.

Kithrand ran lightly across the ash as though he were weightless. He paused when he came to the edge of the first earthen ridge, a barrow as tall as he that wormed its way across the landscape, standards pricking its back as though a dragon had fallen and been buried here. Legions of the Corruptor's dead lay here.

The ground was dry and hardened, with an unhealthy sheen. No green stalks poked their way out of the soil, however fertilized by fields of death they might have been.

They skirted several of these gigantic barrows. The dread weighed her heart heavier and heavier until she could barely walk. Even Kithrand seemed burdened to the earth now. Rowan shot her a sideways glance, frowned, and reached down, scooping her up, carrying her as a young man does a maid he's been courting.

Alorie kicked her feet. "Put me down!"

"No," he said. "Not here. Let me carry you a way."

His face had paled, and the cleft scar in his chin showed more plainly than ever, and she felt his bones, for the journey had worn him down. She stopped struggling, afraid to hurt him or his pride.

Dane glanced over his shoulder and scowled. "Put her down, boy."

Rowan shifted her weight a little and answered, "It's my burden."

"Put her down, I said. Let the earth know what the feet of a Sergius feels like—it's been long enough since the last one walked here." The burly lord stopped, and his heavy body twitched impatiently under his chainmail coat. She heard the anger in his thick voice. He blocked their path.

Brock, striding to the fore, a thin layer of ash coating him to his knees, stopped and turned. "There's been enough fighting here. Don't forget that those buried here still reach out for company."

Dane shrugged. He gave way reluctantly, though Alorie watched him over Rowan's shoulder as they passed, and the lord gave her a look of scorn. It was hidden as Rowan moved beyond the barrow, and she blinked, wondering if she had really seen that expression on the lord's face or not.

The barrows here rose ponderously, blocking out view of the others beyond, each the height of two men, and stretching from tip to tip of the wasteland. A faint mist curled from the still earth. She squeezed Rowan's shoulder and said gently in his ear, "Put me down now. Please."

Reluctantly, he set her on her feet. The ashes were stripped away by an ever-present wind that keened along the harsh dirt. The talismans chimed as the breeze tangled them. The faint tap-tap-tap of their metal edges on the standards that bore them made her shiver. These were the bindings that kept the barrows closed, making the earth into a prison for the evil it had swallowed . . . these were the bindings that Brock said were wearing thin.

" 'Set here on this day in the jaws of death by Myrlianne, lady of the star-shone people,' " Kithrand read, his head tilted back, intoning the runes on one of the standards. Its black tarnished surface betrayed the silver it had been wrought of. His voice rose and fell as he read the names inscribed below, and their hopes, and their magicks, and he sounded as if he recited poetry. It drew her, inexorably, as the flame does a moth.

He paused. "Do you know any of the names, milady?"

"A few. It—it was very long ago."

"Not to such as myself. Five or six generations for you, but the Lady Myrlianne was my grandmother."

"What is . . . what are the jaws of death?"

"This field. They assembled forces, the Seven True Races. Man in all his colors, elves and dwarves"—a wry smile at that—"one of the last times the three stood shoulder to shoulder without fighting among themselves. The earth was prepared, for this was the last stand. Cornuth had already fallen, her bones cracked open and the marrow of the kingdom sucked out. The other lands were conquered, and the armies that stood here were the last of their races . . . if they failed. They plowed with silver and salt and holy water. Ditches were trenched deeply and filled with pitch, to burn the undead that the Despot and the Corruptor drove before them. The prayers had been said, incense burned, gods invoked. Magicks had been brewed and enchantments trembled on the lips of the sorcerers who would cast them.''

The elven lord brushed his white hair from his finely etched face, and he looked at her with eyes that had no white, but burned as blue as the gems on his brow. ''All that wanted was the bait to draw the enemy into the jaws. The last garrison of the High King, and the garrison of the Corruptor himself, led by the High King, provided it. The Despot is said to have laughed when they ran before him . . . a broken army, renegades and dictators. But he and his lieutenant followed, to crush them into the earth. When they came through the Eye of Cornuth, the High King himself closed off the pass behind them. It took all of his powers, both of magic and sword, to do it, but he held it . . . held it long enough for the jaws to close, and the enemy to be brought down. He lost everything so that we might gain everything, including the wisdom to hand the Despot a final death one day.'' Kithrand sighed. ''It's said the Three Secret Races watched to see who would win . . . and that they alone hold the answers we seek, but who but the All-Mother would know if they do.''

Dane grunted. ''A pretty story.'' He spat and brushed past the elf lord, to shadow Brock's footsteps ahead of them.

She stumbled. With surprise, she looked down and saw a yellow-white pointed bone sticking from the grayed soil. Rowan cursed and kicked it, and the spearlike end shattered. The noise echoed throughout the barrows, and once more Brock slowed.

He stood between a narrow passway, two great barrows flanking him. The sky beyond the mountains rumbled threateningly. He did not move, though his dark complexion grew paler. He threw his hood back with trembling hands, and the keening wind made huge wings of his cloak.

Rowan and Alorie joined him, and stopped, too. The standards had been snapped like dry twigs, their runes shattered beyond reading. Closest to them, two of them had melted into now cool pools of black slag. Alorie was aware of the other lords coming up behind her. They gasped in shock as they, too, saw the burrow of the Corruptor, split wide open and empty to the sky.

Dane shoveled them aside and ran to the burrow. He went to his knees, shouting incoherently. Kithrand, who had dared to run lightly over the tops of the other burrows, bent his head, his antenna eyebrows wilted and quivering. Rathincourt merely took off his helm and stuck it under one arm.

"It appears," he said, "that we are too late."

"Not everything is lost," Rowan added. "The final barrow is still closed."

"But for how long?" Brock said bitterly. He clenched his fist. "The Corruptor is gone. When he gains his strength, he'll return for his master. That is the bargain they struck in hell!"

He did not meet Alorie's eye. Her stomach knotted, for she knew without anyone's saying it that Sinobel had failed in its watch . . . that if Sergius had done what he had pledged to do, the council might have been able to keep the Corruptor down yet a little while longer.

Rowan broke away from the cluster to pace the length of the grave. He knelt over a broken standard, then looked back to them, calling out, "There is more, Brock."

"More? What do you mean?" The mage went to his side, Rathincourt trailing him.

"He did not break out of his own accord, as I read the signs. He was broken out, or broken out sufficiently to regain a measure of strength, and then he blasted his way lose. That is why these standards were melted, rather than snapped. And why the earth is disturbed the way it is—"

"What fool would be stupid enough to loosen the Corruptor?" Rathincourt wiped his sweating brow with the back of his hand, regardless of the chill of the wind.

Brock had bent over the sign and now straightened.

"Worse, my lord. This was no fool, and he had powers beyond my imagining if he dared to free the Corruptor."

"Aquitane," Alorie whispered, but her voice didn't carry to those kneeling at the disrupted barrow.

Only Dane seem to have heard . . . Dane with his massive forearms buried into the rubble of the grave . . . Dane with his head bowed as he grieved wordlessly. "All lost," he muttered. Then the massive man stumbled to his feet, and turned to look at her.

Brock rubbed his eyes wearily. "There's something . . ." He dropped his hands. "Can you tell how recently he was broken free?"

Rowan shook his head, his dark auburn hair ruffling in the breeze. He sifted the dirt and weighed it, as though the very earth held an answer for him. Then he looked up. "With the rain . . . it's hard to tell. Perhaps two weeks?"

"Too soon!" Brock swung around. He eyed the pass into Cornuth, the bulk of the last great barrow reared in front of it. Then he smiled grimly. "No wonder the reken have left us in peace! Our ranks were reduced to the last man, and we were driven, not harried here! The Corruptor learned his lesson too well. Kithrand, Dane! Get Alorie . . . we're getting out of here, and now!"

She hesitated as Dane lumbered toward her. She froze, for his face contorted in a twisting expression, like a man in a seizure . . . and yellow-green flame flickered in the depths of his narrowed eyes.

From far away, she heard Brock shout again. The edge of the barrow rippled and folded back, as an obscene image blossomed upward, and she knew the scent and fear it carried with it. The barrow had birthed a malison. The others swung around to meet it, swords drawn. Brock fumbled at the pouch hanging about his neck. Everyone faced the menace but Dane, who bore down on her, a slavering noise dripping from his slack mouth.

Alorie screamed and stumbled backward. The bone fragment that had caught her before stabbed upward now, ripping into her hem, like a hand grasping to stop her flight.

Dane roared as he drew his sword and cocked his arm.

She yanked at her skirt. The fabric refused to come free, and she threw her weight on it, determined to rip herself away. As threads tore, Dane took a last bound, closing the distance between them.

The barrows possessed him. She saw it in the gray of his normally ruddy face. A cloak pin fell, loosening a wild fringe of red hair. It did not fall to his shoulder but rose as though it had a life of his own and stood about the side of his head, wriggling in the air. Spasms rippled through the muscles of his face, and his jaw clicked as he fought for words.

Through clenched teeth, he gasped, "Run." Words gargled in his throat, and she knew that the warlord fought a desperate battle against the hellion spirit that had taken him.

The skirt gave way. She tumbled to the ground unexpectedly as the cocked arm swung. The blade hissed bare inches from her face. She rolled and scrambled up, gathering her feet to run, and the lord caught her arm.

He—it—laughed. The sound whinnied out and ended drowned in spittle. His fingers bit into her like iron spikes. The pain washed through her, reeling her senses, and she felt her knees giving up and wondered if she would faint first or be beheaded before, as Dane's right arm bunched and drew back. The sun glinted off the blade as she watched it, unable to move.

Thunder boomed, and she heard the shouts of the others, and knew the malison flexed its powers to take them. The jaws of death, she thought, were about to close on all of them.

Marshall's growl matched the man's, and his tawny body knocked her down. The lord lost hold of her as the hunter went for his prey, the exposed wattle of throat above the surcoat. Alorie rolled to her knees. Dane struck at the dog, and she saw the sword blade bite deep, severing him, but the dog had no chance to yelp. His jaws were sunk into the throat of the man who threatened his mistress, and closed there, even in the death throes. In the momentum of their fall, the trunk fell aside as Dane fell backward.

Half blinded by the gushing blood, Alorie twisted her wrist and the elven blade slipped into her palm. Silver, Kithrand had said. They had plowed silver into the land as a defense against the evil. Dane wrapped big hands about the dog's head, struggling to free himself and get to his feet once again.

It was now or never. She gripped the hilt and jumped onto the chest of the lord, driving her blade deep into the eye squinting at her, extinguishing the yellow-green flames forever.

Alorie rocked back. A hot mist blurred her eyes as she touched the head of the dog, murmuring, "Marshall . . . good boy . . ."

The wide-open eyes blinked, and the jaws relaxed, letting go of the lord's neck, before they spasmed. The light in the great brown eyes faded, though they remained wide open, staring into his mistress's face. The dog's body lay still on the ground, the decapitation wound pumping crimson into a gray earth that sucked it dry.

She reeled back, sitting on the ground, her back braced on Dane's massive ribcage. The warmth left his body, even as shouts brought her back to the fight waged yet.

The malison reared above Brock. She thought she could make out a form inside the cloud of death and darkness, a skeletal form that shimmered uncertainly. A wing raised and threatened to envelop the Rover mage, to hug him close and draw him in. Rathincourt lay on the ground, his helm knocked to one side. Rowan crouched, his sword drawn, Kithrand behind him, his elven bow nocked and ready to let fly—but Brock blocked the shot.

The wing shriveled into a tentacle, wrapped about the

mage's lean waist, and dragged him inward to the maelstrom of power. Brock dragged an arm free, and she saw the leather pouch in his hand.

Rowan had had such a pouch, she thought dimly, and sat, unable to move or flee, even though she knew she must.

With a yell, Rowan launched himself to his feet and charged the malison. A blue bolt shattered the ground at his feet, and he pitched forward, sword flung aside. His body slid across the ground to the very feet of the shrouded malison, even as Brock drew back his arm.

He threw the open pouch with a shout of words, words that drummed on her hearing though she couldn't understand them. A spray of powder flashed into the air . . . and bit deeply into the substance of the malison. With a screech the tentacle whipped loose from Brock, and the Rover fell next to Rowan's limp form. Great holes ate into the malison, and then it was gone, with a flash and a boom of sound, as though it had never been.

Brock thrust his hands under Rowan and dragged him up. "Rowan!"

Kithrand knelt between the two of them and took the dark auburn head into his lap. He smoothed the brow a moment, then smiled and said, "Never fear . . . the blood runs strong in this one."

"Thank the horn," Brock answered. He staggered to his feet. "Alorie! Where are you?"

"Here," she answered, her voice a dry croak in her throat. She got to her knees and halfway to her feet before he reached her and pulled her up. He threw his arms tightly about her. His warmth flooded her body, and he led her gently away from the dead lord's body.

"What happened?" he whispered, and she smelled faintly the scent of the powers and herbs that had killed the malison.

"Dane attacked me. He must have been possessed. I . . . couldn't get away. His eyes flamed, and his face . . . Marshall went for him, and bore him down before . . . before . . ." Her words stuck in her throat. She swallowed tightly. "Then I took the elven blade and I struck him through the eye. I thought if it is a hellion, then silver—"

"You did that?"

"Yes."

He drew away from her then slightly. At arm's length, he looked into her face, and nodded. "I picked you well," Brock said.

In death, Dane's face had relaxed somewhat, though his eyes had burned away in their sockets.

"The silver knife," the mage added, "saved you both. He may be dead, but the Corruptor no longer has him."

She shuddered. He reached out and took her in again, and walked her back to the others. As she listened to the strong, slow beat of his heart, he warmed her once more, and she thought she understood a little of the love Rowan bore for this stern man.

Chapter 8

"THE REKEN WILL BE BACK."

"There's no doubt of that," Brock answered. "Having followed their master's orders to drive us here, and failing to destroy us, the reken will be back in force. And who knows what else the barrow will issue once it gets dark? Rowan, you have to take Alorie and get her out of here as quickly as you can."

Behind them, Rathincourt scratched his head, fluffing his hair, as he stood looking morosely at the bodies. Dane had been a friend of his from childhood, and his face was now furrowed with sadness. Finally, he forced out, "I can't just leave him like that!"

"Of course not," Kithrand soothed. "Brock, I trust that we are well known here . . . that there is no possibility to sneak out like thieves in the dark?"

The Rover mage looked at the elf, then shook his head, as though words weren't necessary.

"Then one last thing I shall do on this field of death," the other answered. He pointed a slim finger at the fallen man's body, still accompanied by Marshall's severed form.

A blue flame leaped up. Quickly, the two forms were enveloped in the elven fire that burned without heat, cleanly.

Rathincourt cleared his throat and looked away, saying, "Thank you, Kithrand. I didn't want to leave his bones here to be picked over by carrion or . . . whatever might crawl here at night."

Alorie looked away from the funeral pyre, though the flames did not shrivel flesh or cook the meat of the bodies. Rowan took her arm.

"Come with me now. Kithrand has given them the highest honor he can."

At the horses, where Rathincourt's two waiting liegemen of were all that remained of the lord's, Dane's, and Kithrand's original escorts, Brock took up his pony's reins.

Rowan stopped the mage from swinging up. "Where are you going?"

"The pathways to Veil are blocked, I know that," Brock answered shortly. The green in his hazel eyes smoldered. "I have another way to go now, with questions that cannot wait to be answered. I'll either return to the havens or send for you and Alorie. In the meantime, I entrust her to you. Remember the words we spoke on the first morning I sent you after her, and follow them now as you did then."

Rowan dropped his hand from the other's arm. "You'll come back."

"Of course I will. There's the herbs to harvest for my powder that works so well against the malison, destinies to be charted, but, in the meantime, your charge is the Lady Alorie. Remember, Rowan, there's a traitor in our midst, possibly more than one. The Rover life has been a hard one. Not all of us have been strong enough to accept it."

"Do you know who it is?"

"That's one of the questions I'm going to be asking. The other is, who or what is powerful enough to release the Corruptor." Brock settled himself in his saddle and looked over Rowan's shoulders to where Alorie stood, watching them.

She matched his gaze without words. Then, as if in answer to his unspoken request, she came to his side. As Rowan looked away, Brock leaned out of the saddle and whispered gently, "You have one duty to remember, if I shouldn't return from this."

"You have to come back!"

He shook his head and placed a soothing hand over her shaking ones. "If I do not, then you must remember the white unicorn."

A hot mist stung the corner of her eyes. "No. I can't do it."

"You *must*, Alorie."

To be changed forever? "I'll go mad," she whispered, and dropped her chin, ashamed to look at him.

"I don't think so. And you won't be going alone, for I plan to come back and be with you." His fists clenched suddenly about the reins. "The gods owe me a few answers!" His pony threw up its head, squealing, as Brock jammed his boot heels into its shaggy flanks, setting it into a lope.

The two of them watched the mage ride off, his faded black cloak unfurled at his back.

"Do you know what he plans?" Rowan asked softly.

She shook her head, and with her fingertips patted away a stray tear that had escaped. "No. Only that he lied about going to Veil . . . if that's where his mysterious council is, that's where he's going, trap set or not."

"I think so, too." Rowan took a deep breath. "Well, milady. This is a place I don't want to be at nightfall. Let's be going."

The faraway howls of reken haunted every step they rode. Kithrand turned off at the eve of the second day.

He flipped them a jaunty salute, his brows bobbing faintly. "Fare you well, Rover, and you, milady. I have business of my own, and word of the Corruptor's release must be spread." He looked over his shoulder, and she gathered that he listened to the hunt behind them. "I'll draw their stink away from you, as best I can."

"Thank you, Lord Kithrand," Rowan returned. They watched him meld into the forests, even the slim outlines of his horse becoming more and more ethereal as it disappeared.

Rathincourt flexed his shoulders. He'd spoken little
since Dane's death, and now his voice came out dry,
disused. "I will turn aside here, too. Dane's people
must be told and mine as well. I'll leave Dane's men
with you—"

"No. We Rovers travel best when we travel alone."

Alorie sat her pony wearily, but felt the corner of her
mouth curl when he referred to her as a Rover.

Rathincourt bowed from his saddle toward her. "I
will keep your honor, as always, Lady Alorie."

"No."

His eyes widened.

Alorie gathered her courage. "No, Lord Rathincourt,
if traitors know, then honest men must too. Tell them
all that a Sergius survived the fatal attack at Sinobel.
You needn't tell them all you know—Aquitane is too
powerful for that, and you'll need time to build up your
own forces. But tell them I live!"

Gratitude passed over the lord's face, and he nodded.
"Thank you, milady. That news will do good where the
other does ill."

He reined his lathered horse around and waved the
liegemen after him, and they disappeared in the opposite direction. Their going was not silent, as had been
Kithrand's, and she listened to the crackling of twigs
and thrashing of branches long after they were gone
from her view.

Rowan's voice broke into her thoughts. As she turned
to look at him, she noticed the waning light of the sun
brought the red out in his dark hair, and that gold
flecked the depths of his warm brown eyes. He rubbed
his cleft self-consciously as though aware she looked
too closely into him. "Are you sure that was wise to
do?"

"Maybe not." She gathered her reins as well as her
thoughts. "But if I'm ever to regain Sinobel, I must
make allies. You may not have noticed, Rover Rowan,
but I'm a woman, and a woman without an army at
that."

As she rode past him, she did not hear his murmured response, "Oh, I've noticed, all right."

"Alorie."

The whisper was low, piercing her dreams with dagger sharpness, just as she fought a dark passage once more. She opened her eyes, feeling her chest rise and fall rapidly with the same panic in waking she had felt in her dreams. She pushed her hair from her face.

Rowan gently shushed her, and helped her to her feet. He made a motion to listen, and she did so, though her pulse beat so strongly in her ears she couldn't hear for a moment. She held her breath and her racing heart slowed a little.

Boom-boom-doom. She heard the muffled beat sounding, pause, then repeat again. "It sounds like drums," she whispered.

Rowan nodded. "Reken drums," he said.

Boom-boom-doom. Then, from another distance, ba-boom-boom.

"They've spotted us," he told her. He took her fur from her shoulders. Kneeling, he tucked it about the spot on the ground where she had been lying, the sweet grass still crushed from her form, and drew the saddlebags she'd used for a pillow close, until she couldn't tell if someone slept under the fur or not.

Across the glowing embers of the dying fire, she saw another bundle, similarly asleep. He took her hand and drew her away from the tiny clearing, guiding her into the woods, seeing as a cat might see.

"Wait here," he whispered, and backed her to the wide trunk of an oak tree, its leafy branches hanging low around them.

She caught his hand as he turned away. "Don't leave me."

"I'll be all right. Can you climb?"

"Not—not in a long time." She hesitated, memories of climbing the prize orchard trees of Sinobel catching her. Memories of stolen fruit, still green at the stem, staining her fingers as she shinnied back down the bark, hoping she wouldn't be caught, flooded her. "Yes, if I have to."

He pursed his lips and gave a nightbird call. "If you don't hear that, then climb for your life."

Before she could give assent, he deftly freed his hand from her grasp and was gone, blending into the night of dark and shadows and gray patches. Alorie backed up closer to the tree heedless of the tiny knobs and bark that poked into her back.

Reken barks split the air. Growls and howls followed as the beasts ravaged their camp. A pony squealed and bolted away into the forests, leaves and branches crackling under its panicked flight. She heard shouts of surprise and then pain. A war whoop sounded like Rowan, and she knew he had drawn his sword and flung himself into the midst of the reken.

She knotted her hand. The night denied her vision, and so she squeezed her eyes shut.

Clangs and grunts rang out. She heard feet trampling the ground and heavy bodies hurtling into the brush, a cry of triumph, then a quick gasp and another ring of metal against metal.

Something ran past her, cursing under its breath. She caught the stink of the beast, as its leather armor creaked and its thick bare feet beat the ground. It was gone before she could jump away to the other side of the tree.

She kept her eyes open, and backed away from the oak in fear—and into a pair of splayed hands that gripped her shoulders triumphantly. The beast gave a low, coarse laugh and its rank smell enveloped her.

Something cold nicked at her throat. "Don't talk," the reken ordered.

Her scream turned into a hard lump at the feel of the knife. The soldier laughed again and said something over its shoulder to a comrade. Two reken at her back, at least two, she thought wildly.

"We were right. The man was smart . . . but not as smart as us. He put the female right into our grips."

Leather armor creaked and the already rancid smell became overpowering as the other reken moved into sight. She struggled as the first embraced her closer and pulled her back against its chest, which was covered by a studded breastplate that bit into her back.

"Leave the others. Gnorish leads them . . . they're not ours."

The second reken stood taller than she. Its fangs curled heavy lips, and its pelt slid down over its wrinkled brow to its eyes—and it was those eyes, gleaming at her in the half-night, that stopped her struggles. In the depths of their slanted yellow orbs was a cold intelligence she had never figured on. She had come to know the reken well—brutish, with their long arms that hung to their knees, yet supple and swift—but she had never seen into their eyes before. It was all sinews and muscles, yet fluid in the way a river otter or woods weasel was supple. It lifted a hand tipped in thick, black talons and caressed her cheek.

Her skin quivered under the touch.

"Take her head *now*," grunted her captor, and the blade sank farther into her neck, pricking the skin until she fought back a cry, determined not to show them the pain.

"No. Ironhair wants her alive."

"The master wants her dead."

The second reken flicked its gaze away from her face and examined that of her captor. It frowned, reminding her for a faint second of the wolfish Mutt courier they had killed. "No. Ironhair is my master."

The knife gave at her throat even as the arm and hand binding her tightened, and she realized the two reken worked at cross purposes. Ironhair? Who was that? Then she thought of Rathincourt and curled up inside herself, for she abhorred the thought. But what other lord could be powerful enough to control reken and bear that nickname? Not Aquitane, whose hair was blond, as pale as finely spun gold.

The reken leader looked back to her, "We take. You follow. No trouble."

She gave a broken nod, and her captor released her.

She screamed, "Rowan!" with all her might as she kicked, lashing at the reken's groin, then twisted and bolted away as the second tumbled over the prone body of the first. She pitched headfirst into the brush.

"Alorie!"

Rowan's shadowed form leaped over her, sword glinting. He made short work of the reken that drew a knife while the other stumbled to its feet and ran off in the darkness. Alorie watched it go . . . not entirely sorry to see it flee, thinking that it had saved her life, though for purposes of its own.

Rowan, the reken spitted at his feet, pulled his sword clear and called out, "Alorie!"

She pulled herself from under the brambles. "Here."

His sleeve was torn and damp, but he pulled her to his rib cage, under the wing of his free arm, as he wiped the sword blade clean on the bark of the tree. His heart thudded. She could smell the blood on him, thick and pungent, and prayed it wasn't his.

"Are you all right?" he asked as soon as he caught his breath.

"Yes. Two of them lay back . . . they knew you might be ready for them."

"Five came at the fire . . . I got four, one got away. Then this one, and the other fled." He made a noise in his throat. "Five out of seven. Not too bad for a Rover lad."

"Are you all right?"

"A graze . . . flesh wound in the arm. Unless the blade was very dirty, I'll be fine. Medra's got poultices that should clear it up. The ponies bolted, but I don't think they'll go any farther than the brook." He stroked her hair absently as he looked down at the reken body.

She began to shake. Her knees melted into jelly, and she thought she was going to be very sick to her stomach. Rowan dropped his sword and caught her up.

"Alorie . . . Alorie . . ."

She pointed over his embrace at the dead reken. "He

wanted my head. But the other said no, his master wanted me alive.''

The gentle hand stroking her hair moved her head to pillow on his chest. "It's all right now.''

The dizziness fled. She gulped and pulled back, sudden anger flooding her. "The next time you start a fight, you're not leaving me behind! Give me a longknife and we'll stand back to back—but I'll be damned by the All-Mother if I'm going to wait in the shadows, wondering if some . . . some *thing* is going to have my head on a pike!''

Dawn filtered through the woods, and she could see his face more clearly in the graying light. The corner of his mouth twitched. "Well then,'' Rowan said, and cleared his throat. "That sounds fair enough to me.'' He leaned down and stripped a sheath off the dead reken. "Until I can get you a better blade, this should do.''

He strapped the belt around her waist after first cutting two new notches in it to fit her slender figure. He palmed the hilt of the longknife. "I may have to do some explaining to Brock, but I'm game if you are. Let's get the ponies and go home.''

She stood a second as he turned and went in the direction of the brook. The new dawning brought songbirds to life, and the quiet of the darkness gave way to a flood of chirps and scoldings. She brushed the hilt of the weapon with the palm of her hand. It sent a chill through her body, as though she had started something she might not be able to give up that easily.

Chapter 9

MEDRA FROWNED, wiping her hands on a rag hanging from one of her many apron pockets. The movement made the apron jiggle, and its contents clicked and jingled softly against one another. "I don't like what you're doing, Rowan."

The Rover man she knew as well as her own son leaned against the framing of the cooking shed and bit neatly into a crisp greenfruit. With a laugh at himself as the juice ran out of the corners of his mouth, he wiped his lips on his sleeve and grinned. "She asked—no, demanded—that she learn the weaponry."

"You drive her too hard. Every sunset, she's in here soaking her blisters, and I have to wrap her hands for her, doctor the scratches, and check her for bruises and breaks."

Rowan finished off the greenfruit and tossed the core into a basket of leavings for the swine. "She drives herself. I have nothing to do with it," he said softly, and his expression grew serious. "If she were mine, I'd wrap her in lamb's wool and wash her feet in rose-water. . . ." His voice drifted off as Medra's sharp gaze impaled him.

"And that's another matter, young Rowan! I've seen you look at her. Turn your eyes in another direction, if you know what's good for you. Brock has said nothing to me, he keeps his own counsel, but you and I both know he has plans for her."

He straightened and put his shoulders back tautly. "That I have often thought about."

Medra marked the scowl on his face as he left the cooking shed, and she dried her hands again, this time more thoroughly and with a great deal of thought.

He found her outside Stonedeep's gates, at the edge of the trampled meadow they had designated for practice grounds. She was on her stomach, reaching into a thicket, coaxing one of Stonedeep's hunting bitches to come out. He heard the pups growling at her as she did so.

He stood and just watched her, thinking that she'd changed since he found her outside Sinobel in a gray, misty morning only a month or so ago. False spring had come and gone, and spring was here in truth, as heralded by the new life she tried to coax out of the bushes to come and join her. She'd lost the soft blurring to her lines. Her face had redefined into a long oval, her nose with that determined Sergius knot on the bridge, a frown line from squinting her blue-gray eyes . . . eyes that had too often been gray lately. Her long dark cloud of hair she kept knotted tightly at the nape of her neck, despite his suggestion that she cut it off to avoid giving the enemy a handle. Her eyebrows, not arched gently, but a strong bridge across her face, had wrinkled at that suggestion. Instead, she took to wrapping it into a bun and securing it with comb and pin. She'd grown, too . . . the hand-me-down skirt Medra tailored for her now rose about her booted ankles instead of sweeping the ground. She was willowy, but he had been wrong about her. She would never be nut-brown and scratched, hardened and leathery, as the Rover women always got. No. Alorie would always have that quality about her of gentility.

He watched her now, entranced, and finally dropped to his knees beside her. "I'll get one of them out for her."

He reached toward the spotted pups, their milk-white

stomachs bulging, their blue-black eyes narrowed at him. The hunting bitch showed her fangs.

Alorie dropped her hand. She wiggled from under the brush and stood up, dusting herself off. "Leave them, Rowan."

"It's all right—she won't bite me."

"I said, leave them."

He rolled over on his back and stared at her until she dropped her gaze in shame. Her hands clutched at the sides of her full skirt. "I'm sorry."

"You miss Marshall," he said, and got to his feet.

"Always." With a sigh, she turned around and picked up her bow and quiver of arrows where she'd laid them down. She refastened the quiver on her belt. "Another dog wouldn't be the same."

The beat of wings, low and coming in over the trees, stopped her. She nocked her arrow and had her bow up before Rowan could put out a hand, as the bird glided in toward the gates of Stonedeep.

"Something for Medra's pots," Alorie murmured, and drew the bowstring back.

"No, wait! That's a messenger." Rowan stayed her, and they watched the bird circle at the gates.

With an easy, long-legged lope, he crossed the field and held up his wrist, whistling sharply. The bird screeched in response, then glided down and struck his arm, and held there tightly.

Rowan soothed the falcon's feathers. Alorie untied the scroll from his leg deftly before the hunting bird could strike at her as Rowan slipped a hood from his pockets to pull over the bird's head.

She looked at him in surprise.

He shrugged. "I always carry an extra hood and jesses with me. I'm one of the catchers."

Bearing the falcon to the gates, Rowan called out to Medra, who came and took the magnificent bird, bound for the perches. He took the scroll from Alorie and unrolled its tight body. He frowned as he read.

"What is it?"

"War on the boundaries. Rathincourt says that Dane's lands have been overrun, but the people have rallied under Daneson and are fighting back from the hills. Aquitane holds the seaport of Trela'on."

Alorie pictured the long narrow Straits cutting into the land, with Trela'on on one side and Trela'ar opposite it. "If he tries for Trela'ar, he'll run the Straits. No one will dare them without paying tribute."

Rowan nodded. "Not that anyone sails that deep now . . . not with Cornuth fallen, and Sinobel overrun. But Trela'ar is at Cornuth's back. I don't wonder that Quickentree is anxious to secure footholds. The lords, according to Rathincourt, have refused thus far to swear allegiance to Aquitane on the basis of his claim to be the heir of Sinobel." A wry smile twisted the corner of his mouth. "Though our friend says that several are flirting."

"That's a dance that will never grow out of style." Alorie moved away from him and chewed on the corner of a fingernail, unaware of the look of amusement Rowan wore at her words, spoken like a true Sergius.

His amusement faded quickly as he finished the scroll. "Rathincourt has word of armies massing."

"Whose?"

"He doesn't know. One is pitched at the edge of the desert. One is said to be spearheading downward from Sinobel."

"We know whose forces that will be."

"If Rathincourt doesn't know, neither do we."

"It has to be the Corruptor!"

"It could be dwarves from the Delvings. There's bad blood there, has been for centuries." Rowan tapped the scroll. "The others need to know."

"If only Brock were here."

Rowan's frown deepened. They'd not received a single message from the mage, nor had any of the Rovers scouting the various countrysides sent back word that they'd run across his sign. It was as though the mage had disappeared from all sight. It gnawed at him, for

Brock had never done that before that Rowan remembered. Still, the mage had been circumspect in his comings and goings for as long as he could remember. "And what could Brock do?"

She returned the frown. "I'm not sure . . . but spring is deepening, and then it will be summer. If I'm to regain Sinobel, we must gather the backing now. Otherwise, we'll be mired in fall rains with a long hard winter staring us in the face."

Her words brought a grin to Rowan's face, and he gripped her shoulders. "A warrior princess, eh? Now I know why you took to the longknife and the sword so well."

The moment he touched her, he sensed the quickening of her pulse. His laughter stilled in his throat, and his face bent over hers, with that sudden attraction and confidence of a man who knows he has touched a woman who wants him.

Alorie pulled away suddenly and cleared her throat. "I'd better see Madra. She'll be pleased—no blisters today." With a ruffle of her skirts, the girl slipped away from him and out of his view.

Rowan tapped the scroll against the palm of his hand. He'd known from the moment Brock told him to go and rescue her that he was facing the change of his destiny, the coming that all Rovers waited for. The evolution from a ranger back into a guard was his fate, and she was his trust, but he'd not anticipated his own emotions in the bargain. But then, who was it that said the gods diced fairly with any man's fate? By the horn, it was not the same as tumbling a wench for the pleasure of a moment . . . not the same he felt in his heart at all!

He searched for Alorie after dinner. When she told him she couldn't walk with him until her chores were done, he stood by her side, his arms thrust into foaming water to his elbows, and ignored the gibes of Medra and the others in the kitchen until Alorie was free. Medra shot him more than a gibe—a piercing look of her flint-hard eyes, which he ignored.

He escorted Alorie out of the gates, slipping through a barely opened crack. She touched the wooden stakes. "We'll have to tell the gatemaster about this. A reken could get through there easily."

"Only tonight," Rowan said. "I bribed him to leave it ajar."

"But why?"

"Because I wanted to walk with you, and there's no privacy inside. The children will be flocking about us because their mothers sent them outside to harry us."

Alorie looked up at him. She was busy taking the knot out of her hair and loosening the fall about her shoulders. She paused before dropping the comb and pin into the pocket of her skirt. "Is there news?"

"No." It stopped his words for a moment that she asked for news of Brock. He grasped at his courage, found it, and started again. The woods had darkened, and they walked slowly, without light, except for a fine sliver of a moon in the sky. "When Brock comes back, he has plans for you."

"For everyone, I'm sure."

"But it's you I'm worried about."

"Me?" She drew up opposite him and stopped in her tracks, looking puzzled. Then she smiled. "My head, you mean? I think you've been a fine swordmaster. I ought to be able to spit anyone who comes hunting for me now!"

"No," he said again, wondering how she could be so contrary to what he was trying to say without having to say it.

Alorie shook her head lightly. "I'm sorry, Rowan. I don't know what you mean."

He reached out quickly, thrusting his fingers into the cloud of her hair, tangling them at the back of her neck. He pulled her forward as he bent down and kissed her, quickly, roughly, afraid of her response.

His lips smothered a tiny gasp, then her full lips

softened and met his, kissing back. She caressed his mouth, and her body came into contact with his, a burning that met him at his knees and hugged close all the way up to his shoulders as he swept his free arm about her.

They broke apart for breath and stared at each other. Her eyes were wide, and her mouth stayed slightly parted. Then she looked at the ground. "That was a better way to say it," she murmured.

"Only if I have the right to say it."

"I'm a woman without family, lands, or dowry. Perhaps even without honor."

"Don't talk to me like that. I'm a Rover, a condemned man before I was even born, and you're the heir to the High Counselorship." Rowan spun on one heel then, cursing. He added, "Brock will have *my* head for this."

"But nothing's happened. You kissed me, that's all. If we'd met at the Maying Dance, you'd have done the same, and in a line with a dozen others."

He turned back to her. "It's not the same, and we both know it. Forgive me, Alorie, for thinking it might be." He grabbed her wrist roughly, to pull her through the woods after him, back to the safety of Stonedeep.

A rustling stopped him. He pressed a finger across her mouth, muffling her question. A large body moved, cautiously but still with noise, toward them.

In the night, a shadow loomed, large as a man, and Alorie palmed her longknife as Rowan thrust her behind him.

"Quiet, children . . . you'll wake the watch at the gate."

"Brock?" Rowan squinted into the darkness, then grinned. "What are you doing back here, and without coming into the haven? Where have you been?"

The robed and cowled figure laughed, a dry, musty noise. "Where haven't I been? On roads you couldn't have walked anyway, Rowan, or I would have sent for you."

Alorie moved out from behind him. The figure startled and then said, "What are you doing here?"

"We—ah—" Rowan stumbled, but Alorie interrupted him smoothly.

"One of the hunting dogs whelped out here. Rowan's been trying to catch me a puppy, to replace Marshall. She's gotten them well hidden somewhere."

"Ah."

"It's getting late, but I should be able to fix you a warm dinner, if we hurry. And then you can tell us where you've been, and we can tell you the news Rathincourt sent."

The mage waved a gloved hand. "No. I have other business to be about." He swung around to face Rowan more fully. "Look at me, the two of you."

As Alorie tilted her face to look at the featureless depth inside the cowl, Rowan stared into the darkness of the mage. The shadowy figure made a pass, and both froze into place.

For a long time, the mage studied them . . . studied them as though memorizing each and every feature of the two poised before him.

At last, he reached out and tweaked a lock of the girl's hair. "Perhaps I was rash asking for your head," the being murmured. "Yes. Perhaps I was too rash. Sergius or not, it's a fair countenance. Ah, Brock . . . and you would have hid her from me, if you could. And because it is no longer necessary for me to kill, old enemy, I will not. Yes . . . these two might be turned to something far more useful."

The gloved hand, smelling of something old and buried long ago, brushed across Rowan's broad shoulder. The being laughed harshly. "Beware, Brock. This one would like to steal at least one of your treasures. Puppy hunting, indeed." He stepped back and clasped his hands. "When I clap my hands, you will come awake, listening to me and to me only. You will not remember what has happened, until the time comes. Whatever Brock has spoken to you of his plans, all that has changed and must be forgotten. New plans will be forged and we will speak of them again, but whatever Brock has secreted in your minds and hearts . . . that I will sweep away, like this.'' And he passed one hand, palm outward, before them.

And with that movement, Alorie sighed. Her pledge to seek the white unicorn faded like an ill-remembered dream, as the Corruptor obscured her memory, easing her soul.

The being watched them a second longer, then added, "And if you, Brock, slippery weasel that you are, should come back against all the odds, I will leave a wedge in their thoughts about you. Yes. Just in case you slip the trap.''

The being laughed again, startling an owl, which lighted up from its branch and winged away across the woods. The Corruptor spoke, low and intimately, to the two, who, like guileless children, couldn't help listening to him.

Chapter 10

ALORIE WOKE, her heart pounding and her ears roaring. She reached out desperately for the tallow candle balanced on a crude table near her cot and warmed her palm over its bare glow. The candle had nearly burned down. She turned on her side, seeking its light desperately, her eyelids fluttering as she fought to shake off her dreams. Then she must sleep again, quickly, before the candle burned out, or she would lie afraid in the dark. She could get another candle from the storeroom, but Medra would scold her for wasting the precious commodity.

She took her hand away from the candle. Sleeping in the caves of Stonedeep was like sleeping in the womb of the earth . . . almost like being dead. All sound was muffled at night by the heavy tapestries that hung over each niche. Yet a simple hammer might send a ringing through the rock that all could hear. Just such a hammer was used for the alarm, though she'd never heard its voice.

The candleglow flared up as the flame reached the pool of tallow spread at its base, and she sat up in the bed, the furs sliding from her chest. No—it wasn't the last of the candle that lit her room . . . a star burst at the foot of her bed, its fiery glow reaching out, and out. . . .

A figure stood there. She knew him immediately, even before he pushed the hood back from his head and his dark skin gleamed. The green in his eyes sparked from the incandescence framing him.

He put a hand up in warning. "Quiet, milady. None should see me but you, and even this sending is hard for me."

"Where are you?"

He smiled gently. "Not here. I can't tell you more, I'm sorry." The figure approached her side. The signet ring on his hand glowed, the source of the light that brought him. He slid it off his finger and held it out to her. "Take this. Remember all that we talked about. You will have to begin your quest without me, and quickly. Don't hesitate, Alorie. We haven't time."

She reached for the ring. At her touch, the light enveloped her also, and for a moment the two of them were linked by more than touch. She caught pain and fear and determination and knew that he was held by an old foe, a dire enemy. She caught a glimmer of something else, and she reached for it, and was blocked immediately.

Brock smiled grimly. "My mind is not for you to know. Not yet, anyway. Wear the ring always. It will aid you. It will help you as I can't." Reluctantly, he let go and faded into darkness, as the light immediately died.

"Where are you?" she cried out, and the stern voice, faintly but clearly, answered, "Seek the prophecy graved in stone to learn what I haven't had time to teach you. Hurry!"

She put the ring on her ring hand and clutched her fist tightly so the band couldn't slip off her more slender fingers. The metal was still warm. Holding her fist to her chest, she lay back under the furs and blinked at the darkness.

Only a tiny orange glow held it at bay. Somehow, Alorie realized, that was enough. With a sigh she closed her eyes and found a peace in sleep.

Rowan came off the hunting trail, his throat tight

with anticipation, and he feared the worst as he approached the gates of Stonedeep. His catch dangled at his belt, skinned and blooded. The scent of death tingled his nerves, warning him of more. Rarely had he felt what Brock often used to. Rowan depended more on his eyes and ears and the solid feel of a sword or bow in his hand, but today, without being horned in, he knew that danger awaited him at the haven.

He broke through the grasses in the late-afternoon light, and saw an enclave waiting for him. Corey, Ashcroft, Tien, and Medra each waved an arm. Tansy was at their backs, kneeling on the soft dirt and drawing something there that Dalla nodded over earnestly. Then he saw other Rovers from other havens, travel-worn, lying on the ground, wrapped in blankets and cloaks, propped up on their elbows, talking also with Tansy and Dalla.

He swallowed the tightness down. Travelers would normally have been taken to the hot springs first, and fed, before meeting.

Medra nodded her head as he handed her the catch. Ashcroft clapped his shoulder. "We were just about to sound the horn."

"What is it? This looks like a council of war."

"Worse." He waved his hand. "Gather, fellow Rovers, in the grove. We have a table prepared for you."

Alorie sat alone at the table, her back ramrod-stiff, her hands knotted upon the tabletop. As he stepped around her to the opposite side, she flashed a look at him of anger and fear. She knew nothing more than he did, he decided, and he seated himself.

She poured him a cup of cool spring water and pushed it across as the other Rovers, some of them tousle-headed with napping, came to the council. He drained the cup, hoping to ease the lump in his throat, but though the dryness of past days' hunt washed away, the anxiety did not. He poured himself a second helping from the pitcher and drew it close, and forced himself to wait. Medra returned from the cooking shed, wiping her hands on one of the rags hanging from her apron. She would not meet his eyes as she took a seat on the bench at the table's end.

Ashcroft cleared his throat. "We had a messenger this morning, and today many of you came into our gates at the haven of Stonedeep, having been sent here by a similar messenger days ago. We have been forgotten these many decades by the fellowship at Veil—cast out, dishonored, family and lands taken from us. Yet something has occurred in this last fortnight which jogs their memory. They've sent for us to gather and wait, for one of them will appear and talk with us."

Corey ran his hand through his pewter-colored hair. "They do us too much honor," he said, and irony flavored his words.

Medra snorted. She crossed her legs, and her apron chimed softly to the movement.

Rowan looked at Alorie, but she'd withdrawn her hands from the tabletop and balled them in her lap. The bridge of her Sergius nose was pinched white, and she frowned slightly as she watched Ashcroft intently. She'd not taken in her hair yet that day, and the fragrant drift of it seized his gaze. He suddenly desired to take hold of it and draw her close as he had that spring night not too many days ago, when they had walked and talked and kissed, and last spoken to Brock on his mysterious path which took him away from them again. He sighed, then looked up, his unspoken thoughts having interrupted Ashcroft.

His brother looked at him solemnly, then the corner of his mouth quirked. The Rover held out a tiny silver bell. "I am instructed to ring this three times, and a member of Veil will come to tell us grave news, and we will make decisions here. I am also told that none of this would have been necessary had the heir to the High Counselorship of Sergius been taken to Veil, as she should have been."

A faint murmur paused him again. Tansy, her usually

cheerful face solemn, bent to the table, using a small dagger to clean her nails.

"Shall I ring the bell or shall we hear news of the road first?"

"Let the mages at Veil stew in their own juice," Tien said. His slant lids could not conceal the angry flash of his eyes. "They've had no use for us before. Dalla and Tansy bring word that we should hear first."

"That's right," Corey seconded, his deep voice rolling out of his slender chest. "News of the road. We Rovers must look to our own."

Ashcroft inclined his head briefly. "Then let's hear it."

"I found signs of a battle along the Paths of Sorrow." Tansy plunged her dirk into the wooden table. "Not fought with sword or bow, but with fire."

"Magic."

"I think so. And this was left in the ashes." She tossed out a smooth pebble, and Alorie leaned forward. She sat back as the pebble rolled belly-up to show a runic B scratched there.

Rowan couldn't control the tremble in his hands as he reached for the object and held it up. "That's Brock's, all right," he said and let it drop as though it were still warm.

Ashcroft dropped his formal phrasing. "Who else knows Brock's sign?"

Medra stretched out her hand, and the pebble was passed its way down the table to her. She winced as it dropped into her palm, then examined it. She nodded wordlessly and rolled the stone back to the head of the table.

"I'll go after him," Rowan said.

"No! You know better than that. No, Brock has chosen to do what he's chosen to do. You can't help him."

Alorie tilted her face slightly in question as Rowan looked to her and then to Ashcroft.

"He left a Rover pebble as sign. He wouldn't have done that if he didn't expect one of us to come after."

"And one of us did," Ashcroft answered calmly in the face of his brother's vehemence. "Tansy was traveling the forbidden trail."

The woman looked up. "I had reason."

"The best in the world. Dalla tells me one of your children was taken by reken raiders from the Kilarnen haven."

A strand of hair broke loose as she nodded and forced out, "I found her and brought her back. She was just a baby—" Her voice broke and she bowed her head over the dagger she had buried in the tabletop.

Medra placed her arm about the other's shoulders. "She'll be all right," the older woman soothed. "She won't remember it harshly. The mages have seen to that, and the flesh heals even faster than the spirit. She'll be all right."

Alorie shivered violently in dawning realization of what the two women talked about. "Not because of me—" she stammered.

Corey glanced at her. A vein throbbed at his bony temple. "No, girl, not because of you. Reken have been harrying us since the barrows were filled. But bear the guilt for what happened to Brock, if you want to. *That* I will blame you for."

"Enough! The Lady Alorie is our guest here."

"I consider myself one of you," she said faintly. A high blush tinged her cheeks.

Rowan slapped his hand palm down on the table. The noise startled a flight of sparrows seeking shelter in the grove at the advent of dusk. "Brock left a sign," he said. "He expected to be followed. No Rover goes down a trail alone unless he wishes it."

"I haven't given my news yet," Dalla said patiently. "Perhaps you should listen, Rowan."

He turned to her and shrugged, giving way.

"I too saw the lightnings in the sky. I was answering Tansy's call for help, though I followed a different

group of raiders. They combed the battlefields of the
Seven True Races, looking for whatever treasures they
could steal from the dead. I captured one. He'd been
seared by magefire and told me of a duel he'd witnessed
. . . and described the mage. It was Brock. It could
have been no one else."

Rowan saw Alorie's eyes widen in surprise. Few
besides himself knew that the man had few of his
powers, having been stripped of them by the council at
Veil. He reached quickly for his cup of water and
spilled it, sending a flood of water across the table
toward the girl. He stood up quickly as she jumped
away from the bench.

He bent over her skirt, pretending to pat it down,
even as she muttered, "Oh, get away. It's all right. I'm
used to being wet."

"Always on my account, right?" He stepped close
then, as she smiled, and whispered, "Brock told you of
many things that no other Rover knows," and stepped
away, while Tansy clicked her tongue and said, "I see
Rowan is making another conquest."

Ashcroft cleared his throat. The silver bell showed in
the half-light as he held it up. "I think it's time to do as
we were bid."

He rang the object three times, each chiming note
hanging on the air with a piercing tone until all three
merged together and yet hung on, a supernatural note.

Alorie seated herself again as Rowan stayed on his
feet. A black hole swirled at the head of the table.
Ashcroft staggered, as it threatened to suck him in, and
then fell back, bumping Corey's shoulder, as the Rover
reached up to steady him, and with a *whump!* something fell onto the ground.

A wiry man, bald, with a fringe of brown hair about
his pate, jumped up, dusting off his richly embroidered
clothes and suede breeches quickly.

Tien let out a low whistle and remarked, "He must
be a successful mage—or at least he seems well dressed
for his efforts!"

The mage turned about and glared at the gathering. "You waited long enough to summon me."

Ashcroft, back on his feet, bowed his head in respect. "We waited for our fellows to arrive, as your council requested, mage."

"Then I will proceed, for time is very short. We have received the word that the Corruptor has escaped the Barrowlands. This eighth day past, one of our colleagues fell in battle with the malison. We give you our condolences for the death of the man you know as Brock."

"No!"

Murmurs of disbelief turned to roars of protest as the mage spread his palms in supplication. "We found the body on the Paths of Sorrow. We know that he intended to come to us, for reasons of his own, and we share your pain. In the coming struggle against the Corruptor, he will be sorely missed."

"When?" said Alorie faintly.

"Eight days past."

"That's not—possible." Her face paled in the twilight. She put out a hand to Rowan, who caught her, and braced her swaying body as she stood. She pressed her fingers so tightly into his hand that he sucked his breath in pain and looked down to see what bruised him.

Brock's signet ring, on her slender fingers, cut into his flesh. She met his gaze with a stricken look of her own.

"Last night," she whispered, and took her hand away and tucked it in the pocket of her skirt, so that no one else might see.

The mage from the council of Veil frowned at the two of them. Medra stood briskly. "Let's get these lamps lit," she said and bent toward them.

Rowan put his arm about Alorie's shoulder, giving the impression of comforting her, while his thoughts whirled. Why would the mages of Veil lie about finding Brock's body . . . if Alorie had seen him last night and been given his signet ring? "She's faint," he said. "I'll walk her a moment. Wait for us."

He took her away from the table, and as soon as they were out of earshot, she looked up.

"He can't be dead!"

"Why would they lie?"

"I—I don't know. A sending came to me last night. He was like a shadow in a fire, but I'd swear he was alive. He left me this, and said I was to hurry with my quest, that I was to seek the engraved prophecy."

Only a little of what she said made sense. The prophecy he understood. Only a few knew it—those who had journeyed to fallen Cornuth to reach its last standing wall, whereon the words were etched. Brock knew the prophecy. Its teaching was a sacred duty. Every Rover knew of it—though few knew exactly what it said. He tucked a heavy wing of her dark hair behind her delicate, shell-like ear as she bent her head in thought. "Are you sure?"

"I know his ring. I know that I woke with it this morning."

"Then he sent it beyond death." Rowan sighed heavily. "Alorie, I don't know what plans he had for you, except that the last of the House of Sergius is one of the keys."

"Then I had better find out, hadn't I?" She gripped his arm tightly. "Take me back to the council. I want to hear what the mage has to say."

They returned to find Tien matching words with the mage, who, flushed bright in anger, had just turned to Ashcroft, demanding due respect from this motley lot of Rovers.

Ashcroft laughed without humor. "Respect is hard won from any Rover. Take it that we are ready to listen to you, and leave it at that, Cranfer."

The mage rubbed the back of his neck until the flush left his baby-round face, then took a deep breath. "Then you must all listen well. The Corrupter has risen—"

Corey snickered at that, muttering, "It was we who told you."

"—and the time has come to see if the prophecies hold true." The mage looked at Alorie and held her with his dark brown-eyed gaze. "Are you the Lady Alorie, granddaughter of Sergius the Third and daughter of Nathen Sergius?"

"I am."

"Then Brock meddled well, in that much. Had he taught you the words or said anything to you?"

"Only when he appeared in my grandfather's court and asked for me, saying that I was . . . necessary. And later, he told me to seek the engraved wall."

Tien's head snapped to attention. "A girl take the journey to Three Towers and Cornuth? It can't be done."

Tansy twisted her dagger into the wood in front of her, her hand curved tensely white about the hilt.

Cranfer's eyes took on a vivid glow and he clasped his hands together. "Not alone—no. This is what we anticipated. We have called forth a company of valiant heroes to guard her on her quest . . . the bones were rolled, the thunder read, the sacred wells looked into. There's no doubt in our mind. Alorie must seek the blade that engraved those words and then was driven into the rock, to stay until a chosen one retrieved it. That sword alone can drive the Corruptor back."

"That blade was damned."

"A traitorous weapon, yes, but its time has come to redeem itself. It failed the High King; now is the time for it to restore the High King. And the prophecies hint obscurely at the last of the House of the High Counselor to do it . . . when moon overshadows paling sun, evil everlasting shall be undone . . . or something like that." Cranfer cleared his throat. "I was never that good at memorizing."

A sense of wrongness nagged at Alorie, but as all eyes rested on her, she nodded tensely. "I'll try."

"Now for the company—"

Medra stood abruptly, interrupting the mage. "Things

of this import take time," she said. Her thin-lipped smile took the edge off her words. "Meanwhile, the gate must be closed against the night."

Dalla rose. "I'll do it, and take the first watch." She broke into an easy lope across the clearing, headed for the stockade gate, which already stood in deep purple shadows.

The Rover woman never saw the arrow that struck her, driving her back from the edge of the closure. The council of Rovers heard its whistle and the sickening thump as it pierced her body, and rose to its feet in one movement, Cranfer pushed aside, as they rushed to defend Stonedeep.

Reken whoops and snarls came out of the night. The wooden gate swung open wide, and Alorie saw dark forms boiling over Dalla's dead body. Rowan grasped her elbow as he raced past, and pulled her to her feet.

"The caves!" he yelled, drawing his sword and propelling her in the far direction.

She palmed the hilt of her longknife as she raced. Pigs squealed in their pens as reken brawled among them, their swords making short work of the noisy swine.

Medra's lean form jumped ahead of her. "The children! Keep them away from the creche!"

Alorie pulled her blade. Something dark and furry blundered into her at the caves' mouth. She drove the longknife deep, and the thing growled and tumbled at her feet. She leaped over it and joined Medra at the grate, pulling it shut across the only known entrance to the caves of Stonedeep.

Alorie took a deep breath as she sagged against the grating. Medra glabbed her by the collar and pulled her back roughly.

"Are you stupid? The grate won't stop an arrow!"

"I'm sorry. Rowan . . . Tansy . . ."

"They'll fight outside the caves to protect us. They won't come inside unless there's no way to fight free."

"If we're besieged."

"Something like that." Medra took down a large lamp, lit a small pottery one, and then blew out the larger. The tunnel dimmed instantly.

"What about the caves above?"

"None of them come through, at least as far as we know." She made a face as she warily spied on the battle outside. Alorie tried to ignore the shouts and barks and screams of pain. She concentrated on Medra's voice. "We lost a few Rovers exploring the back caves."

"Lost?"

"Forever." She patted her apron. "You stay here and guard the grating . . . I saw your work with the longknife. I need to get clean rags and needles for stitching when the wounded come in."

"All right." Alorie waited until she disappeared around the bend, then let herself go, sliding to her knees. She looked at the blood on the longknife and tried to associate it with death. A dull ringing clamored at her hearing, and then she realized it was the alarm hammer, sending its message throughout the walls of Stonedeep.

Chapter 11

MEDRA MOPPED her forehead with the back of her hand, smearing the grime and blood into a welt across her brow. "Help me drag him back into the side cave," she ordered Alorie briskly, then leaned down to a still form.

Alorie stifled a groan of weariness. The only light in the tunnels was from the tiny pottery lamps, the big lamps having been put out when the raid started. She didn't know who she grasped and dragged out of harm's way, except that he was wounded and his chest rose and fell in quiet gusts of life. She rolled him beside Tien, who wakened and tugged at the pressure bandage on his forearm.

"Hist," Medra warned. "Leave it be, Tien. You'll make it."

"The reken—"

"Have overrun everything but the main grate. Lie still. If you must use the last of your strength, save it until they breach the tunnels."

The Rover smiled weakly, nodded, and lay back. His eyes flickered shut.

Alorie caught up with the tall woman's big strides. "Will they?"

"Maybe. Maybe not. Rowan's still out there, and Ashcroft, and Tansy, and Corey. And a few of the others. Reken are stinking cowards." Medra interrupted herself with a spit to the side. "They'll not fight us if too many of them fall."

But they were still fighting, Alorie thought to herself, as she rejoined Medra at the grating. They'd been fighting most of the night. A pile of them lay to the side of the caves, and that hadn't stopped them. No, these reken weren't like the others she'd seen, slinking and cowardly. A greater purpose drove them forward, hacking away at the last defense of Stonedeep.

A slender shadow lunged at them, with a hoarse cry, even as a spear thunked into him and bore him down.

Medra cursed and bent to the grating pulley. "That's Corey! See if you can get him in!"

The Rover crawled across the bloody ground, and the meager light from the lamps showed his face etched in pain. Alorie bent double and dove out from under the grating bottom as it squeaked up. She gripped his hands and wrists.

"Help me," he said feebly and wriggled with her effort to pull him back.

Yellow fangs and gleaming eyes flashed in the night. Two reken fell on him, grasped him by the ankles, and pulled him roughly from her arms. Alorie tumbled onto her backside and sat breathless until Corey screamed.

She pulled her longknife and jumped forward, aiming by smell rather than sight. Glowing eyes dodged away from her, but she struck home, her blade skewering one of the reken. Corey kicked his body away. He rolled and kept on crawling toward the safety of the cave as the second reken snarled. Alorie took a breath as the creature hurtled through the night at her.

Her blade reflected the silvery moon a moment, and in that moment she saw the beast clearly, as though it had been the full light of day. She pivoted to her right and struck at its throat, her wrists carrying the weight of it as it impaled itself with a gurgle. She swiveled as her longknife turned, and the dead reken dropped off it onto a pile of its fellows. Without a thought, she grabbed

Corey by the collar and hauled him into Stonedeep after her.

He lay on one elbow and blinked up at her in the dim light. He smiled wanly. "That's how I like my nurses," he said, and coughed. "With teeth and a real bite to them!"

Medra ripped off his vest and tched, silencing him, as Alorie quickly lowered the grating into place. True to his heritage, the Rover had already been badly wounded. The spearhead had broken off in his collarbone, where crimson seeped out of his shirt. Medra shook her head. "You'll live, Corey, but next time don't be so heroic. Come in sooner to get patched up."

He nodded and rolled over onto his stomach so she could get at the spearhead.

Alorie's stomach turned, and she faced back to the cave mouth, unable to watch Medra work on this victim. She felt the longknife's weight still warm in her hand, cleaned it, and returned it to the sheath.

She must have slept, having fallen to her knees and slumped against the cave, for she came awake suddenly. A faraway dawn grayed the night.

More shouting. She thought she heard a horn from the direction of the stockade gates. The fighting carried on, but her mind stayed on Rowan. A flicker of weak magefire flared in the distance.

"Hello the haven!" Rowan's voice! She stumbled to her feet.

A figure reeled out of the darkness, hands clutched to his flanks. She cried aloud, "Wounded coming in," for she knew the clothing, though it was still too dark to see his face. She fell on the winch to reel the grating upward.

Medra came up behind her and she called out, "That's Rowan!"

The tall woman bent down and scrambled under the grating before she had it waist-high. Alorie cranked furiously, her face bent to her job, knowing that Medra would bring the Rover in.

She wedged the wheel and straightened, as Medra reached the staggering fighter. The figure in Rowan's clothing broke apart with a snarl and a bark. Two reken jumped out at Medra. Six more boiled out of the shadows. Their weapons glinted in the paling of the moon, and their pungent odor rolled over Alorie. Medra struggled between the two as the second swung its blade with a vicious whine.

Crimson droplets sprayed the air as Medra fell. She rolled in the trampled grass and cried out, "The children, Alorie! Go protect the children!"

No chance to drop the grate. Alorie pivoted. Reken boiled into the cave mouth, and Alorie took to her heels, with the raiders after her. She heard their footfalls. Their hot breath grazed her back, as she flung herself into the labyrinth of Stonedeep. One fell in the dirt. She heard its grunt and cry and knew one of the wounded had come alive for one last fight. She doubled her efforts, knowing she must reach the creche first, so that the women there could barricade the cave and make a stand.

Something whooshed past her shoulder. It clattered to the tunnel floor, and she kicked it as she ran over it. Metal rang out. A throwing dagger perhaps. It sent her pulse racing in her ears. She stretched out, running harder, knowing that her back represented a target the reken couldn't miss. With a gasp, she slid around a corner and doubled back into a second tunnel. For a moment, the pursers were left behind, and all she could hear was her own rasping breath and the thunder of her boots.

Once she reached the nursery chambers, she was finished. She would make her stand there. No Brock or Rowan would appear to save her. Marshall's furry body would never make a last leap to stand between her and death. She fought to swallow, her tongue like a wad of cloth in her mouth as she breathed desperately. Behind her, the tunnel filled with the barks and stink of reken again.

The stone rang with the hammer-sounded alarm, a pounding that jangled at odds with the rhythm of her pulse and her steps. She flung herself down the last corridor and filled it with her shouts.

"Raiders! Save the children!"

As she slid to a halt, lanterns flared to life, and she found herself facing the cave opening to the creche. Chairs and a table filled the opening. Beyond it she glimpsed the pale faces of the mothers, holding hoes and rakes, one a harvest scythe, their knuckles white as they gripped their weapons. Behind them, four of the older boys crouched, holding daggers and skinning knives.

Calinthia put her hand to her mouth. "Alorie! Have they broken in?"

Alorie nodded. The women began to dig down the barricade, to let her in, and she waved frantically at them. "No! Leave it up! I'll fight out here."

"But milady—"

No time. A dirk whistled through the air, digging into a chair leg next to her shoulder. Alorie grabbed a kettle lid from the barricade and turned around to meet the reken, her longknife in the other hand.

A second dagger clanged off the pot lid as she faced the raiders. In the glow from the nursery, she saw her enemy clearly for the first time in the light.

She shuddered. Not human, no never, not even close to human. Feral and rank, they slowed, watching her, their eyes aflame with the excitement of the chase and the kill. Two of them dropped to all fours, long-backed and supple, their flanks heaving as a low snarling filled the chamber. She closed her eyes briefly, then forced herself to watch as they took stock of the tunnel and the barricade.

The leader reared back up to its full height. Blood and grass stained its studded leather armor. A crimson ax filled a loop on its belt, but it carried a sword now and tossed it lightly from hand to hand, licking its fangs as it watched her.

It waved an arm to the reken behind it. "Get the girl

first," it ordered, its voice harsh in the silence. "Then we'll get the meat."

Alorie clenched her teeth in horror. They referred to the children as meat! Sweat poured down her forehead, and she wiped it quickly on her sleeve, dropping back into a fighting stance. She'd missed a drop, and felt it trace its way from her eyebrow down her temple, where it hung wetly on her cheekbone. Then his words struck her. The reken had come after her. Would not even have followed her to the creche, except that she'd led them. She forced the thought away, but it kept returning.

The reken leader grinned, opening its jowls wide, its red tongue lolling out. "Where's your armor, warrior? We shall go for your knees first—are you ready for us?"

Alorie fought to keep her hands from trembling as the reken fanned out behind their leader. She scanned the group and saw no bows, so she was relatively safe for the moment. Then, boldly, she picked the dagger out of the chair leg and the second one off the ground, and tossed them back over the barrier to Calinthia, who wiped them off before handing them back to the older children.

The reken leader laughed. "You are bold, girl. I shall call you Little Tooth in honor of your longknife."

Human words sounded unspeakable in its throat, oiled and harsh, but she understood it well. She put her chin up. "I bite."

The reken laughed louder, its furred russet chest rippling with its humor. "We shall see!" It waved one of the raiders to her left. The reken dropped to all fours and leaped, snarling, at her.

Alorie moved to her left, as Rowan had taught her, but kept her guard on the right as well. Her longknife glinted as she saw a shadow there, twisting toward her. She lashed out, pushing her shield into the attacker on her left as she cut to the right.

The first reken fell, its snarl gurgling into silence, and she kicked it solidly, the body flipping over and thudding into the cave wall. The second had somersaulted back from her block and rejoined the raiding party, blood seeping from its muzzle.

The leader stamped a foot. "Well done, Little Tooth! You know us well."

Alorie stopped listening, realizing the reken baited her, trying to distract her. She gripped the kettle lid tighter, aware of just how frail a shield she held. But one lay dead, and a handful faced her . . . though she could hear shouts now in the corridors, human voices mingled with high-pitched whines and snarls.

The reken heard too, their short ears flicking forward and back. The leader barked something in its throat and they surged forward, Alorie stepping back until the chairs and table gouged her back. She could never keep all of them at bay. She gripped the longknife tighter. A vision of All-Mother flickered through her thoughts, and she wondered if her soul would be harvested by her soon, or if she would lie fallow in the dirt, waiting.

She parried the first blow and dodged a second, meeting a third with her blade, as Calinthia called out behind her. A reken fell, one of their own daggers buried in its chest, and a Rover boy shouted triumphantly, "I got 'em!"

No time to think. Her arm wove a deadly dance, each glancing blow sending a thrum of pain into her shoulder, as she gritted her teeth and met the reken attack. Her skirt ripped and she stumbled over the hem, and the shield clattered away from her arm as an ax tore at it. She jumped back, panting, and saw the reken faces snarling in front of her.

The leader raised its sword in half-salute. "You fight well, Little Tooth, but now it's time—" Its voice broke off in a gargle of pain, and it doubled over, a battle-ax sunk deep into its back.

The remaining reken whirled in their tracks. Alorie stumbled forward, stabbing at the flank of one of them. It turned back to her, met her blade, and they fought furiously, while the other two jumped at a second foe.

She caught a glimpse of a tall, brawny fighter swinging a broadsword as her reken went to its knees, the longknife in its throat.

She pulled the knife free as reken heads rolled, and she and the unknown warrior stood in crimson dirt, staring at one another.

The warrior grinned and bounded over the fallen bodies, to grasp her in an immense hug and twirl her around, his laughter echoing. "What a woman!"

Her senses whirled as the breath crushed out of her. The swordsman released her as she gasped. His chest was nearly bare, covered with vest and studded armor, and only wristlets protected his vast arms. He wore breeches, and leggings, and shin guards of worked bronze from ankle to knee. His hair, held back by a leather thong, curled in ringlets of sable about his ears, the same color as the hair that curled profusely on his chest and over his arms. He smelled of smoke and grass and horses, and though blood splashed him, he seemed unhurt.

He took in her assessment of him with the same broad smile. "They call me Gavin. The mages sent to my holdings, saying there was need of a hero, and a quest to fallen Cornuth. I could do no less than answer. And you, Rover woman? We could comfort each other, if only for a night, before I give my allegiance to the girl I'm to protect."

Alorie staggered back and sat, unexpectedly, in one of the chairs used for a barricade. The longknife drooped in her hand. She searched for words.

Another shadow ranged up behind Gavin . . . a strong, slender form, with dark hair that the lampglow tinged with fire. Her heart skipped a beat as she struggled to her feet.

"Rowan!"

A blanket flapped about him, wrapped about his body. His bare arms and torso looked pale next to the magnificent bulk of Gavin, but Alorie thought she'd never seen a more beautiful sight than the half-naked

Rover who jumped fallen reken to pull her from the
barricade. This embrace was one that didn't dance her
about, but pulled her tight as though he might never let
go, even in death. Rowan breathed, finally, in her ear,
"You're safe."

She answered, tightening her own grip about him.

Cranfer's hand shook as he mopped his brow. He sat
in a high-backed chair and wrinkled his nose as the
burial fire of reken grew higher and higher outside the
Stonedeep gates. But even the stink didn't take away
the mage's pleased look. "Our call for champions proved
timely," he said yet again.

Gavin flexed his massive shoulders and tried to look
humble as Medra, her forehead bandaged tightly against
the flesh wound she'd received, poured him another
goblet of mead. He downed the drink.

In addition to Gavin, four newcomers sat at the haven
table, each from a far-flung region of the Seven True
Races. They and their men had fought through the siege
at the gates, breaking the reken at last. Rowan had told
a story, amusing now, of being waylaid and knocked
cold, to wake up finding himself stripped of all but his
boots (which reken couldn't wear) and his knit drawers.
He fought his way into the caves wearing nothing more
but the addition of a tattered blanket. Tien asserted that
the reken laughed themselves to death.

Rowan sat quietly now, his fingers laced tightly with
Alorie's, their hands held under the table. She felt his
warmth as she leaned against him, though he was dressed
now, as though she could feel the heat of his bare skin.
Every nerve in her tingled alive. Cranfer kept shooting
her glances to see if she was alert and listening to his
babble about the long road to Cornuth.

Cranfer ticked off his fingers. "We have Gavin
Bullheart, son of Flaxendown, the farmland heart of our
lands."

"Where, no doubt," Tien whispered, "they used
him to plow rather than horses or oxen."

Ashcroft hid a snicker in his goblet. Gavin turned and smiled at Alorie, having not heard, with a childlike look of pleasure and pleading on his face. She ducked her face.

"From Bylantium, seaport and bazaar of the thousands, comes Duke Lathum."

A thin, sallow-faced man bowed, his lanky brown hair flopping over his brow, hiding the scars of acne that pitted his face. He added, "I'm a trader and a sailor, not a hero . . . but I think I may be of some use."

Rowan stirred. He whispered in Alorie's ear, "I know him. He's a good man. Quick with a sword and even-tempered."

A round-shouldered black man nodded at his name, "Crust, of Sobor, sent by Lord Rathincourt, for the aid of Lady Alorie."

He flexed his shoulders. The broadcloth shirt strained and rippled. "I'm a farrier, milady. Good with animals and hot metal. The Lord Rathincourt apprenticed his son with me, to teach him silence and discipline."

Alorie smiled widely, liking Crust instantly. Then she added, "But where's his lordship?"

Cranfer, frowning at the interruption, said, "He's raising an army, such as it is."

Sobered, she sat back and listened to the rest. Kithrand she already knew, but the elven titles Cranfer rolled off his tongue at the elf lord's introduction set her aback a little. She'd no idea that Kithrand was so ranked among the elves. She felt a little awed, until the lord caught her glance and gave a roguish wink.

The silver-haired lady sitting at the end of the table turned her pointed chin quickly to interrupt Cranfer. "I am Viola, a mage and a weaponmistress. I rode the leagues to gather up these heroes, and I am inclined, having viewed the Lady Alorie, to stay on and finish the job."

Alorie looked at the mage, startled by the dulcet

tones, thinking of the needlelike claws hidden within a cat's velveted paws. The woman had never struck her as a mage . . . she resembled the fallen Dalla, lean, quick, dressed in breeches and shirt like a ranger. The woman caught her staring and smiled, a curve of thin lips that did nothing to warm her violet eyes. Alorie shivered and looked away.

Cranfer made a tower of his fingers as he put his hands together. "That's five."

"I'm going," Rowan stated.

"You're a Rover. You've been exiled from the duty of a guard."

"Then you'll need a scout. Either way, I'm going. Don't forget, mage Cranfer, that the Lady Alorie's very needs herald the return of my people to their lost honor."

"Perhaps." The mage let the word linger before he began to speak again, but a deep bass voice cut through his words.

"And there's me."

Alorie jumped to her feet, jostling Rowan, who groaned slightly. "Pinch! Is that you?"

The dwarf climbed onto the bench's end, his cheeks flushed with pleasure. "Aye, milady. I heard the news and rode here as fast I could, though by the looks of the bodies stinkin' outside your gates, not fast enough. Forgive me."

Kithrand stood and pushed away from the table. "I'll not travel with a dwarf," he said in a tight voice.

"Hist," Pinch answered. "And who said I wanted to travel with a flighty elf? But it's the lady I'm worried about."

The elf lord's antennae danced in agitation, and he flung his silken cloak over his chest, the end flipping over his left shoulder. "Their hearts are as black as the bowels of the earth they mine."

"Say you. But I say the word of an elf is like the fluff of a seeding flower, pretty to look at, but gone the minute an ill wind begins blowin'. Men are nothing to elves, say I. Here today and gone tomorrow, begging your pardon, Alorie.''

Kithrand drew in a deep breath, about to argue further, and Alorie interrupted.

''I say, with the Corruptor freed, that the Seven True Races have to stick together. You're both friends of mine and I need your help.''

The elf faced her. His antennae jiggled quietly to a stop, and he looked somberly at the tabletop. ''Very well,'' he announced. ''But I warn the dwarf to keep his distance from me.''

Pinch laughed. ''Never fear.'' He placed his ax on the table, a big beefy weapon that even Gavin admired. ''Now let's plan the road.''

Rowan drew Alorie to her feet and away from the questers as they leaned over the tabletop, looking at a parchment Cranfer unrolled. He walked stiffly from the flank grazing he'd received, but he adjusted his gait to hers. At the gates, he stopped and turned to her. ''I know a sun-warmed pond, with sweet grass to lie on, and thick woods to guard.''

His eyes asked her more than his words did, and she looked into his face hesitantly. She touched his forehead gingerly, where a red-and-purple bruise mottled his scalp.

''I thought you died last night, and I didn't know what to do.''

''And I thought the raiders had plowed through you like kindling and I was going to pull the hearts out of every one of them.''

''Really?''

''Once I got my clothes back.''

She laughed as he made fun of himself, then put her finger over his lips. ''Is this pond a place where we can be alone?''

''Very.''

She knew for sure then what he asked of her, and warmth flooded her body. ''I never—''

This time he hushed her. ''I know,'' he said. ''And

I'm not sure we will .. but I know I want to be alone with you, just for a while . . . before things change so much we'll never have the chance again.''

Alorie leaned against his chest and gave him her hand, and answered softly, "Then take me with you.''

Chapter 12

KITHRAND REINED his stumbling horse to a halt and leaned over its lathered withers. "We'll be at the barrows in the morning."

Alorie shivered in spite of herself as her horse fetched up against Kithrand's and she fought to halt it. To no one in particular, she said, "Do we have to go through the barrows?"

"It's the only way to get to Cornuth from this direction."

The elf lord frowned, his antennae knitting close together. "The horses are nearly done for. We'd best camp tonight."

Alorie felt the trembling of her beast under her and knew that Kithrand had run his horses close to death, to make the time they needed. These tall, fine-boned animals, twelve in all, had been brought by Kithrand for the company to ride, cream of color and blue-eyed. They snorted at the touch of mortal hands upon their flesh. The extras carried packs, a burden they accepted no more readily than men. She dropped a hand to hers and stroked its neck gently.

The faery horse shook its head and ceased its trembling. Its nostrils cupped wine-red against the chilled late-spring wind as Rowan nudged his mount close to hers.

Gavin shook his head and gathered his reins. A crude fur rested upon his shoulders, his only concession to the biting wind. He looked at Rowan with a frown. "Give me the word, milady, and we'll spend the night at Sinobel. I'll clear it for you.''

Viola laughed sharply. The big farmer squared his shoulders and pretended not to hear her tone.

A sudden vision of the circled city strewn with death made Alorie clutch her reins tightly. Rowan kneed her leg. ''I won't let you go back,'' he said.

She opened her eyes and saw the look in his, once so frightening and now so welcome. It warmed her.

Viola kicked her horse, and it surged between their two mounts. The silver-haired woman with the young face tossed her head and eyed her coldly. ''A storm is brewing,'' she said. ''And my skill tells me that it is sorcery-sent. We would be very wise to take shelter immediately . . . an ice storm in these woods could be the death of us all.''

''I agree,'' Kithrand said. He looked at Rowan.

The Rover inclined his head slightly. ''Then I have scouting work to do. Pinch!''

The dwarf, a tiny man hunched on the withers of the white faery horse, waved a gnarled hand. He pulled out of the rear, where he was as far from the elf lord as he could ride. The two joined together and rode down the forest, while the remaining riders bunched together.

The cold wind grew even more chill, and Alorie pushed her chin into the collar of her fur, seeking to warm her breath. Gavin pulled his sword halfway from the immense sheath on his back, then took his hand down, his eyes traveling alertly over the expanse of forest.

In the four days past, his blade had come between Alorie and reken three times. There was no doubt he was born to fight; and in her he'd found his cause. Yet, it troubled her. She'd never seen herself as a symbol for which men might die, and the role bothered her, yet Gavin would not be turned aside. Kithrand had finally taken her hand and told her quietly that men need a cause, and that she would wound him worse if she denied it to him. Yet, even as they stood bunched now in the woods, listening to the wind whistle about them as though seeking them, she could feel his eyes upon her, always watching.

Duke Lathum's voice reached her, as he told a story to Crust and Viola. "So the woman returns to the wizard to have her fortune told, and he tells her, 'Madam, I have bad news and worse news.' 'What is the bad news?' she asks, and the wizard replies, 'You have one day to live.' 'By the All-Mother,' the woman shrieks, 'what could be worse news than that?' And the wizard replies, 'I was supposed to tell you yesterday!' "

Crust laughed in his rich baritone, and even Viola chuckled. Alorie found herself grinning, though her teeth grew cold at the baring of them. The sallow-faced duke had proved to have quite a sense of humor, and was a fair juggler to boot, though Alorie often wondered what possessed him to become a party to her quest.

Thunder rumbled darkly overhead. She could feel the heaviness of the air and looked up through spread green branches to see the boiling clouds overhead.

Kithrand ducked his head under his cloak. "Here it comes!"

The pelting drummed the trees and leaves, silver pebbles raining, muffled a little underfoot. One of them stung Alorie's hand, and she yelped. The faery horse threw up its head in protest as the hail poured down all around them.

Crust fought his mount for control. It backed under a wide-spread evergreen, which shielded it from most of the hail, though the tree's needles looked sprinkled with gems. The dark man glowered up at the sky. "Never heard of hail this late in the year."

Viola's eyes snapped darkly. "It will be worse," she promised, "unless the Rover finds us shelter."

"Never count on a Rover and a dwarf," Lathum warned. He held his cloak up with both arms, tenting himself and his horse. "Begging your pardon, milady," he said to Alorie as she swung to face him abruptly.

She opened her mouth to protest the slur, then re-membered her own grandfather's feelings about Rovers. She closed her lips tightly and kicked her faery horse closer to Kithrand, who had also sought shelter under a pine.

The pelting stones paused, then stopped. Thunder rattled the skies again. Alorie rubbed her horse's shoulder, where a glancing hailstone had cut the flesh and a tiny droplet of blood welled up. As she looked about, the white stones littered the ground, some as large as her fist. She wondered if Viola was right, and if some mage had sent the storm after them on purpose. Who could be powerful enough to control the weather? She shivered, wishing again for an uncountable time that Brock had lived to guide her.

The trees shook. Rain began again, cold rain, and the wind whistled down. The sky filled with sleet that hung off the trees in sheets, freezing where the wind touched it. Viola cursed and kicked her horse out of shelter.

"Move, now, or we'll be frozen here in our tracks!"

Gavin kneed his horse to the fore of Alorie. "I'll breast the worse for you, milady," he said. Kithrand let him ride by, and then followed. The howling wind grew louder until they had to shout to hear one another, as the ice and snow came down, blanketing them even as they forged ahead in it.

Alorie narrowed her eyes against the blast. It stung and bit at her, snow-wasps, until her nose went numb and her hands felt as though they could crack.

Ice hung off the furred shoulders of Gavin, who continued to grin into the wind as though it was his destiny being handed to him on a silver platter. His faery horse put its head down, and whinnied now and then as though in pain. Its hooves slid for footing as the sleet mounded up, and the ground became icy.

Alorie lurched and tumbled headfirst when her horse went down under her, squealing and kicking. A hoof grazed her, and she ducked and scrambled away from it. The horse flailed to regain its feet. Kithrand spoke a soothing word, and the creature quieted, then gathered itself and stood.

She heard a sharp crack in the woods behind her and twirled, hoping to see Rowan or Pinch rejoining them. Instead, a black shadow loomed out of the white blizzard, and she let out a scream as it raised an equine head and the spiral length of its horn pierced the wind.

The black unicorn's eyes blazed. It reared, snorting, hot breath a gusty steam upon the frozen air. The storm lulled slightly. Viola hissed a word, then her voice fell to low chanting. Alorie guessed she prepared a spell, and backed up, away from the black beast, as its forelegs touched ground again. It pawed up a mound of ice and trumpeted angrily.

It charged at Alorie. Duke Lathum passed her by with a swoop, his sword out, yelling, his cloak snapping at his back. The faery horse slewed to a stop. It frantically tried to pivot and run as the dark unicorn swerved and found a new target. Alorie stumbled backward, and Kithrand grabbed her arms and threw her upon her horse any which way, where she tried to straighten herself.

The swarthy man laughed. His voice sounded brittle in the frozen landscape. "This beast is worth a fortune in Bylantium!" he called. "Leave it to me!"

The dark unicorn pulled up, half reared, and charged again. Lathum switched his sword to his left hand and pulled out a loop of gleaming rope.

"An elven catch," Kithrand said, under his breath. "The man's a fool to try to capture that demon! Lathum! Don't try it!"

Alorie shoved her boots securely into her stirrups. The storm let up, and snow flurried gently about them. The duke urged his mount to meet the black creature's fury.

She screamed, and the duke turned toward her. The wind drowned her words, ripping them away from her as though never spoken. "The horn! Look out for the horn—"

Lathum twisted back to meet the unicorn, his face in a fierce kind of joy as he stood in his saddle and twirled the golden rope about his head. The white blizzard cloud half obscured the unicorn, but Alorie knew well the terrible length of the beast's horn, though it was barely visible. Lathum seemed unworried. He let go of the loop too late, a gasp hissing from his slack lips as the horn pierced his body through, lifting him from his horse's back as though he'd been lanced.

The unicorn plunged to a halt, heavy hindquarters bunched under him. His proud neck bulged, but he carried the man's weight on his horn. Lathum squealed, hands and feet kicking.

His death agony echoed in the woods. "My God!" he cried. "Save me! Kill me first!" he pleaded, waving his thin arms, dancing in the air. Then his body jerked to a final spasm.

Alorie looked away, licking her iced lips. When she looked back, the unicorn had lowered its head, dumping the body onto the ground. With a growl, the beast tore at the dead man's throat.

Kithrand gasped. He slapped Alorie's mount. "Get out of here! Now!"

Viola sat with pale face, her spell long since finished and useless, her hands slack upon the reins. The elf lord spurred to her side and shook her. "Ride! Now, while we can!"

Crust brushed past them, caught up Alorie's reins. "Let's go, milady!"

They passed Gavin, who sat transfixed, his sword in his hands. His wide eyes took in the sight of the blood-drinking, flesh-eating unicorn. His blue lips trembled, but he stammered, "Give the order, and I will slay it for you."

"I order you to run," Alorie managed. "Like the rest of us!" She whipped speed out of her horse, as the icy wind slapped at her face once more.

They ran for it, the howling wind tearing at them and the rain coming down, frozen into arm-long icicles on the trees. Branches cracked and fell from the weight about them, and yet, borne under the ice storm, she thought she could hear yet the growling and slurping of the unicorn as it devoured its victim.

Chapter 13

THE SCREAMS OF AGONY and smell of fresh blood lent wings to the faery horses. They plunged headlong into the blizzard, which picked up new strength and pelted them again with rain that froze in curtains of ice wherever it touched.

Alorie pulled her furred cloak up to the bridge of her nose and blinked painfully against the cold wind. Her lashes felt stiff. Kithrand pulled his horse to a sudden halt as a blackness loomed against the pale fury of the ice storm. His horse slewed to its hindquarters, forelegs pawing the air in protest.

Crust put himself between the elven lord and Alorie, as she stood in the stirrups to see what accosted them from the woods.

"Kithrand! Hold your bow!"

It was Rowan's voice, strained and nearly drowned out by the storm, but Alorie pulled her fur down and grinned. The darkness sorted itself out into the man and the dwarf and neither dwarf nor elf seemed to notice that they halted side by side on the trail.

"You're running into the storm," Rowan said. His breath gusted in white clouds.

"We have reason," Kithrand answered shortly. He held his hands up to his face and breathed, warming his lips, nose, and antennae. "A black unicorn stalks the trail behind us."

"Ye've seen it." Pinch took his knit cap off his blond head, knocked the ice off it, and replaced it.

"It skewered Duke Lathum, and we left it devouring its prey."

"Devouring—" Rowan curbed his horse to a stand-still, wind and blizzard or no.

"Did you find shelter?" Viola asked impatiently. The cold had washed her face of what little color it had, the flesh tones grayed like the silver of her hair. Only her eyes remained alive.

"No. But we know where we can go, if there's no turning back."

Pinch's cheeks burned red. "No!" he protested. "I'll no let the lady go in there."

"We haven't any choice." Rowan looked over the group. "We're leaving the trail and turning northwest. Stay close to my horse's crupper—we can't go after those lost in the storm."

"Where is it," Alorie asked slowly, "that Pinch is afraid of?"

"The Delvings."

Kithrand's head swiveled to the unseen range of mountains. "The true races have had no allies from there in my lifetime."

His words fell among them in the strange quiet, for the storm had lulled as though it, too, listened to the elf lord.

"Rovers have been in, and out again. There's no-where else to go if the dark beast cuts off our retreat."

Pinch shook his head. "Better to be in the open. Down in the Delvings, there's nothing but darkness and old stone, wicked stone, laid open by greedy hill dwarves. I like to see what I'm fighting!"

"So do we all," Gavin said. Ice glazed his fur, and his lips shone bluish in the half-light. "But with the Corruptor free, old wounds should be healed. I say we take the chance—staying out here will be the death of us all!"

Viola nodded briskly, and Kithrand kneed his pony to

join Rowan at the fore. Pinch's silver eyes gazed deep into Alorie's face, and then he looked away, ashamed.

He did not turn his horse to follow after until all the others passed him.

Kithrand dropped back and talked to Viola in low, eager tones, which Alorie only half caught, as the wind tore them away. The snow and rain stopped. The trail turned to a slick and dangerous slush under the horses' hooves as the elf lord tried to convince the mage to try her powers against the weather.

Viola shook her head. ". . . each has certain talents . . ."

Kithrand pressed. "Can't take no for an answer."

"—disaster—"

"Then why are you riding with us?" Kithrand's voice rose in anger.

Viola looked over her shoulder and saw Alorie watching them. She pulled her hood and cloak tightly over her hair and faced back away. "I have my time," she said, and reined her horse away from Kithrand abruptly, even as the faery horse whinnied in protest.

The hail pelted them ceaselessly. The rain gave way to ice in the chilled wind as they left the forest and began to climb across barren hills toward the mountains of the Delvings. The faery horses nickered in shrill pain, and their cream coats became splashed with crimson welts. Alorie put her arms up for protection until her wrists were as battered as an old shield, and she no longer cried out, for each new hit was a welt on top of an old wound.

Suddenly, the wind stopped, as they crested a ridge. The hail clattered and rolled away, white rock on a brown hill, and melted into rivulets.

Viola, a large bruise the size of a hand under her right eye, tilted back her head, then slowly dropped her hood as she looked into the sky. "We're out of his range," she said slowly.

Kithrand jumped from his mount. He walked from horse to horse, touching their muzzles softly and speaking a gentle word to the beasts, for the animals had taken the worst beating of all. Alorie felt hers tremble at the elven lord's touch, but when he moved on, the horse held his head a little higher and his trembling stopped.

The sharp-eared lordling stopped finally at Viola. He looked up at her, saying, "I suppose healing is not one of the talents you possess either."

She glared down at him, and pink stained her otherwise pale face. Then she answered, "As a matter of fact, it is a borderline ability." As she rocked back in the saddle, she began a chant. Each word was precise, though Alorie could not have repeated it, the sound dropping into the quiet day as a pebble is dropped into a spring, and the ripples of the magic ebbed over all of them.

When she had finished, she slumped over the withers of her mount, and Kithrand reached up quickly to steady her. Viola pulled away. "Leave me alone!"

Kithrand, his mouth twisted in a bitter smile, returned to his horse and swung up. Crimson no longer stained the faery horses, but welts still webbed across their hides. "Ah, well," he said heavily. "Half a healing is better than none."

And Alorie stretched. She felt stiff and bruised, though better. She looked at the mage. She wasn't sure if she had truly been partially healed or if Viola had manipulated time, and her wounds were now several days older and more bearable. Had they stood frozen on the ridge while the days passed?

Her glance flickered down into the woods, where ice still blanketed the ground. No, her mind told her. It's not possible. Yet . . .

Gavin rode near and flashed a smile. "Have you ever had a stone from the dwarven mines, milady?"

"No." Her horse fell in next to his mount.

"I've seen one or two. It will be my pleasure to see if I can get you one."

Pinch twisted in his saddle. "Touch nothing down

there! The land is cursed. The stone, the metal, every-thing! Touch nothing, take away nothing."

Gavin nodded indulgently toward the dwarf, but he looked back to Alorie. She shrugged. "Give Pinch his due," she told the swordsman.

Gavin touched his hand to the hilt of his sword and then to his forehead in quiet obedience. She kicked her horse and rode forward, aware that his eyes burned at her back.

The sun was dipping toward the far horizon when they paused on a ridge and Rowan dismounted, eying the two forks of the mountain pass he'd chosen. The wind had risen again and tore viciously at his cloak, worrying it like a dog with a bone. Viola had spoken only once, and that was to say the storm tracked them, and they would soon be caught up in it again.

Crust spoke, rare words from the quiet, dark black-smith. "The pathway remains unchanged."

"Maybe not. If we go down there, we can skirt both the Delvings and the Barrowlands, until we reach the Eye of Cornuth. Then the only way through is at the Barrowend, where the Despot rests." Rowan rolled the leather reins in his hand. "It's a treacherous way."

Kithrand slid down to the ground. "Then let an elf skim it, and see if it's fit for travel!" He was gone, in a flash of gray and green, hardly seen.

Gavin got down too. With his short sword, he hacked at dry bushes, gathering wood for torches. Pinch watched him warily.

"I'll no be a-traveling at night."

Rowan looked at him, and his expression was one of anger. "You'll do what you have to to escort the Lady Alorie."

Pinch blanched. He closed his lips tightly. Then he said, "None of you know what you're riding into. None of you!" With that he reined off the trail and sat, his back stiff as a poker, refusing to talk to anyone.

Viola dismounted, staggering with weariness and catch-ing herself on the stirrup. She smiled vaguely when she caught Alorie watching her. She waved. "Get down yourself, and get your sea legs. Riding all day is hard on you."

Alorie shook her head. From the ache in her ankles, she doubted she could stand if she got down. "I'm fine," she said.

A shout from down the mountain drowned her reply, and then sharp howls. Rowan and Gavin both vaulted to their horses, but Viola had trouble holding hers still, for it began to circle in fear, as the eerie belling grew louder and louder.

"Reken," Gavin said girmly, as he pulled his sword out.

"No," Rowan told him. "Wolves, maybe."

Kithrand raced up the ridge, his white-blond hair streaming behind him. "Run!" he shouted. He whistled sharply for his mount.

Crust reached down and with one hand picked up Viola and threw her across her mount's back. Alorie's horse reared and bolted toward the Delvings, down the far purple side of the ridge, as the shadows of dusk reached for her.

A flash of eyes, and a dark furred body leaped at her, and red-gummed fangs snapped. She kicked, hard, though the movement tore her boot loose from the stirrup. She fell forward suddenly, pitching onto her horse's withers. The wolflike creature yelped and rolled into the dirt. She thought of the courier they'd killed in the forest outside Stonedeep, who'd been warped and twisted, and fought to regain her stirrup.

The beast she'd kicked down wore leather armor.

She straightened in the saddle long enough to pull her longknife free. No one ran ahead of her; all the others pounded at her heels. She gripped the faery horse tightly as it gathered its stamina for the headlong race down the mountainside.

Like a white cloud, they blew down off the peaks, she and Kithrand's magical horse, and the howling gained at their heels. She hacked down one creature and ducked as another leaped, sailing past her shoulders. Its foul stench wafted over her. Not Mutt, not wild dog, not wolf. Corrupted.

Pinch's mount drew even, bearing its lighter load. The dwarf clutched the white mane dearly. His ax, bloodstained, rode with him. He looked to her, as black soot and orange flames stained the edge of dusk ahead.

"The Delvings! And the gates are closed."

A horn blasted down the pass, and Pinch cursed, then added, "Milady, they're already under attack!"

She remembered the rumor of an army massing at the edge of Sinobel. "There's no choice."

A maw widened at the pit of the pass. Great stone teeth closed that maw, and through its gap, she sensed an army kneeling, bows in hand, glittering by torch-light, looking down the pass. The faery horse jumped, sailing over a body. As she looked, she saw the familiar reken sprawled beneath in ebony-shadowed dirt.

"Open the gates!" Pinch cried out. "Auld heim! Open the gates!"

The white horses flew downward toward the gate. Either they would open, or the company would be smashed by their momentum upon the stone teeth. Their hoofbeats drummed in a deafening echo.

She saw a flurry of action throughout the parapets cut into the mountainside.

Pinch roared, his mountain dwarf's bass voice unmistakable. "Open up, I say, for the House of Sergius!"

With that, the legions of reken waiting in the mountain pass came to their feet, howling. Arrows hissed into the air, and Alorie ducked over the neck of her horse as they narrowly whizzed past her.

The stone jaw began to inch open.

"That does it," Pinch muttered. "Now hang on, milady!" His fear of the Delvings swallowed whole by his fear of the reken masses, he drew his ax from his belt.

They charged at the line of bowmen. Kithrand's beautiful steeds, cream-white in the black of night, raced so

quickly across the battlefield that no reken could hold
an arrow to them. Almost as one, the wave of horses
jumped and sailed over the bank of archers: Alorie's
mount and Pinch's, Kithrand, Viola, and Rowan on
their withers, with Gavin and Crust at the flanks. In the
silence, Alorie heard the sound of the bows being
stretched.

Then they tumbled to earth, their flight hurtling them
toward the stone jaws of the Delvings.

"We've made it," Pinch exulted. He swung his ax
freely, knocking aside bodies charging his flanks.

The maw reared in front of her, torchlight coloring
the teeth bloody. She heard the arrow strike and her
mount stumbled, with a shrill whicker of pain, going
down. She felt herself in the air, falling, falling, toward
the obelisk of mountain in front of her.

Chapter 14

"CATCH HER!"

Alorie made herself go limp and squeezed her eyes shut, waiting for the crash against the stone teeth of the gate of the Devlings. Instead, she thumped into several small but chunky bodies, their studded armor biting into her furred cloak and body, oofs and grunts heralding her arrival.

She lay stunned until the forms began to kick and wiggle under her. Rowan reached her first and pulled her off the pile of dwarves.

"Alorie!"

"My horse—"

"Gone. But the packhorses got through." A thunderous grinding drowned out the rest of his words, but she smiled as he drew her close, and they had no need for words as the gate clenched shut again.

Gavin dismounted from his lathered horse and scowled at them, and looked away quickly as Alorie looked over Rowan's shoulder. He fussed over his horse instead.

The dwarves surrounded them, dirty, sooted, a few of them splashed with the black blood of reken, their weapons gripped tightly in their hands.

"Who called for the gates to be opened? And who are you?"

Pinch squirreled off his horse. His blue knit cap he swept away and held in his gnarled hands, his silvery eyes glinting in the torchlight that illuminated all of

them. As Alorie broke loose from Rowan's protective
hold, she saw hundreds of dwarf soldiers watching them
from beyond the circle of light, their faces grave and
tired.

"You may not know me, but you know my looks.
I'm Pinch, from the Gutrig Downs."

The dwarf he addressed stood half a head higher,
with a massive pair of shoulders any human would be
proud to own, and a wasp waist cinched tight by his
swordbelt. Thick brown hair curled his well-formed
head, and only a small patch of beard crossed his square
chin. Young and vigorous, the captain of the guard
looked down at Pinch. "We know you. If we had not
acknowledged the common kinship of the Seven True
Races, we would never have opened the gates to you."

The captain's dark eyes flicked away. "Gripe,
Pepper—take their horses to the stables. Hairfoot, come
with me. Our guests may find it dangerous to linger
here at the jaws."

Even as he spoke, a reken arrow arched through the
narrow teeth and clattered harmlessly to the stones at
their feet. The dwarf kicked it, and then ground the
arrow to splinters beneath his boot.

"Damned good archers, the bastards," he muttered.

The company slid to the ground as waiting dwarves
took the headstalls of the faery horses, though Kithrand
first spoke lilting words of elvish, else not one of the
horses would have suffered dwarf hands upon it. Even
at that, Kithrand's own mount snorted fiercely and pawed
the ground as a lithe young dwarf boy, Pepper by name,
reached for his bridle.

Too young to wear a beard, yet geared fully in battle
dress, the apple-cheeked dwarf boy grinned. "Ye fear-
some charger," he said, and bowed in respect. "Let me
tend to your needs after your trials."

The cream-colored stallion pricked his ears forward,
then shook his head and snorted again, mildly this time.
Then he lowered his head so that Pepper might reach
his reins.

Gavin laughed heartily as the horses left the gates. He slapped the ice off himself and his furs, and checked his broadsword, and caught Pinch's eyes. "Well, short warrior. The reception here doesn't seem to be as dire as you thought."

"You're not inside yet," Pinch muttered, but the big-muscled swordsman didn't hear him and turned away, to follow a bowlegged sergeant called Hairfoot, who disdained wearing boots and whose large, hairy feet slapped across the stone as he escorted them inside.

Darker than night was the mouth of the mountain that swallowed them. Alorie blinked and leaned a little on Rowan's arm as he guided her after Hairfoot. The torchlight shrank and cowered before the might of the stone that thrust away all light of day or night and pressed down about them. Alorie pushed a heavy strand of hair from her face uneasily. She had the feeling of being sniffed, touched, probed, though no one walked close to her except Rowan at her side. He looked down at her, his face pale in the washed-out light.

She remembered then Pinch's warning about evil stoneworks, and shuddered.

"Here in the warrens," the captain said, and his voice echoed, "the main army is being quartered. Stay close to Hairfoot."

Hairfoot swaggered down the middle of the great cavern, its ceiling beyond the reach of the meager torches the dwarf carried. He'd had two of them, but thrust one into Gavin's hand, and now the barbarian carried it high. The captain followed with one of his own, and those three burning circles shed little illumination upon the halls of the warrens. They passed through a portal, and the darkness gave way to a blast of light, a shimmering that bedazzled all of them, and they halted in their tracks with cries as they hid their faces.

"Douse the torches, quickly," the captain ordered, and the torches were ground in the dust.

Pinch alone watched calmly, his eyes gone deep and

mysterious. The lights flickered, the blazing abated, and Alorie dropped her hands from her eyes.

A thousand jewels blinked back at her, their fire set off by the torches, and now quieted. Not dark, these caves, no, never, not when the slightest ray of light would be captured and reflected a thousandfold. Pink, yellow, and blue, the shafts brightened the warrens, and Alorie became one of the first to know that dwarves did not walk in eternal darkness as the stories told.

The stars twinkled down, but never went out as the group walked among them.

Dwarves came out and watched them . . . mothers with babes in sacks on their back, bakers with aprons dusty as they worked, armorers, and more. They watched in curiosity, then disappeared back into their tunnels and caves as the strangers walked past.

Another portal, and this cavern more gemmed than the others. Alorie and Rowan looked up as they passed below. He pointed silently. She glimpsed the teeth of a grating above them, and knew that it could be lowered at any time to keep the enemy out . . . or themselves in.

An immense fortress rose carved from the stone, outlined by gemlight. Guards leaned from its parapets. Big enough to hold most of the population of the mountain, Alorie recognized it for what it was, the inner sanctum of the Delvings, its last stronghold as well as its capital. With a shudder and a groan, two massive wooden doors shielded with plates of bronze, etched and carved with the names of a thousand kings, opened inward.

Hairfoot bowed and stayed at the doors. The captain of the guards, who'd been pacing their rear, now stepped forward briskly. Even Rowan and Gavin were hard pressed to keep up with him as he strode past and guided them into the great hall. Baskets of gemstones threw out a dazzling light rayed by a few tallow candles.

Guards thumped their fists to their armored chests and bowed low as the group walked past. Kithrand's antennae bobbed in amusement as Pinch grunted and saluted back.

"I never thought to see it," the elven lord said, "but it appears that here in the Delvings, blood does run thicker than molten gold."

"Don't count on it," Pinch growled, his deep voice nearly drowned by Gavin's laughter. He looked up at the huge swordsman and his brow furrowed, but he said nothing else.

The group halted in front of a carved throne, its back a winged sun, the throne empty, though countless kings had worn grooves into its arms and seat.

"The king will be with you in a moment," the captain of the guard said, with a twist of a smile. He walked to the side of the throne as they stood waiting. One of the guards came to him with a bucket and a cloth and cleansed his face and hands, then removed the heavy breastplate and held a glimmering surcoat while the captain shrugged into it.

Then he ascended the throne and sat, smiling grimly down upon all of them. "I am King Bryant. Tell me now why all of you have come."

All but Alorie and Viola went to their knees and bowed their heads. Alorie dropped into a deep curtsy, and the silver-haired mage inclined her head in respect before the dwarf king.

Kithrand got to his feet first. "I am Lord Kithrand, of Charlbet, and these are my companions: Crust, smithy and liegeman to Rathincourt of Sobor; Viola, enchantress of Veil; Pinch, free sword of the Gutrig Downs; the Rover Rowan"—at this last, Bryant nodded and said, "Of him I have heard," but Kithrand continued smoothly as though unaware of the interruption—"Gavin of Flaxendown, sometimes known as Bullheart; and the Lady Alorie, heir to the High Counselorship of the House of Sergius."

At that, Bryant's intense gaze rested on her, and he leaned slightly out of the throne. "Last of the house?"

"Yes."

He sat back with a sigh, his face lined in thought. As long as he stayed silent, so did they. The moments seemed to run into a river of endless time, marked only by the winking of gemlight. At last the dwarf king stirred. "That explains much, though not your presence. We sent for allies and expected an army."

"The Delvings sent for help?" Kithrand's astonishment overwhelmed his normally bored expression.

The dwarf king looked at the elf lord. He gave a short laugh. "Even in your lifetime, elf, such a thing has not been done, eh? Well, we have our reasons. The reken boiled out of Sinobel, an endless army, from behind walls where we had once been led to believe allies might live. Sergius the Third treated with us from time to time . . . even attended my father's funeral a handful of years ago. In fact"—and his dark brown eyes sought Alorie's face—"the dwarf kingdom had been led to believe that a marriage of alliance might not be unthinkable. My grandmother was a human, too, and some of that blood runs in my veins as well."

A shock ran through Alorie as she looked into the handsome face, mated to a stunted body, though when he strode by her side, she had known he was her height, a giant among his own people. She could not meet his gaze longer and looked downward, aware that Rowan shifted uncomfortably beside her.

"Now, however," and Bryant looked away, "we understand events of great import begin to worry at the world. There are kingdoms beyond my own that I must consider."

"The Corruptor has been freed," Kithrand said.

Bryant nodded gravely. "I have heard. That is why I sent for alliance to the other races, but we were besieged before I heard from my messengers. Of the five runners I sent out, two heads were returned to me. I had a little hope that others might have gotten through."

"But why," Alorie asked, "why would the reken be attacking you? The Delvings has long held itself separate from the others. No one could anticipate a threat from your armies."

Kithrand choked, but Bryant laughed at her. "Indeed . . . no one in all the kingdoms could possibly think that the Delvings might come to anyone's aid. That is why we left you to the reken, eh?"

The familiar heat of blush warmed her cheeks, but she held her ground. "Would the gates have been opened if the king himself had not ordered it, and a dwarf had not ridden among us?"

"Perhaps not." Bryant scratched his chin thoughtfully. He looked over her head to tall, silent Crust in the background. He pointed at the blacksmith. "Perhaps you could decipher the mystery for the lady."

Crust cleared his throat and flexed his big arms. "The forge, Lady Alorie. I would reckon that the beasts have come after the forge. The kingdoms war among themselves . . . soon weapons and armor of any kind will be at a premium. Old blades have grown brittle. Forges of yesterday lie cold, most of them. Only the Delvings still blazes."

In the shocked silence that followed, Alorie murmured, "And just as no one would figure the Delvings would march in aid, no one would figure the outside kingdoms would come to help the Delvings."

Bryant's eyes gleamed with ironic humor. "A Sergius heart, indeed. Yes, milady, and though I sent, and hoped, it appears that none will answer. We must fight, not only for ourselves alone, but for the welfare of the Seven True Races. If our forge is taken by the enemy, none but the enemy will be equipped for the wars that lie ahead. And if you did not come here because I called, why did you come?"

"Cornuth," Alorie said, though Rowan gripped her arm in warning. "I have been sent to read the prophecy written upon the Three Towers."

"And desperation drove you to my doorstep, because the way to Cornuth is blocked along the normal roads."

"Yes."

"And what will you give me if I show you the way?"

His dark brown eyes stared into hers, gripped her, held her, and she knew what he wanted. She swallowed. "I cannot give promises, your highness, that may be impossible to keep."

King Bryant stared into her a moment longer, then noticed the protective way Rowan moved beside her. He sat back. "I see. Then I will help you however I can, and that will be little indeed. The way to Cornuth underground, you may find, is possibly more treacherous than the roads above. We're under siege not only from without, but from within."

"Where?" asked Kithrand tensely, but Rowan, lifting his chin boldly, was ready with the answer before the dwarf king.

"From the Pit."

"Yes. You know it?"

"Brock told me of it once. A bottomless hole, to the very depths of the earth, he thought."

"And that you must pass before you reach the tunnels that will lead you to the Eye of Cornuth."

A murmur ran through the company, and Pinch slammed his fist into his open palm, muttering, "I knew it!"

Bryant stood, and signaled a guard. "Go find Pepper in the stables, and bring their packs." He turned to Kithrand. "You will have to leave your horses here, but I'll keep them well for you."

Kithrand shuddered and said, "Show them the light of day as soon as it's possible."

"When the reken are gone," the king answered. He motioned to them. "Sit and rest. I'll have food brought, and then you can be on your way."

Materializing from the quavering shadows of the hall, dwarves came carrying every manner of chair and stool. A long line of them brought out a table from the side wall, a massive wooden table polished by centuries, and set it in front of the throne.

A swan unfolded wings to embrace Viola's spare frame as she sat down. A tiny smile curved her lips, as she caressed the chair. "I had forgotten," she said, "the cleverness of dwarven handiwork."

"Then we have been shut away from the world too long," Bryant answered wryly. He watched as Alorie sat in the curve of a splendid seashell, all pink and coral.

He indicated the chair closest to him. "Sit, kinsman, and give me news of the Downs."

Pinch chewed a lower lip, then finally did as the king bade him, though his opaque eyes gleamed with disapproval. Alorie watched him perch atop a toadstooled chair, his knuckles white as he gripped the edge of the table. What was it he feared so about the Delvings? Was it the Pit?

Gavin took out his dirk and cleaned his nails with it while waiting for the table to be set. He eyed the glowing gemstone basket far above his head, and Bryant turned from a word with Pinch, as though the man's thoughts attracted him, and said, "The stones are worth little aboveground, swordsman. They are simple quartz."

Gavin flushed guiltily and returned his dirk to his wrist sheath. He took advantage of the appearance of trenchers and food to change the subject.

And, indeed, no one did more than eat for quite a while. Though the dwarf king apologized for the quality of the table, the fresh fruit and cold meats and vegetable puddings drew out appetites that had been discouraged by days of dried jerky strips and water, except for an occasional rabbit. Even Pinch relaxed enough to loosen his belt and eat heartily.

By the time they had finished, the dwarf lad Pepper had puffed in, laden with all their packs and dragging a small handcart with those he couldn't carry. He grinned when Rowan tossed him a pear and bit deeply into the greenfruit.

"Thanks, my lord," he managed between chunks.

"No lord I," Rowan answered, "but you're welcome."

Pepper pointed at his clothes. "A lord of the road, you are," he returned. "Master Brock told me stories when he visited."

The dwarf king's eyebrows rose as the banter drew his attention. A cold wind had breached the great hall, and she drew her cloak about her shoulders.

Pepper looked about the group, unaware of the stir he had begun to create. "Where is the good mage?"

Viola's hair swung lankly as she turned to the conversation. "Dead," she said flatly. "On the Paths of Sorrow."

Bryant dropped his dagger. It clattered about the goblets, drawing eyes to the king of the Delvings. With a flush, he retrieved his knife. "That's sad news indeed." His eyes burned into Alorie as he stood up from the dining table and backed to the throne's platform and began to ascend it, still watching her. He laughed without humor. "The first guests inside the Delvings in a king's lifetime, and they bring ill tidings—"

An alarm crashed through his words, jerking Rowan and Gavin to their feet, nearly tipping the table over.

"The gate! The gate is breached! A war party over the gate!"

Alorie pushed away quickly. She grabbed her pack and slung it over her shoulders, and checked to make sure the longknife hung at her side. She bumped shoulders with Viola, who was doing the same.

Bryant, not waiting for his attendants, tugged on his breastplate over the surcoat, as the great hall flooded with his guard.

"How many?"

"A hundred, lord, before we got the gate down. Someone came through and worked the winch—"

"You'll know better next time," Bryant said, and pushed his way past the red-faced guard, who bowed low before him with the news.

"Your highness—"

"Yes?" He swung around impatiently to the dismissed guard.

"No reken, lord, not all. A human, fair with cold eyes, leads them, tall, wearing the dark blue of Quickentree."

Alorie thought her heart pounded to a fatal stop. The breath clutched at her throat. Aquitane! The arrogant lord here inside the Delvings!

Rowan pulled his sword free and took her hand, jogging her into movement. With that touch, she breathed freely once more.

The Rover faced the dwarf king, a little taller, perhaps, but both were noble in stature. "Show us the pathway to Cornuth."

"The invaders—"

"—may well be on our trail."

Bryant looked at Alorie. He nodded then, as if he had made up his mind to something. "This way, then, and quickly."

The dwarf king put on a brisk pace. Pinch resorted to running to keep up, as did Alorie and Viola. Crust and Gavin took up the rear, while Kithrand stayed with Rowan.

The gemstones faded into twilight. Horns and hammers behind them rang out, and Bryant shrugged into his armor. He stopped once, and turned, caught by the sounds of battle.

"I should be with my people."

Hatred rose in Alorie's throat. Would Aquitane do to the Delvings what he had done to Sinobel? She half turned on the pathway, and felt a brand across her hand. She opened the clenched fist with a gasp, to find Brock's signet ring alive with fire, scorching her finger.

"Magefire," gasped Viola. She stared, hypnotized, at Alorie's hand. In the dusk of the caves, the gemstones picked up the eerie glow and reflected it.

Kithrand put his hand out over the ring, quieting it, and the pain evaporated. "Use it against the enemy," the elf lord said. He added a sentence of elvish which she grasped for and almost understood, before the melodious words melted away.

Rowan blocked the dwarf king. "I can guarantee you that Aquitane is after us first, and the forge second."

"The human lord heads the reken army?"

"Perhaps. We're not sure."

"Then what does he want, to risk his life before his troops have broken my army?"

Rowan said nothing. His lips pressed together thinly.

The dwarf king looked at her, and she could not meet his gaze yet again. "He wants the last of the House of Sergius. He wants Alorie."

"Yes."

"He'll never have her!" Bryant's resolve blazed across his handsome face, and his jaw squared off. "The Pit sends evil to harry us . . . let's see if we can draw Aquitane into the trap meant for us! Quickly then, and keep your silence. What comes out of the bowels of the earth to chew on dwarvish bones might like yours as well!"

Chapter 15

Because rowan loved her, the entire company was in danger. She could tell that as they moved through the Delvings, for his attention was directed at her. She knew, and so did Kithrand and Viola and possibly the others as well, and she didn't know what to do about it. Yet, how could she stop him? For she wanted that love, and returned it, and would no longer have felt whole without it. But it blinded the Rover now as he moved through the twilight, and she followed after, wondering what she could do.

They had lost all sense of night and day following the dwarf king down into the bowels of the earth. What few gemstones remained flickered the barest light from their torches. She stumbled often on the path, Rowan throwing his hand out to steady her. King Bryant stopped once and looked over her shoulder and then Alorie realized that they had gone so deep that the war horns could no longer be heard. She knew that he wondered about the fate of his people . . . if that one hundred who had breached the gate had opened it to a flood of reken soldiers.

He signed his breastplate and muttered something. Then he looked at her and turned back to his original path and led them deeper and deeper to the bottomless hole known as the Pit.

A pressure on her ears was relieved when she yawned suddenly. A heavy scent rose from the descending trail in front of her, a thick sulfurous scent that made her cough and choke and press her hand to her nose.

"We're nearly there," the dwarf king warned. He pulled his sword from his scabbard.

"What attacks from the Pit?"

"We don't know what it is. Huge, long, and low, it crawls up. It's never left behind survivors, but we've seen the tracks and carcasses. Multilegged, almost like a spider or such. It doesn't always come up. We never know when it will attack."

"And what makes you think we can draw it to Aquitane?"

Bryant looked sharply into Rowan's face. "I think it'll come to the noise of the fighting. It's a beast, after all . . . and it's got to feed on something."

A strange odor wafted up and tangled itself about the pungent scent that choked all of them. It was animal, and Kithrand stopped dead on the track even as Pinch bumped into him. His antennae flicked, catching the light, and Alorie thought fleetingly of an alarmed butterfly.

The elf lord pulled his bow first, rather than his sword. "I think it best to stay as far away from *that* as one can."

Pinch disentangled himself from the elf's heels and growled, "I didn't want to come here in the first place."

The heat and light flared from her ring again. Alorie dug her hand deep into the pocket of her riding skirt, but she could feel the warmth, though this time it did not burn her as it had before. Magefire, Viola had called it. Did she have a power she could throw at the Pit beast? Or even better, flame at Aquitane . . . traitor Aquitane, who deserved to die more than any simple beast out of the dark did.

The noise of Crust freeing his sword sliced into her thoughts. Alorie balled her hand tightly, savoring the power, and hurried after Rowan. Viola began whispering methodically, and Kithrand swung around, snapping, "What are you doing?"

The silver-haired enchantress looked at him. "Don't you wish to know what it is you face?"

He gripped his bow and ready arrow tightly. When he nodded, it was with a stiff-necked movement, as though he didn't wish to give in to the mage.

"We are caught," Viola intoned lowly, "between the arm of the Corruptor and the minion of an even older evil. Caught, elf lord. Neither will be ill-used as the king thinks to do."

He caught his breath. "A seer. So that is her power. And your advice?" Kithrand added gently. Her voice had gone flat, and her eyes rolled back. He motioned for Alorie to be quiet.

The others shifted on the rock, leather armor creaking faintly, and behind them, the pulse of trailers could be heard through the stone. Crust and Gavin turned to face the rear, their swords at ready.

"One only will be tested here," Viola prophesied. Then her head jerked back and she might have fallen, but Pinch braced her up. She shook her long, dangling hair in embarrassment and said bitterly, "I hope the elf lord got an earful," before she pushed past them toward the bottom of the trail.

Gavin flexed uneasily, then caught up with Kithrand. "I'll lead in."

Amused, the lord said, "What makes you think this task is yours?"

"The mage spoke of testing. I am a farm lad, good with a sword—but not good enough for men to follow me, yet I know that this is what I was meant to do. I must prove myself."

Kithrand gave an ironic bow and let the huge swordsman past, though he watched with dancing amusement as Gavin did so. Alorie raised her hand and Kithrand caught it, stilling her yet again. "In the days to come," the elf lord told her, "many of us will do what we have to do. We all answered the summonings from Veil for reasons of our own."

She looked deep into the ageless eyes of the elf and

felt her thoughts grow dizzy, before he released her. But he hadn't worked any magic on her . . . it was the effect of looking into a soul that looked young, but saw into immortality. She lowered her hand, and Kithrand kept hold of it as they started once more into the twilight of the cavern trail.

Gavin broke into a run. They followed on his heels, as the narrow path widened suddenly and swerved, and the dark opening of the bottomless hole opened up before them, in a vast cavern hung with swords of rock and crystal. Their flight startled a flock of bats, and the women screamed involuntarily as the squeaking beasts flew into them.

Alorie glimpsed furred faces and leather wings and tiny, sharp white fangs. They grasped her hair with their blind claws and yanked as they flew, striking anyone in their way.

The thunder of the bats' startled retreat would tell the pursuers exactly where they were.

Bryant pointed with the tip of his sword. "That way!"

Sudden illumination from above, a dozen torches or more, set the gemlight afire, and the red-orange cast shone down on the vast pit below. Bryant's shadow loomed behind him as he pointed the way.

Gavin stood at the edge of the pit, looking down. He kicked a stone over. It rattled and echoed downward, but none of them heard it hit bottom.

Rowan hurried them past. Alorie paused, drawn by the sight of the swordsman waiting for a foe to appear, to challenge him. In the still, warm, foul air, his half-bare torso gleamed with sweat. Yet Gavin did not stir, oblivious to the danger from above as Aquitane and his men drew near. A strange passion stirred his features.

"Come on, Alorie!"

"One moment longer," she answered absently, as Viola and Crust brushed past her.

"By the horn!" Kithrand cursed, and let his arrow fly, aiming above them at the descending path.

A man screamed once, then tumbled downward, his pierced body falling in midair, somersaulting into the Pit.

He screamed again as he slammed into the side and slid down to his death. The cry reverberated throughout the cavern, and the crystal swords hanging above trembled in agitation.

Arrows hissed through the air, striking rock near Alorie's boots, sending up puffs of dust. She glared back as Rowan grabbed her shoulder.

"Get out of here—now!"

"I—"

Gavin's glad cry interrupted her response. His shoulder muscles bunched fiercely as he raised his sword. "There it is!"

A dead silver gleaming, two huge antennae pushed over the rim of the Pit, and then legs tipped with sharp claws gripped the edge, and the beast scuttled up.

Long and low and shaped like an arrowhead, the insectlike monster paused. Gavin backed away in spite of his intended courageous stand, and held his sword across his chest in guard, his jaw dropped open in surprise.

The beast reared up, its hundred legs beating against the air. Then its fangs clacked in a furry maw and Alorie choked. The remnants of a man's torso and an arrow dribbled from the Pit spawn's jaws. The tail it reared on whipped around, and she spied a wicked dart, liquid from it staining the earth, and it sizzled.

"Gavin! Forget it! Run!" she screamed. Her throat ached.

Rowan pushed her behind him.

"Where are you going?"

"I'm not going to let him face that alone," the Rover said. He grinned at her. "I'll be back."

"No!"

Another flight of arrows were loosed, these aimed at the Pit beast. They bounced off the creature's scaled

body and fell about Gavin in a hail. The swordsman did
not flinch, oblivious, frozen in his own fear.

Rowan danced in, legs curled about him as he stabbed
at the exposed flank, the flat head of the creature still
looking upward, entranced by the aura of light shining
down on it from Aquitane's men.

His sword punched a hole, and dark crimson gushed
out. The beast curled and flipped its tail, sending Rowan
sprawling near the edge.

Gavin unfroze. With a war cry, he lunged at the
beast. His blade cut through the maze of legs and
etched across its underbelly. He danced back, grasped
Rowan by the collar, and pulled him clear, just as the
edge of the Pit crumbled a little, sending a shower of
dirt and pebbles downward.

The beast roared. Quartz shattered overhead and tumbled below, and the earth quivered as another roar
answered from the Pit. Gavin stepped back as the creature struck at him. He dodged the fangs and returned
the blow with a solid thrust of his great sword. Blood
spurted once again, and the swordsman slipped in it as
he gathered himself for another cut. Gavin caught himself and threw the sword like a spear, straight into the
pale wattle of a throat below the fangs as it came for
him again.

With a bellowing, the creature reared up and fell
backward into the Pit.

Answered again, the cavern trembled.

Rowan caught up with Alorie. "Let's get out of
here!"

She dug her heels in. "That's Aquitane up there!"

"And something even bigger down there! Now,
Alorie!"

"I want Aquitane!" She lifted her fist and uncurled
her fingers, and Brock's signet ring flared on her hand.
As the ground buckled under her, she fell. The spear of
magefire veered away, splattering against the side of the
cavern.

Bryant reached them, and he and Gavin hauled the

two of them to their feet. He grasped her quivering hand. "Destroy the Pit, and you'll destroy the forge! Down below, in another cavern, we use the heart of the mountain."

"It's not the Pit I want," she gasped and fought to get free. She looked up and saw the party of men and reken following them, their faces illuminated by the gemlight and torches they carried.

Aquitane was close enough to see her face as well. He paused, one arm ready to signal a wave of archers.

"It's not up to you," Rowan said hoarsely.

She stood, looking across the Pit into that face that she hated, and knew that he knew she could destroy him. The moment gripped her, like the moment she had stood on the landing above the great hall, and seen her father and grandfather slaughtered. No . . . she couldn't murder the way he had.

The ring's fire turned icy, and she shrugged out of their grip. The edge of the Pit rippled and gave way again, and they all gasped as they saw the claws that tore at it, as a second beast dragged itself from the bowels of the earth.

Alorie aimed her hand suddenly at the ceiling of the cave. Magefire lashed out, and a curtain of stone fell, shielding Aquitane and his party from the beast and blocking his pursuit of them. The rockfall continued. Crystal spears pierced the monster, and with a scream, it hurtled back into nothingness, as the four of them turned and ran after their fellows.

Chapter 16

"ARE YOU SURE?"

Crust shifted his weight uneasily, broadcloth shirt rippling, and he rubbed the back of his neck with a massive hand. "No, miss, I'm not sure . . . but I'm a smith, and if the forge needs working, then here is where I'm meant to be." He glanced back up the mountainside, the early-morning breeze drying the sweat on his brow. "Besides, the king says he needs a good climbing partner to get back into the Delvings. I reckon we owe him that."

She smiled gently at that and nodded. "I guess we do."

Bryant sat on a boulder overlooking a green valley, studiously ignoring their parting. She turned from the giant black man then, and went to him, putting her hand on his shoulder. Below them, sitting around a campfire and eating fresh stream fish, the rest sat awaiting her.

The dwarf king met her eyes. She studied him, the desire inside her to memorize him, for some unknown reason. His hair curled in the teasing spring wind. She thought that despite the fact he was a dwarf, he was a handsome being, and she did not find repulsive the notion that once her grandfather had considered him a suitable mate.

He seemed to read that in her eyes and covered her hand with his own broad and gnarled one. "I hope that this meeting will be well remembered by you, Lady Alorie.''

"I can't thank you enough for your help. I hope—'' She swallowed tightly, finding words difficult. "I hope you regain your kingdom quickly.''

"With Crust to help me climb, we'll be in a back way soon enough. Then Aquitane and his reken had better be on the run.''

"You won't kill the lord.''

"No. I will give him enough rope to run back to his master, and then someone—you or I or Rathincourt— will yank that rope tight. The time of the High King and the Despot is near, milady. The Seven True Races can't afford to fight among themselves.''

"I will tell the outside that the Delvings is a staunch ally, one to be reckoned with.''

He inclined his head and withdrew his hand. "Thank you, milady.'' He stood and beckoned Crust. "Let's have at that hillside, before the sun gets higher.''

Alorie stood back and watched the two, dwarf and giant among his kind, and black man giant among his, shoulder a pack and measure the golden elven rope between them that Kithrand had given them.

Not wanting to see if they climbed or fell, she turned her back and ran lightly down the trail.

"There it is,'' Rowan said, in low triumph. "Cornuth!''

They stood, dusty and foot-weary, overlooking the ruins of the fallen city. It was midday on the day before that, they'd heard triumphant horning from the Delvings and known that the reken had been beaten off and the forge secured. Kithrand still held hopes that his horses would come to him once freed by King Bryant, a dozen no more since Alorie's had been shot from under her. No one dared say to the elf lord that it was unlikely any horse could cross what they'd just come over.

Where the dire army had marched, chasing the High

King through the Eye of Cornuth to what would become the Barrowlands, the land had been cursed. Dread things crawled it by night and day, and Gavin, his great sword gone in the throat of the Pit beast, had more than redeemed himself with his short sword. They had left a bloody path behind them of beasts that ought never to have lived in the first place.

Alorie shuddered, and swept her hair from her sun-burned face. Behind them still, something trailed and tracked relentlessly. Though she'd never seen it in the shadow of gnarled trees, she felt the dark unicorn at their backs. She could sense it.

Rowan held out a hand to her and helped her onto the crest. "See, there it is—Three Towers."

"I see only one."

"The others have crumbled. But we'll find their spires there yet . . . it takes a long time to beat down stone."

"It must have been a huge city."

"Yes. When we're there, you'll see the Straits beyond."

Alorie lifted her chapped face to the faint spring breeze, already cooler than it had been. She'd never seen the ocean and found it difficult to imagine, water stretching beyond her as far as she could see.

Pink and gold and blue, the stone buildings beckoned past broken walls and gates. Even as she watched, something immense pulled itself from the alleys, crawled over the top of a building, and disappeared into shadows. She shuddered.

Rowan blinked too, then grinned. "We'll find a way to stay clear of that, whatever it was."

"There'll be reken down there," Alorie said. "We may be walking right into the hands of the Corruptor."

"He's not down there."

"Oh no?"

Kithrand had leaped up onto the crest beside him, and the elf king wore an excited expression. "No, milady—having been buried so long, he fancies life! Yes, he's probably surrounded himself with clear water and green meadows. That's not to say it will be dull in Cornuth.''

She looked at him. ''I think I underestimated you, Lord Kithrand. You appear to enjoy a good fight.''

His antennae wavered as he looked sharply at her, then a faint blush appeared on his alabaster skin. ''Sometimes an elf needs a brush with humans to feel alive again himself,'' the elf muttered.

Gavin jumped and balanced himself with them, his short sword in his hand. ''What do you say, milady? Are you ready to take Cornuth?''

She laughed. ''Taking it is hardly what we have to do. Rowan says we must sneak in, like thieves in the night. There are things there we don't want to disturb.''

Gavin's eager expression faded. He replaced his sword and brushed his dark hair, grown unruly over the long journey, with his strong fingers. ''Then you won't be going after the sword of Frenlaw, as Viola has said.''

''Where did you hear that?'' Kithrand drew himself taut, and his white-blond brows frowned together.

''The mage has told me. Alorie is to read the engraved prophecy, and then true to that prophecy, take the sword that graved it from the stone where it was sunk, until its time.'' Gavin shrugged his shoulders. The scab off one of his battle scratches across one bronzed biceps flaked. ''You'll need a man to wield that sword, milady. I hope my performance in the past days has not disappointed you.''

''Never, Gavin,'' she said, finding her voice. The sword had been rarely mentioned, and to all purposes, it was the prophecy she sought. Brock's apparition had said nothing to her of the sword. That part of the quest came from Veil's interpretation, and she'd all but forgotten about it. ''The blade of Frenlaw has a terrible reputation.''

"Aye . . . but not until he melted down the steel and reforged it on the sacred hilt. Before that, it was rumored to have been a gift of the gods themselves."

Kithrand relaxed. He crossed his arms, as the wind toyed with his fair locks. "You know your folklore well."

Gavin looked at him, and the childlike innocence that so often veiled his face faded away. "I know what all of you think of me. That I think no farther than I can plant my feet in front of me. Maybe so. When my father planned for harvests in seasons yet to come, I drew circles in the dirt and attacked cities with my men of straw. I see things differently than others do—but this I swear to you, I know my destiny." He looked over all of them, and his gaze fell away to the hollow behind them where Viola and Pinch sat, resting weary feet. "That's more than most of you can say."

With his thumb hooked in his swordbelt, Gavin jumped off the crest and made toward the city of Cornuth.

Unabashed, Kithrand yelled after him, "Stay to the groves. We want to surprise the enemy."

"Honestly, how can you talk to him like that?"

The elf lord shrugged and took Alorie's hand. "He bared his soul to us, and I'd like to think the big lug thinks we didn't take him seriously. It will help him save face later."

Rowan rescued Alorie's hand from Kithrand. "I like to think we'll make Cornuth well before dark!" He helped her down from the crest and added, "You get Viola and Pinch."

The elf lord bowed. "Of course, milord. Whatever you say."

Alorie caught up with Rowan's long strides. "Does he always do that?"

"Do what?"

"Mock us."

"Elves are known for their sense of humor, Alorie. Besides, I think it keeps him from taking us too seriously. After all, you and I are a relatively short chapter in Kithrand's life.''

Alorie lost her breath keeping up with the Rover as they ducked into the woods that flanked the open meadows approaching the gates of Cornuth. As at Sinobel, the open area was several leagues wide, giving gate sentries a clear look at the approach. And as at Sinobel, the nut orchards running parallel to the road had gone wild and grown vastly, and now they provided the necessary cover to get within hailing distance of the ruins without being seen.

The woods brooked no trespass. The branches thrust and fouled their steps as if they were alive, mouths and eyes in dark burls of bark staring at them. Viola more than once snatched at her long silver hair and glared at an errant twig as though it had pulled her locks on purpose. Alorie cracked her shin on low-swinging limbs and snubbed her toe on hidden roots that erupted from the soft earth.

Pinch had the worst of it. He was too short to clamber over the obstacles of fallen logs, and more than once Gavin had to come to his rescue, lifting the gnarled dwarf by the scruff of his neck.

Alorie put out a hand abruptly to halt a whipping branch aimed at his eyes, and took the brunt of it across her palm. The lash stung her, and she put her palm to her lips to ease the pain.

"Let me see that," Rowan said and captured her hand. With a twinkle in his eye, he kissed her bleeding palm.

"Ah, spring and youth," Kithrand commented. The elf lord balanced lightly on a tree limb above their heads. "Young love and all that." He smiled at Alorie's blush. "Did you think we didn't notice? But I might remind you, brash Rowan, that Brock had plans for this young flower."

Alorie snatched her hand back at his words and stalked angrily past the two of them, with Pinch grumbling in her wake, but she heard Rowan say, "I've had enough mockery, Lord Kithrand."

"I daresay you have. Nonetheless, though your brave mage is dead, his ambitions still live." The branch snapped as Kithrand sprang from it to another, as at home in a tree as a squirrel.

The elf lord disappeared in the woods ahead of them, scouting.

Gavin retraced his steps through the brush, where he'd made as much noise as a bear tramping ahead of them. "Kithrand says we're nearly there, and it's time to break cover."

Rowan's face had not yet calmed, and he brushed a lock of wayward hair from his forehead. He took a deep breath.

Crouching under the last of the heavy branches, even as they rustled and crackled above their heads, they crept from the forest. A stretch of meadow ran in front of them, broken only by the upheaved stones of what had once been a king's trading road, now thrust aside by simple weeds and grass. A clump of wildflowers swayed in front of Alorie.

Pinch pulled his battle-ax free and rolled the haft between his thorny palms.

"Is there no other way to enter?"

"Not that I can see." Kithrand dropped lightly to the ground beside her. "We could wait until dark."

"No," Rowan answered. "I want to see what I'm doing, and the prophecy will be hard to read by torchlight."

Gavin, taking heed from Pinch, loosened his short sword and swung his arms, stretching his muscles.

They started across the meadow, the soft green carpet comforting under stone-bruised feet. She thought she heard a brook's voice in the shadows behind her, and turned, thinking first of a cool drink. She froze, as the shadows moved.

The dark unicorn trotted from the woods. The sun

glinted off his onyx horn, and he bared his teeth, sharp and canine, like a wild animal. His tufted tail lashed the air, and his mane crested his thick, proud neck. At Alorie's muffled sound, her companions stopped and swung around.

Rowan grabbed Viola's sleeve. "To the gates! Run!"

Gavin picked Alorie up under his arm, and she kicked wildly to be set down, knowing there was no way the swordsman could outrun the horned beast.

The unicorn reared and trumpeted. Pinch spread his booted feet and swung his ax back over his shoulder in readiness for the charge. Then another sound came from the forest, a clarion answer to the first.

Like a snowy cloud, a white unicorn moved out of the woods. He tossed his white mane and pawed the ground in challenge. Ringing their leader pranced the eleven cream-colored faery mounts. Kithrand gave a shout of joy.

"By the horn," Pinch breathed.

Gavin let Alorie slide to the ground. She fell to her knees and watched the two beasts circle one another, wary stallions sizing up their opponents. What point and counterpoint in the creatures, each the eclipse of the other! Where the dark unicorn carried a rank scent of carrion and death, the white smelled of green grass and wildflowers. The white horn glistened from his broad forehead, catching the rays of the sun and spiraling them out in glory. He came to a stop opposite the dark beast, and Alorie saw his hide quiver, as though the creature he fronted offended him. The long tips of horns came near to touching, each nearly half the length of the animal that carried it.

The black beast lunged. The horns clashed and rang as they parried off, and the white reared, striking out with hooves of fire, as the black charged into him. The two whinnied in anger. Bucking and snapping, the unicorns fought.

"Come on," Rowan said. "Let's get out of here."

"No," Alorie said. "We can't let it be killed!" She

raised her hand, but the signet ring was blackened, dormant, as it had been since the day at the Pit.

A crimson tear opened up on the white unicorn's flank, and the stallions disengaged. The white beast held his head proudly even as the dark lowered his, eyes slitted, and began a low growling.

Gavin took hold of her once more, saying, "Like a true soldier, he's buying us time." He threw her over his shoulder.

"Put me down!"

The huge swordsman ignored her, and crossed the meadow in bounds that jarred her teeth into her skull. She glimpsed the others following on his heels, the two unicorns bound into eternal conflict beyond. The dark struck, and the white fell, then rolled and got back to his feet and trumpeted again, call strong and clear and noble.

Alorie saw no more through the tears in her eyes.

They crawled through dusty broken rock, and the wind keened after them, searching them out, as the late-afternoon sun slanted into Cornuth and set it ablaze. The blue stone took on a purplish shade.

Viola wore a careful nonexpression as she wove her way through the ruins, leading them onward, for as a mage, she'd been once to Cornuth, and was the only one of them to be sure of the way. Gavin guarded their backs as Rowan guarded Viola. Pinch hobbled beside Alorie, who finally had muffled her crying and had nothing left but a swollen face.

The dwarf patted her hand. "There, there, girlie. I tell you, the true beast will win."

"And my horses will be waiting for us," Kithrand added. "I don't relish walking back through the Eye."

She didn't answer him. Their voices sounded too loud in the fallen city, and she remembered too well the sighting she'd shared with Rowan. Then a blackness fell across her, and she looked up to see a tower shading them all, and Viola standing at its base.

She pointed. "There is the reading."

Alorie joined her, and the men made a half-circle, their weapons ready. She stepped forward, squinting, at the crude runes in the stone. "But this is a language . . . I don't even know this!"

The silver-haired mage never flinched. Her stern hand remained pointing at the wall. "There is the prophecy," she said.

Alorie swallowed despite her dry mouth and throat. She walked close and kneeled, to better examine the stone. Half in shade and half glaring from the sun's rays, the letters were obscured by dust. She reached out and brushed the fine silt away carefully. As her fingertips touched a rune, it seized her . . . a power dragged her in and she could not move her hand away. Her lips moved, and her voice shouted aloud words she did not understand, and the signet ring once more blazed on her finger.

Her finger traced the prophecy, graving it once more, her arm straining, and Alorie felt the sweat on her forehead run down her temples to pool along her chin and neck.

It controlled her, not she it. She knew not what she said, but the words roared from her and echoed in the ruins until she had moved the entire length of the wall. Then her hand dropped wearily to her side, and the sound died away.

When she turned, she saw tearstains on Rowan's face, and Gavin had clasped his hands to hide his, and Pinch stood looking downward, noisily blowing his nose on his sleeve. Kithrand stood frozen, as pale as ever, the mockery drained from his face.

Viola smiled thinly at her. "Now take the sword."

Buried hilt-deep, the sword of Frenlaw glimmered at her. Alorie took a deep breath, then reached out and grasped it. The metal warmed instantly to her hand. She braced herself and pulled—

—and the mystical weapon came free.

Alorie tumbled back, the empty hilt in her hands. The blade, still buried in the wall, turned to a molten river and trickled away into the dust.

She stumbled to her feet with the empty guard in her hand as reken drums broke loose, and enemy soldiers hurled over the walls at them.

Gavin sprang forward, his sword ringing as it cut into three of them. Viola grabbed her hand. "This way out!"

Pinch took out a reken as it charged her, blades in both paws. Its head rolled in the dirt, still grinning.

Kithrand froze, unable to get his sword out of his sheath in time. Bow forgotten on his back, the elf lord sprinted after them, shouting, "Run!"

With a shout, Rowan took their flank, his blade dripping black blood. Gavin dropped back behind him, and the two swordsmen covered the group as they fled.

Outside, in the green grass, Kithrand gave a piercing whistle. The faery horses appeared, fresh and prancing, and he threw himself aboard the lead stallion. Alorie gave Viola a hand up even as Pinch tugged at her knees.

"Get yourself on, milady!"

She looked over her shoulder at the edge of the ruins, where reken boiled out like bees out of a hive, and Gavin and Rowan turned and made a run for them.

She wrapped her hands tightly in the horse's mane until it squealed and tossed its head in pain. Pinch leaped aboard Viola's mount and clutched her waist tightly.

Alorie looked to the elf lord. "Do something! They'll never make it."

He cleared his throat, his chest heaving as he tried to breathe, and shook his head. "I might strike one of them."

Gavin put his head down, his mighty legs pumping, as Rowan, his shadow, kept pace.

Alorie saw the arrow that struck him, slicing into his

leg. He went down with a sharp cry, rolling in the trampled grass of the meadow where the white beast had fought the black and no sign remained of either.

Cursing in elvish, Kithrand leaned over and whipped her horse across the rump. The mount gave a startled leap and bolted, as she saw the reken overwhelm Rowan's fallen body.

The wind tore her sorrow from her in a single word: "Noooooo!"

Chapter 17

"HE'LL NOT be dead, milady," Pinch said, as they pulled the horses to a rest, and the fleet elven mounts stood with their heads lowered, gusting in huge sobs of air.

Alorie felt numbed, as though her heart had been ripped from her chest and nothing left behind. She looked, unfocusing, over the green valley. Cornuth still hugged the southwestern horizon, but she recognized little else that she saw.

Kithrand leaned from his horse, his dagger in his hands, and he cut her hands free from the horse's tangled mane. She looked down, bewildered. In her right hand, cutting into the skin, she clutched the empty hilt of the sword of Frenlaw.

She threw it to the ground. "The damned thing is still cursed. So there you are." She tilted her head back and shouted into the wind, as if it could hear and understand her. "Here's your precious quest. The prophecy is read and the sword recovered. What of it? What good will any of it do now?" Alorie looked back to the ground and her voice stilled to a whisper. "I don't remember any of it."

"But we do," Gavin answered. He threw his leg over his horse's withers and leaped to the ground. He approached her after he had picked up the hilt and tucked it into his heavy leather belt. "You told us of the High King . . . the last days of his reign, when the Corruptor turned against him, and betrayed him . . .

and of his blindness to his errors, but his devotion to his people. You told us how Cornuth fell, and the Eye of Cornuth was filled with a blasphemous army. We heard how the jaws of death were sprung, and the promise that was made to the Raltarian guard to be restored in honor one day when the High King came again, and regained all that he had lost—and more.''

Alorie leaned over her horse's neck, as though all energy had drained from her body and her spine could no longer carry her weight. She felt the animal's warmth from its lathered hide, fine veins standing up through the satiny pelt. She turned her head, laying her cheek against the bare spot where Kithrand had severed the mane. ''You knew all this before.''

''We were told it was promised. Hearing the promise itself . . . well, now, that's another thing,'' Pinch said gruffly. He cleared his throat. ''You told about dwarves and elves and the four humans . . . and the Mutts. You told us that even the counselorship for the king would fall, and when the last came to the last, what we would face. It's not a bright time ahead, lassie—but we can see to the end now. They've given us a chance, the gods have.''

Alorie blinked. A tear trembled at the edge of her lash, and all the world took on a blurred, rainbow cast. ''You knew that,'' she repeated dully.

''Not all,'' Viola said. ''No one has ever been able to read the complete engraving.''

''Then you tell me exactly what it said.''

She looked down, her face hidden behind a veil of silver hair. ''No, milady. You see . . . each of us heard something a little different, depending on our part in the final prophecy.''

Kithrand had his back turned on them, looking out over the stretch of ground to Cornuth as though his very life depended on it.

Alorie brushed the tear from her eye and sat up. ''What did yours say, Kithrand?''

The elf lord glanced back guilty. He shook his head. "I don't remember, Alorie. The reken attack . . . "

" . . . came later." Alorie had no desire to argue with him now, but she knew he hid something from her. "What now?"

"We keep riding." Gavin tore handfuls of grass from the trampled ground and wiped his mount down vigorously. "They will trail us."

"No." The elf lord looked away again, his voice thickened. "Rowan is still alive . . . or he was when he was taken. No, the reken will think they have a hostage. They will think that we'll return for him, and then they'll have all of us."

"But we won't." Shock iced fingers through her at the sound of Kithrand's words. "You turned and ran for your life, and left him there, and not one of you plans to go back! Gavin—"

The dark-haired man looked at her impassively. Then he said, "Though I hope someday to be the man to carry the sword that fits this guard, I can't, milady. Rowan and I both knew it might take our lives to guard you. Give him that, Alorie. Give him the right to be a man, whatever the cost."

"Noble talk."

Viola kneed her mount viciously. It lunged into Alorie's, nearly unseating her, for they all rode bareback. The mage swung before she could duck, and fire cracked across her face.

"Grow up, last of the House of Sergius! Do you think we're children, pretending to dice as the grownups do?" Her pale expression flared. "You're no virgin girl child anymore."

"No." Alorie glanced to the ground as her horse pawed it restlessly. She felt her long dark hair stroke the warmth of her cheek where she still felt the blow. No one had ever dared strike her before. "Do you think . . . do you think he'll live?"

Gavin mounted. "Who knows what the stinking reken

will do? Well, Lord Kithrand . . . no one here knows the trail but you.''

With a tired movement, the elf lord pivoted his horse. "That way then . . . to the sea . . . but not to Trela'ar. Woods elves say that the city is already taken.''

"Aquitane again." For a moment, Alorie felt she should have killed him when she could.

"Perhaps. But I don't think so. Duke Lathum of Bylantium, before his ill-fated end, confided to me that the Straits, though risky traveling, are still open. Trela'on, held by Aquitane, even makes enticing offers to free traders, such as no port taxes. He'd do no such thing if he also held the sister city. We'd be at his mercy then.''

"Maybe we should go back to the Delvings. Crust could make a new blade for this—''

"No.''

That response came from all gathered around her. Alorie looked in surprise to Pinch, Gavin, Viola, and Kithrand. "The prophecy again.''

"It says that we must seek the answers to the questions the sword of Frenlaw asks.''

Viola pushed her hair from her face brusquely. "Leave that to me, Kithrand—but first, I think we should put as much ground between Cornuth and us as we can. Rowan gave us an advantage we're fools to waste.

The horses rested, Kithrand led the way. Alorie felt the wind in her face, and followed, trying with all that was left of her heart not to think of the seawind Rowan had promised.

Viola insisted on being on stone. They had ridden up and down the seacoast for the better part of a day looking for the stone she wanted when they reached it. It rose, like a table, from the dunes and twisted sea grass, a slab of blue-veined rock that had withstood the wind, rain, and high tide, its surface only becoming more polished with time.

Alorie, dismounted at last, her legs stiff and weary, watched the image as she paced the structure. Her long, elegant fingertips stroked its polished surface. Unheard vibrations played a cold chill down Alorie's spine, and she looked away. What did Viola want?

"This will do," the mage announced flatly.

"Good." Kithrand looked up from the fire he'd kindled. The dunes built up here, giving a little grace from the ceaseless wind. The other rocks stabbing into the open gave shelter. It was a defensible spot.

Not far away, as the ocean sucked back, Pinch and Gavin tried their hands at spearing fish for dinner. So far, they'd spitted two.

With both hands, Viola tucked her hair back from her face. She smiled at the sight of the gnarled man and the great farmer dancing in the foam, jabbing at shadow fish in the water. Alorie thought with surprise that Viola was almost beautiful when she smiled. The humor vanished suddenly as it had come, as Viola sat, tucking her knees up, and pulled her saddlebag over. She took out one of her books of magic and began reciting an endless litany of basic spells, for a mage tends to lose a spell once it's been spoken. The effect was one of pulling a curtain around her, separating herself from the rest of the party.

Alorie looked away. Her faery horse raised its muzzle from grazing the sea grass. It sniffed at Alorie's face in inquiry, and she rubbed the soft muzzle. Mollified, the horse drifted back to its companions and continued cropping. Never had she felt more alone in all her life. It wasn't fair. She'd lost all.

"The sea tends to make one melancholy."

Alorie started as Kithrand spoke and settled next to her. His elven garb showed the stains and wear and tear of the journey. He no longer seemed so grand or ethereal, though his jewels still shone brightly in his braided coronet.

"Is that it? Or is it the death that life hands out?"

"I wouldn't know about that. Elves know very little about death."

She looked at him. "You see it all around you, every day."

Kithrand stared away. "Perhaps it's there . . . and perhaps we don't care to watch it."

"Like Rowan."

He didn't answer her then. The surf roared, and a bird gliding past gave its mournful cry, and Pinch shouted with childish glee as he caught another morsel for dinner. Alorie lay back against the sun-warmed dune, and before she knew it, she slept.

After the dinner, they sat around and licked their fingers shamelessly. They had no water, but Viola had conjured up a bag of wine, which, though she said it was a sham, tasted good even though Alorie still thirsted. In the morning, Kithrand declared, he'd put his antennae to dowsing and find fresh water.

The light slanted low across the dunes, and the wind crept in with a reminder of fog. Viola lifted the wine bag, took a last pull, and tossed it to Gavin. She stood and dusted her hands on her clothes.

"Now we see how well each of us listened to what Alorie read three days ago. You asked me once, Lord Kithrand, what my part was in this quest. Mark me well."

She placed a branch of the fire at each corner of the stone table, and then hopped onto its surface and sat cross-legged. Her lips moved as she recited a magick, and then she opened her eyes wide and looked at all of them.

"You need answers to the questions of the sword of Frenlaw. Only an oracle can answer. That ability has been given to me."

With a movement so quick that no one could catch her wrist, she held up an arm and slashed it with a stiletto-thin blade. Crimson pumped into the dusk, splashing down on the altar.

"So long as I have blood to let, I may speak the truth. When it is gone, I will be done."

She slumped back, her eyes rolled into her head, and she spoke. "Ask me."

Kithrand licked his lips nervously, then said, "Tell us about the sword of Frenlaw."

"As always, you ask the wrong question, but we shall answer. As the sword was given to the Seven True Races, so shall it return. The gods have seen that it must be forged anew. Six from Cornuth will do the task. Once forged by the burning sea, the sword must find a hand to wield it, and that hand must be firm, for it will be tried, and will meet darkness. This is the destiny for the sword of Frenlaw."

Gavin trembled. He reached forward to stay the blood-letting, but Kithrand restrained him, saying, "She knew this." The swordsman cleared his throat then. "Who will take the sword? Can you see who?"

Pinch said, louder, "What about the burning sea? I never heard of forge underwater. What are you talking about, Viola?"

"The last must . . . make a beginning," the sage gasped. She twisted up, endeavoring to look out at them. "She must please the gods twice. The gods watch for you."

She twitched then, and the flow of blood slowed to a trickle, pooling darkly upon the stone.

"I've heard enough!" Alorie screamed. She climbed onto the stone table. "Kithrand, grab her wrist. Staunch the wound. She needn't die! The sword isn't worth it!"

But the wrist she grasped was sticky with blood, and the flesh ice-cold. She peered into dead eyes, as Viola fell back and looked into a sunset she could no longer see.

Chapter 18

REKEN STINK filled the air. The oil of their coat permeated everything, even the skin of water they handed him from time to time, though the fever that burned in him made him gulp it despite the taste.

They tilted the litter, dumping him to the ground, where pain burst through his leg and he doubled up in agony. He dug his nails into the dirty bandage swathing his leg and stifled his cry. Fire lanced and swam through his vision.

"Get up and walk."

Rowan rolled onto his back and squinted, trying very hard to see in the night. Yellow slit eyes glared knowingly at him. "I can't—I can't walk like this."

"Your friends are not coming back for you. Orders say you march with us. Get up and walk!" The ruins of Cornuth illuminated the reken soldier's back, a black broken skyline against the night. Rowan saw scores of reken climbing the wall and dropping to ground, where they loosely formed squads and began to march.

"The wound is putrefied."

The reken leaned close, and the heat of the torch seared Rowan's face. He jerked back, flat on the ground, as the soldier wished while the beast looked at his bandaging. The reken sniffed, and its muzzle wrinkled in distaste. "I can smell it, man." It kicked, and as Rowan screamed, the reken laughed to see the man rolling in the dust at its feet. "March. Either you will

191

lose it, or the wound will open and clean. Either way, you will march!''

He moved away, leaving Rowan to gasp and gather his senses. The reken knew he no longer had value as a hostage, yet they kept him alive. Kept him and planned to move him with their army.

Paws tramped past him. Rowan rolled to his side and pulled himself up. His right leg buckled, and he forced it under him, as the wound throbbed. The soldier was right. Either it would open and drain . . . or he would lose the leg and perhaps his life with it.

Waiting for the putrefaction to take him might be easier than waiting for the reken to torture him.

Rowan started after the line of torches.

Sometime in the second day, the reken halted. Rowan staggered into one of them, half blinded by fever. The creature turned on him, snarling, and knocked him into a rank of soldiers at his back. When he got up, he saw what they stared at on the far horizon.

''The sea,'' a reken growled. ''I can sniff it.'' Its hackles rose under its studded armor.

''Elf fire. It burns with elf fire.''

Rowan mopped a curtain of sweat and dirt from his eyes and squinted. He saw the blue blaze. It reminded him instantly of Kithrand at the Barrowlands, and his heart pounded for a second as he thought hopefully of rescue. He stifled it, knowing he'd been left behind so that Alorie could succeed in what she had to do.

The reken leader reached out and grabbed him by the nape of the neck. ''Elf friend! What do you know about this?''

''An army of elves paces you.'' Rowan laughed and spat the dust from his mouth.

The reken showed its red-gummed fangs and hit him across the face, then dropped him to his knees. He knew, of course, that the beast would not believe him no matter what he said.

But the reken barked something to its fellows, and the creatures showed their teeth to the sea and gathered

their weapons uneasily. Rowan looked at his leg a
moment, saw fresh, clean blood staining the bandage,
and hobbled after them. The wound had broken and
cleansed itself. Now all he had to do was heal—and get
his hands on a weapon.

That was before they camped outside Trela'ar.

He'd been to the fallen seaport once, with Brock, and
knew its outlines against the dawning sky. As he collapsed and clutched a waterskin gratefully, he recognized the structures. Like Cornuth, Trela'ar no longer
existed to rule the Straits of the Seven True Races. But,
like Cornuth, the ruins attracted those who would seek
power and conquer. Directly across from Trela'ar lay
the sister seaport of Trela'on, which Aquitane now
held. A horse could breast the distance from Trela'ar to
Trela'on in half a day . . . except that the waters ran
fiercely deep, and were wild, like the ocean the Straits
were birthed from. It was said that in the old days a
magefire weapon existed that could shoot from one city
and attack the other . . . greatly discouraging piracy on
the Straits.

And the dungeons of Trela'ar were legend.

A reken tugged on the waterskin, and Rowan hugged
it to himself greedily, taking another long pull. The
soldier threw him a bag of jerky and took away the
water, draining it itself.

"What are we waiting for?"

The reken eyed him. Rowan thought it was the same
leader who'd paced him throughout the three-day or-
deal. The Rover was beginning to tell one reken from
another, just as one hunting dog is alike and dissimilar
to another. This one had a broader forehead and a
grizzled muzzle, and a nick out of its left ear.

The reken grinned in feral humor. "A master comes
for you."

He reeled back. A malison!

The other soldiers rested on their haunches. Barks
and snarls filled the air as Rowan looked out over them.

Weapon or not, he jumped to his feet, bowling over

the reken commander. He ran, hobbling on one leg and driving with the other, footsore and lung-burned from the heat. He ran, hoping that one of the reken would drive a spear into him from behind, giving him the mercy of death.

They caught him easily, trussed him like a pig, and dragged him back into camp, laughing at his pleas.

It was there the malison found him.

Rowan woke. At least, he thought he woke, thought he'd been sleeping. The dust and heat of the day gone, stone cooled him now, rock coated with the slime and misery of centuries. It encircled him, blinded him. He put out a hand, unsure if he really had his eyes open or not . . . or did the malison take those, too.

He began to shudder and found himself unable to stop. He hugged himself, like a small frightened child in the dark, and the shuddering went on for a long, long time. Then he slept again in the dark . . . if it was dark, if he had his eyes. He was too afraid to touch them to see, and there wasn't a place on his body that was not raw, on fire, mutilated.

"Ask, and I will take away the pain."

Still dark, yet Rowan saw the being, a gray shadow against the black of the cell. He turned away, not wanting to see, and hugged himself again, crouching in the corner like one of the rats.

"It is all in your mind, my friend. Ask and you will be free of pain."

"And what do you want for that?"

A dry laugh, like the rustle of a dead twig on the ground among dead autumn leaves. He knew that laugh well by now.

"You ask, and I answer. I ask, and you answer."

"No."

"Very well." The malison drifted away. It disintegrated through the rock as though it had never been.

Rowan waited for it to come back, for repercussions.

Nothing happened. He straightened from his crouch on the ground, though his skin screamed at the movement.

If he was not truly burned . . . He flexed cautiously. Limbs that felt shattered responded.

And with that answer, he asked himself another question, one that he did not want to face. If the malison could crack him like an egg and sift through his mind, what was he still doing here?

He didn't have time to think. A handful of reken came for Rowan, their muzzles slit in vicious grins. They stood in blinding torchlight at the door and cast light on the squalid hole he'd been hiding in. They tied his hands behind his back and marched him down the corridor and then up, up and up and up until a glimmer of sunlight and fresh air trickled down through holes in the stone and mortar, and he blinked, and knew where they'd brought him.

Now the torture began.

Rowan had a second to take a deep breath as they caught him up and plunged him upside down in a stagnant well, holding him by his ankles. The black water devoured him, but he was a good swimmer and not afraid of water and could hold his breath for a long time.

He didn't worry until the iron fingers at his ankles loosened, and then his boots were twisted and pulled off his feet. The worn, thin knit stockings came next. Fire blazed along the soles of his exposed feet.

Then the heat branded him. He opened his mouth, gasping with the pain, and the black water roared in, choking him. He thrashed wildly, choking and convulsing, drowning while his feet flamed.

That pain he knew was real as he crawled back to his cell. The reken paused for him every now and then, kicked him in the flanks and waited until he crawled some more. They threw his boots in after him when he reached the cell and curled in the corner gratefully, but he couldn't put them on. He'd never be able to wear his boots again.

He'd probably never be able to walk again on the charred lumps he knew as his feet. He coughed, and spit up black water, and vomited it as far away from himself as he could.

"Ask, and I will take away the pain."

"And give me back feet?" Rowan made an ironic noise and turned his face away, but the malison seemed to encompass all of the dark cell.

"If you ask." A pause. "You don't believe I can?"

Rowan said nothing. He tried to think of sunshine and green grass, and a mug of well-brewed beer.

"Yes, I see now how this must be done. I will heal you now, and then, later, when you are truly desperate, you will be ready to answer my questions and beg for my aid . . . because then you will know my power."

"No!" Rowan jerked his feet under him, afraid then, but the creature touched him with dry hands, dry as a snake is dry and slightly warm. It pulled his legs out, and the excruciating pain of the fire went away as it stroked his wounds. Without seeing, Rowan knew his feet were healed, without even a blister to show he'd been tortured. He began to cry. The malison faded away.

He didn't cry for joy. He cried in the horror of the thing that had been done to him—for what would be done to him the next day, or the next, until he broke and did what the malison wanted of him.

Chapter 19

"AWAKE NOW!"

Alorie started, to the feel of claws on her arm. She rolled, her longknife twisted under her, and tugged desperately at its hilt, but the soft brown eyes looking down at her stilled her cry.

"Missy awake now?" The Mutt reached out again and pawed at her with its stubby, padded hand.

The sea roared, and the gulls called fiercely as they wheeled overhead in the morning light. She blinked in surprise. Where had the Mutt come from? Alorie patted the being's hand. "Yes, I'm awake."

"Good." The Mutt straightened. He was a soft brown-and-white pinto, and the pelt over his face was long. She'd forgotten just how doglike the Mutts could be. "I am Jasper. The reken are coming, and we've come to warn you and lead you from their path."

"Coming from where?"

"Cornuth. They march to Trela'ar, as always." The Mutt's eyes teared sorrowfully. "We are the sons of the sons of Cornuth. We prepare to fight when our fathers' fathers could not. You must trust us and come with us quickly. The elf fire drew us. You're in great danger."

Around her, Kithrand was already whistling up the horses and Gavin was carefully obscuring all sign of the fire. They'd been surrounded in their sleep by the group of Mutts on donkeys, their long gray ears flopping in the uncertain morning.

Elven fire still blazed over Viola's body. Alorie looked, in morbid fascination, and saw that the mage had changed very little. The rock slab made a perfect funeral pyre.

"The fire won't burn out until tomorrow night," Kithrand said. "It is done that way with elves—two days of honor." He'd come up behind her softly. "Be wary, milady," he added in a lowered voice. "I've never seen Mutts wear arms so aggressively before."

And as she looked back to Jasper, she saw that every one of the group wore leather armor and mail, and carried his weapons with authority.

Jasper waited at the head of her horse.

Pinch had already mounted, his jaw tight. The early-morning fog made his blond curls even tauter on his head and chin. He'd mourned hardest for Viola, and as Alorie's gaze swept him, he looked away.

"She died for me," Alorie said quietly.

The dwarf's gaze shot back to her, the color of his eyes so like the color of Viola's hair. "Nay," he said gruffly. "Don't grieve yourself. She died knowing that we have victory in our hands—we've got the sword. She'll miss the hard times ahead, but she foresaw the victory."

"Missy." Jasper bent with his hands clasped to give her a leg up.

She grabbed a handful of mane and, with his help, mounted. The faery horses crowded her. Now there were only four riders and still eleven horses. Kithrand leaped up. He said to Jasper, "You may ride the horses, if you wish."

Jasper grinned, his red tongue lolling from between sharp teeth. "We prefer the devil we know to the devil we don't." He swung into his saddle and kneed his beast. It sprang into a gallop, leading the way east down the beach, water spraying from its hooves.

On a sandy knoll, the reken with the nicked ear halted and threw up a paw. This reken was Nork, the commander. He'd earned his masculinity through years of service to the malison. He, like his masters, hoped someday to have his ferocity and courage breed true. His fellows immediately sank to their haunches, winded by the march, as their commander dropped for a moment to all fours and fluidly ran forward over the dunes.

Gulls screeched, and the tang of salt air stung the reken's nostrils, which flared wide with exhaustion and were sunburned from the last week's campaign. He did not begrudge his soldiers a moment's rest, but he determined to investigate the elf fire as soon as he could, to settle the matter. Having spotted the fire on the horizon, though the captured man had jeered at him, he had reported it dutifully to Ayah, and the master now sent him to determine what caused the phenomenon. Nork took the detail as a matter of honor.

The sun speared his sight with heat. He blinked and squinted tightly. The elf fire did not bother him—it burned coolly—but as he slunk close to the stone, what lay upon the natural altar gave him pause. He went back to his legs, though his spine ached. The masters taught them to stand early, and punished when a reken soldier did not, but he had little liking for it. Yet now he grasped the advantage. He could see better.

A woman lay inside the blue fire, a woman of power, to be given elf fire. His muzzle split in a wide grin. He looked back to his tired troopers and barked sharply.

"Gather wood. I want a litter made. The master will be pleased with this one."

While they scampered to do his biding, he hunkered down and assessed the elven fire. It would be difficult, but with any luck, he could extract the body and quench the fire without losing more than one of his troopers. He growled in satisfaction and signaled a drummer, then squelched that signal. No, he would take her to the malison himself.

"And you've never heard of any burning sea?" Gavin said to Jasper again, as he sat back comfortably, a large joint of cold meat in his hand.

Alorie ignored the questioning. For the first time in days, she felt safe, secure, in a haven of sorts, though the Mutts told her Trela'ar was only a day's hard ride away. The reken did not bother this tiny stronghold, believing the Mutts to be as Mutts had always been, and indeed, even with Jasper's militancy, the stronghold could be easily overrun if the reken army wished. The Mutts lived here because the reken suffered them to, and they had taken advantage of it.

The table was light on vegetables, but the meat was good and well spiced, and the drink a tangy wine. Pinch had had too much already and sat back, in his cups, humming a low dwarfish tune to himself that made Alorie blush if she sat and picked out the words, so she'd stopped. She tilted her head, rubbing her tired neck, and looking at the ceiling of driftwood and thatching. A little bit of sunlight came in, dappling her vision.

". . . but there is a forge, indeed. It's still used a little by the army, mostly for shoeing, but it's there, banked, always smoldering, at the edge of Trela'ar, next to the quarry."

Kithrand's brows danced as they always did when the lord was excited or amused. He didn't look amused now as he leaned forward on his elbows. "Is it watched?"

"No. They sometimes don't come for weeks, except to replenish the fire. If you have weapons you need tempered or repaired, I can get you in." Jasper sat with a confident look on his doggish face.

It's the eyebrows, Alorie thought. Dogs have eyebrows that give them expression, and so, of course, do Mutts. Lazily she reached for her goblet of wine. "What makes you think so?"

"They use Mutts to run it, from Trela'ar. All of us look alike to them. They'd never notice."

"What about the others? Wouldn't they give alarm?" Servants tend to keep their loyalties, for one reason or another.

"Not with a knife stuck between their ribs," Jasper said.

Kithrand and Gavin crossed glances that Alorie didn't miss. Mutts talking casually of killing their kind had never been run across before. Gavin said diffidently, "That would be murder."

Jasper stretched his hand on his table. His thick nails, like his pelt, were mottled brown and white. "No, my friends. This is soon to be war. I have heard . . . the Corruptor is free again. Don't treat me like your hunting dogs, or your humble servants. I am a different . . . animal."

"No one has thought you were an animal."

"No," the Mutt agreed. "It takes one of the Seven True Races to plan a murder . . . or a war." His wide brown eyes flickered over them. "You're in trouble. You need a guide to Trela'ar, and I'll go. The Lady Alorie hasn't told her story, but I know the name. Is she from Sinobel? Is her house the holder of the High Counselorship?"

"Yes," she whispered.

"Then she is the one I've been waiting for. To her I will offer the service I owe my High King." He pushed himself from the table and went to his haunches. "If you will take it, Lady Alorie of Sergius."

"I will, Jasper—though you may not like the service I will ask of you."

The Mutt's gaze flickered. It was obvious he hadn't expected that answer from her. He got to his feet. "That's settled then."

Gavin spit out a piece of gristle. "But what of the burning sea?"

Kithrand shrugged, answering, as he sat back with his goblet, "A forge is a forge. Oracles are often couched in riddles. Viola said six from Cornuth, but now it's just the four of us. As for the smithy, it's close to the sea, and that's good enough for me."

"You're a poet and don't know it." Pinch giggled, before falling over on his face.

Alorie kicked away from the table to take the dwarf

up and help him to a corner, where he curled up and
went to sleep. Before he closed his eyes, she saw the
shrewd light in the silvery orbs, and walked back to the
table, wondering just how drunk the gnarled man really
was. She stared thoughtfully into her wine and listened
to the Mutt explain the route to Trela'ar to Kithrand
and Gavin. When the sunlight faded, she excused herself and took a little walk outside the compound.

Perhaps it was the sea again, or the wine, but she
found herself fingering Brock's signet ring on her hand,
and thinking over the loss of her companions and Rowan.
Her family's death now seemed a faraway thing. There
were times when she heard something and stored it
away, thinking that when she returned, she would have
to tell it to her father, and then suddenly remembered
that he was gone now.

She sat down in reverie and leaned her back against a
green sapling. Spring was drawing to a close. Soon it
would be summer. The Fivemonth was nearly spent.
The responsibilities Brock had placed on her overwhelmed
her—and yet, despite what she did, she seemed no
closer to understanding her role or what she needed to
do. Hurry, he'd said. She rubbed her forehead, and the
darkened ring, long dead, took fire.

The hooded face within the aura looked at her and
said, "Where are you?"

Alorie stiffened, losing her voice and words for a
moment. "I—I'm near Trela'ar. I have the sword of
Frenlaw, but it's useless."

The countenance smiled slightly. She caught her breath.
"Brock—Brock, they told me you were dead!"

"I? But you know better. Tell me what you're doing
. . . it's not what I instructed you to do."

She blinked. Had he forgotten? "I read the prophecy,
as you suggested. The sword—that came from the council at Veil. I brought the sword out of Cornuth. Rowan's
gone . . . the reken have him—"

"I'll take care of him," the image said smoothly.
"What's wrong with the sword?"

"There's no blade. We've got to try to reforge one."

The image wavered. She rubbed her eyes. The likeness of Brock faded, then flared again. "Good. Then come to me at Trela'ar."

"Are you there?"

"I . . . will be." The aura flickered and waned, and she reached out to it, as though she could save it, and the countenance ran through her fingers like water. Though the ring became still, the voice whispered a last time, "Come to me at Trela'ar."

"You will ask me this time," the malison told Rowan, as the reken dragged him kicking from the cell.

The Rover bowed his shoulders. They overpowered him, though he fought like an ox in the corridors, the malison having done its deed too well, and when healing him, healed his whole body. The hard days on the journey and the arrow wound in the thigh were ancient memories to his young and now vigorous body. He shrugged, and one of the reken lost its grip and slammed against the corridor wall.

Rowan grinned.

The malison moved around them, a shrouded being within a cloud, and it formed pseudopods and reached out.

"I can make what they are going to do even more terrible."

Rowan ceased to struggle. The soldiers let go of him. The malison faded once more into the stones of the dungeons.

"Why do you take orders from . . . from that?" Rowan said, as they marched him forward.

The reken looked at him. "Because we fear it," the being answered, and fell in line with him.

Sombered by the response, Rowan quieted. Instead, he took stock of the levels of the dungeon, and the stonework, and he planned. By the time they reached the torture chambers, his mouth was dry, but his mind still quick. Whatever the reken intended to do to him,

Rowan intended that he should be gone from there before they had the chance.

He halted when he saw the litter to one side, and the wan-faced woman lying upon it.

"Viola!"

The reken blocked him from her.

"What are you doing with her?" Rowan dug in his heels, for the woman lay as still as death itself. He didn't know how they'd gotten the mage, or what they planned to do, but he tore his way through the guards.

Viola sat up. She turned her delicate face to him and combed her silver locks with her fingers away from her eyes.

"Where's Alorie? Do they have all of you?"

The enchantress smiled thinly and stood. She wavered a moment as though her legs couldn't quite hold her weight. She raised her hands to him, and after a hesitation, the reken let him get close enough to touch her.

Her flesh was as cold as ice, and he flinched, but the woman had him then, and bent him to her, and smiled wide, and then he saw the blood staining her pale gums as she fought to pull him close.

Ungraven! Rowan tore away from her, flesh ripping from the backs of his hands, and fought the reken, which now jostled him close. He knew what the Ungraven mage could do to him . . . he knew now what his torture would be, as she drained his body of all blood, and supped delicately on the carcass that would be left. No, he wouldn't die—the malison would see to that—no more than Viola could ever live again, despite what the creature had done to her. How had they gotten her . . . how had she died, and where? What about Alorie?

With the same inhuman strength she'd shown, Rowan tore a sword off the nearest reken. He swung brutally, and the blade thunked deeply into flesh. He staggered, but kept on cutting. The Ungraven dropped to her knees and went for the fresh black blood, her silver hair falling into it as she lapped it up.

Rowan fought his way out of the torture chamber, found the corridor empty, as the screams of the Ungraven's victims multiplied, and went upward, searching for freedom. If Alorie was in Trela'ar, he would find her.

Chapter 20

GAVIN LAUGHED AS he tried to fit one of the small patchwork Mutt saddles to the back of his proud faery mount. The horse sniffed suspiciously and danced in the marshland. "Hold still," the strapping farmer said, and slapped the horse's withers. The horse snorted and did as it was bade. The leather saddle, worn flat as a blanket and repaired a thousand times over, would be far too small for Gavin. "As long as the stirrups hold," he declared, "I will ride like a king."

"I'd rather sleep like a peasant." Alorie yawned. She came out of the compound, feeling stiff and wrinkled.

Jasper paused in saddling Alorie's horse and looked to the dark sky. His sharp face wrinkled, and he sniffed deeply. "There," he said. "Now you'll see your burning water, Lord Kithrand."

The elf lord followed him curiously as the Mutt took him across the field and pointed to the shoreline.

The dawn came up, and its pink-gold rays sparkled across the water. Alorie came up quietly behind them.

"Close enough for any oracle," Kithrand answered. He clasped Jasper's shoulder. The Mutt grinned, showing those sharp white teeth again.

"Will the rest be as close? There aren't six of us anymore, only four."

They swung around to face Alorie. Kithrand cleared

his throat. "Milady, Jasper's only concern is to get us to the forge. The rest of our needs—"

"He's pledged himself to my service. There are only a few of us left . . . we'll need Jasper and more to carry the sword where it will do the most good. He should know what we're doing."

Gavin and Pinch came up behind them, leading the saddled horses, except for Kithrand's stallion, which pranced freely after, his cream tail like a banner behind him.

The Mutt's grin evaporated. He placed a hand on his swordbelt. "Don't think to use us unwittingly," the creature warned.

"Never," Alorie said.

Gavin nodded. "He has the right to know, Kithrand, as do they all."

His antennae twitched in annoyance on his brow. Then the elf lord laughed. "I'm persuaded. We did more than journey to Cornuth to read the wall, Jasper—we took away with us the sword of Frenlaw. It's been prophesied that the sword will lead us against the Corruptor."

The Mutt's eyes took on a fierce, blazing joy, and he lifted his pawlike hands. "The sword! Who carries it? You must have an elven spell on it to keep it hidden."

Gavin pulled the bladeless sword from his belt.

The light died from Jasper's eyes, and he reached toward it, then pulled back his hand. Then he nodded. "Now I know why you need a forge. Then we'd best hurry, for it will be night before we find it."

He paused to help Alorie mount, then strode past them to his compound, where his donkey waited for him. So also did his mate, a Mutt female with silken gold hair that feathered lightly about her wrists and ankles as well as tumbled down the back of her head. She held two hawks on one wrist.

"The messengers are ready for the elf lord," she said

shyly as they rode up. "But they won't know where to fly. I don't understand."

Kithrand took one of the hawks from her, saying, "They will know where to go." He took the hood off and stared into the creature's golden eyes until it quieted. "Can you scribe, Lady Alorie?"

"Of course."

"Then dismount long enough to take up ink and pen for me. There . . . she has paper waiting for you."

Alorie slid down. Her pack rested by the table, for Jasper's mate had insisted on replenishing it herself and had been secretive about it. Alorie sat and grasped the pen impatiently. Trela'ar called her . . . Brock and Rowan in Trela'ar . . . but she stilled the pulse that wanted to race in her.

"I think we should let my kinsmen at Charlbet know that the sword is found, and that they should join Rathincourt's army. Also, to notify King Bryant of the Delvings, if he should care to send aid. Agreed?"

Gavin and Pinch nodded even as she already scratched out the wording. She flushed as she paused. "It won't be in elvish."

"They'll understand. And as for the second hawk, I'll send it to Rathincourt himself. You were asleep by then, but the three of us decided last night that we should cross the Straits to Trela'on, and go overland from there."

"That's Aquitane's holding."

Kithrand's mount shifted weight under him easily, a reflection of his rider's emotions. "We'll keep you from his hands. Chances are he never made it out of the Delvings, anyway."

"And from there?"

"To Dirtellak," Gavin said. He puffed out his chest. "To protect the Tellak River."

The Tellak, old man river of the lower kingdoms,

feeding a hundred hundred miles and more of land, with fingers stretched out to all his children, a broad, mighty river that rolled unceasingly, flooded in high rain, wiping out villages by the score, yet treated with respect by those who depended on him. "If the Corruptor goes for the Tellak, we'll be paralyzed."

"Not quite, but I agree with Bullheart's strategy. Sooner or later, there will be a battle at Dirtellak."

Pinch scratched his side. "It wouldn't be a bad place for Rathincourt to quarter the army."

Alorie bent over the paper. "Then he should meet us at Dirtellak." She scratched the words out quickly, as a shadow passed over her, but when she looked up, she saw nothing. Dirtellak was south of Trela'on . . . perhaps it would be a good idea to keep Rathincourt face to face with Aquitane, to remind the usurper lord of the power she could flex if she had to. And with the sword . . .

Deftly, she tightly rolled both scrolls.

Kithrand fastened his to his bird and tossed it in the air, jesses trailing behind it as it took wing. With a piercing whistle, it circled and took off, toward the sea.

The second hawk he held a moment longer, then it followed its companion.

"Will it find Rathincourt?" Alorie crooked her neck until she could no longer see the hawks in the lightening sky.

Kithrand grinned. "If my memory is any good, he couldn't mistake the lord . . . unless Rathincourt's snow-white mane has fallen since we parted ways last."

The mention of the lord's hair brought back a disturbing memory to Alorie, and she bent to get her pack, determined not to let her expression be read. Ironhair . . . an iron-haired traitor within their ranks. She'd grown used to being the target of reken soldiers and had not thought of Stonedeep for days, and she wondered fleetingly if she'd ever see the haven again.

Jasper's mate put a soft hand on her arm. "Please, milady. We . . . have a gift for you."

She straightened and followed the Mutt around the corner of the huts, where several others waited, their ears pricked in shy anticipation.

They handed her a length of white cloth without a flaw in its threads, woven soft enough for a gown. She hesitated to take it with her trailworn hands, but they pressed it into her palms.

"Thank you. I . . . don't know what to say."

Jasper's mate smiled. "It came from long-ago Cornuth. It was to be the nightdress of a famous lady, or so the story says. We had many bolts, and use it for our pups, and celebrations. This is the last length, and we want you to have it. It will fit in your pack?"

"Yes, I think so." She'd have to fold it many times, but she'd carry it as long as she could. Impulsively, she hugged the Mutt. "Thank you all." A piercing whistle interrupted her. "I have to leave."

"All-Mother watch you," the female whispered and let her go.

Rowan hugged a broken stone wall and ignored the rumblings of his stomach. Troops moved past him. They'd been moving out of the seaport all morning and into warships anchored in the harbor, and he followed them cautiously, looking and listening for word of prisoners, or important captures, but had heard nothing.

He despaired of hearing news about Alorie. These reken came from many dens, all over the upper lands and to the west beyond the Delvings. Soldiers never ceased to grumble, but their main thrust now was to the docks. Something big was being readied, and it seemed to have nothing to do with their tiny party coming out of Cornuth with the sword of Frenlaw.

He gripped his own sword at ready now, an ill-kept, nicked, and battered reken weapon. Either the legend-

ary sword was of no importance to them, or the matter
had already been handled.

He swept his hair from his brow and pressed tightly
against the ruins, as another pair of reken came past.
These two argued loudly.

". . . barfing my guts out over the water."

"Orders are orders."

A bark of amusement. "Today. Tomorrow the malison will have changed their mind again."

"Ours isn't to know."

"I know that I marched long sweaty days under
Aquitane to get Trela'on . . . now they want us to go
and burn it." The creature growled. "And I would,
happily, if I could march to do it. Don't like boats!"

They passed out of his hearing range, arguing about
what booze best prevented seasickness.

Rowan came out of the shadows, thinking that Aquitane
had picked traitorous allies. As his stomach cramped
again, he saw a singleton reken soldier weaving down
the ally, a full pack banging against its back. With a
grin, the Rover faded back into hiding, without wondering if the reken ate anything he could stomach. The
sword glimmered. Eat and drink, first. Then he would
return to seeking Alorie.

Jasper came back to her side as the sea breeze whipped
her heavy hair from her shoulders. He replaced a knife
in his sheath after cleansing the blood off. "The forge
is ours."

She looked away. Another death. Her horse stamped
under her before trying once more to lower its head to
crop the salty marsh grasses at the edge of the beach.
She couldn't see the ocean line from the depths of the
quarry. Trela'ar beckoned. 'Come to me at Trela'ar,'
Brock had said. And Rowan would be with him. It
would take the better part of the night to get the forge
hot enough to work with, and they had yet to locate the
metal with which to make a new blade. She'd have
plenty of time to brave Trela'ar and get back.

Gavin cleared his throat. She nodded to him then, and the big man leaned over to the Mutt. "Where can we find scrap metal . . . steel, good steel?"

"Nowhere. The forge has been cleaned out. It's been used recently. I would say the reken are fully equipped and getting ready to launch a major attack. One of my spies tells me that at high tide this afternoon, five major warships sailed across the Straits."

"Pray our hawk gets to Rathincourt." She kicked her horse then, turning her heart away from Trela'ar.

Mutts worked the smithy. The bellows roared and the flames grew hot, and they stoked them hotter yet. Jasper supervised the moving in of fresh barrels of water to cool the metal, and Gavin himself bowed to the anvil and moved it closer to the fire.

"I wish now we'd not let Crust go," Kithrand observed.

"I can make the blade," Gavin said. "I apprenticed myself to a smithy once because I trusted no weapon I hadn't tempered myself."

The sky darkened. Night would hide the smoke from the forge a little, but not the heat. Alorie turned to Trela'ar and stifled a cry.

The ocean flamed. Not near, but across the Straits . . . she could see the water boiled in crimson flame.

Pinch hobbled to her side. "It's Trela'on," he said. "Trela'on is burning. And that's what Viola meant . . . that we would be here, on this night, while it's attacked. Not a pale sunrise or sunset coloring the sea."

"We've got to find the metal. Jasper—"

But the Mutt had stripped off his leather armor, to work at stoking the fires. His eyes glittered. "I know where metal can be had."

"Why didn't you tell us of it sooner?"

The Mutt paused. Naked, in the twilight, he looked more than ever like a rangy dog, stretched out and made upright, his features humanized, but his hide as silken as ever. "I trust you no more than you trust me. We need each other, but I have seen the look in your eyes, Kithrand. What dog would murder so casually? Our weapons are our *life*."

He signaled his men and pointed at the ground. "Your swords."

The Mutts stopped their tasks and found their weapons. As they filed past Jasper, without hesitation each of them dropped his blade. Metal rang as they piled up. When they had done, half a dozen swords lay at Jasper's feet. He gathered them up and handed them to Gavin. "They are old, but worthy. My people brought them from Cornuth when they fled. I like to think that among them might be a sword used in the High King's service. Melt them down. Use the metal for a new blade for the sword of Frenlaw."

Alorie touched Kithrand's arm. "There's your six from Cornuth. Not six people . . ."

But Gavin frowned. "Your arms—"

Jasper snapped, "You've given your service and your lives for this. Are Mutts allowed less? Take them!"

The great farmer smiled then, the muscles on his arms bulging with the weight of the swords. "For Gavin Bullheart," he answered, "your friendship was always good enough. For the sword of Frenlaw, only the best."

He returned to the forge and the great melting kettles, the Mutts trailing along behind him to work the bellows and continue building the fire. The two-sided building glowed with their efforts.

Kithrand went for his bow as hooves suddenly pounded along the beach. "It's a patrol!"

He shoved Alorie down, but she rolled out from under his knee and got to her feet, pulling her own longknife. "Protect the forge. I'll draw them off the beach."

She vaulted her horse and kicked it, hard. It squealed in anger and raced off across the dunes. She heard the reken yelp of triumph as they spotted her and came after. She leaned over her mount's neck and whispered words in elvish that Kithrand had taught her. The horse whinnied and stretched out, its hooves barely touching the sands.

By the burning sea, the sword would be reforged. Gavin would carry it triumphantly across the Straits to Dirtellak. Her part was done. Now, now, she would follow her heart and go to Trela'ar!

Chapter 21

"GO AFTER HER!"

Kithrand licked his lips nervously. "You must be insane," he responded to the big man. "I haven't enough arrows to attack what's left of the reken army holding that city."

Gavin flexed his shoulders and looked down at Jasper's man. "You're sure they caught up with her?"

The Mutt nodded, his spotted pelt rippling. "She bolted right into them. I thought the horse would carry her free, but it stumbled in the sand. She held on like a burr, and it righted itself, but they had her."

Pinch hefted his ax. "The Mutt and I will go. An elf is little enough protection for my back, anyhow."

"I won't tolerate your words, little man."

The dwarf's gaze glimmered harshly at him. "You don't have to, lordship. Nobody's said much about it, but we all know you took to your heels and ran at Cornuth. If you'd held your place with the rest of us, Rowan would still be with us." He pulled a donkey close and mounted it. "Gavin needs to work the metal. Perhaps your lordship could take a turn at the bellows."

With that, the dwarf kicked his heels into the startled beast, and with a grunt, it bolted into the night. Fluidly, Jasper swung aboard his mount and followed after.

A darkness stained the elf lord's face as he stared into their disappearing backs. Gavin took care to say nothing as he plotted the forging of a sword.

Alorie breathed hard as the reken surrounded her.
The horse quivered and shook himself, but stepped
soundly, and she forced herself to quiet. He'd not broken anything. She wrapped the reins about her hands
and loosened his mane.

The lead reken's eyes smoldered, and it grinned.
"We've been looking for you, milady," the beast said,
as it reached over and tore the leather from her fingers.
"The mage sent us."

Surprise widened her eyes, and the reken added something over its shoulder with a guttural bark.

She was even more surprised when not one of the
patrol left to investigate farther down the beach. Satisfied with her capture, they wheeled and returned to
Trela'ar.

A fallen city, but not destroyed like Cornuth, it graced
the natural cove. Trela'on's burning illuminated it, and
she rode in to an eerie orange glow. She could even
smell the ashes on the night air, along with the sea. It
must have been magnificent once. Now crude drawings
obscured the beautiful stonework and natural erosion
had brought its gates down. Handfuls of reken guards
threw gaming sticks and stones and fought among themselves. The patrol garnered one or two curious glances,
and then the soldiers returned to gambling.

Alorie shivered in spite of herself. She rubbed her
signet ring yet again, as if to reassure herself that Brock
lay hidden somewhere in Trela'ar. How Brock had
persuaded reken to aid his efforts, she had no idea . . .
but she hoped that he had made it to Veil and regained
his powers, and now waited to ply them. Any man who
could get past the walled circles of Sinobel . . .

The patrol faded into the interior of the city, drawing
closer and closer to the immense fortress that overlooked the harbor. She looked at it, slits of windows in
the towers, dead black eyes watching the rest of the
city. That part of Trela'ar did not have a glorious
history. The dungeons of Trela'ar had been an abomina-
tion on the face of the earth.

Her neck flexed so that she could continue watching it even as they rode past.

In the shadows of the fortress, the city lay quiet. No reken prowled here. The patrol rode another block and then halted, waiting, in a darkened street.

A cowled figure stepped out of the night. Black-gloved hands waved over the reken's faces, which had gone slack and motionless.

"Go and forget," the man said.

The reken pivoted their mounts and rode off, leaving her alone in the street. The signet ring warmed and lit up the night like a beacon.

"Oh, Brock!" she cried, and threw herself off her horse and into his arms.

She drew back from the embrace uneasily, even as the man shrugged off his hood and pulled his cloak back. In the faint moonlight, she could barely see his face, though she searched for it. "Where's Rowan?"

"He's safe."

"The other reken never even looked at me coming into the city. They thought I was a prisoner."

He nodded. "Tell me about the sword."

Alorie swallowed. The uneasiness built in her. She couldn't name what she felt, but it wasn't happiness at the reunion. She stepped back and nervously fingered the ring. Then she caught at the feeling and pulled it in, and her heart stopped momentarily.

A scent wafted on the air. She couldn't name it, didn't know where it had come from, except that it hung, heavy and soulless, and she knew its odor well . . . like a brother to that of the dark unicorn.

She blinked and stepped back again, and the faery horse whickered uncertainly.

"Come, Alorie. I need to know."

"I—don't have it."

"That I can see."

He held out his gloved hand enticingly to her, and she wondered who she faced.

"Wh—where's Rowan?"

"They're looking for him. They should have him soon. I have a rather short leash." And the man smiled, and she knew from the shape of his teeth that it wasn't Brock she talked to.

"Oh, my *God*," she cried, and pulled the ring from her finger and threw it at his face. She caught hold of her horse's mane, endeavoring to mount it.

The man screamed in pain and hate as the ring flared up. Magefire touched him, white molten light that blazed in his face, and the countenance of Brock blazed and left in its stead another face . . . one she would see in her nightmares as long as she would live.

The Corruptor reached for her. The faery horse cried out in pain, unable to bear his presence. It lashed out, a hoof grazing the man's thigh, and he went to his knees. The horse lunged past him, carrying Alorie with him. She kicked and tried to swing herself up.

The night rang with the being's cries. She heard reken drums and knew an alarm had been sounded. Sobbing, she let the horse drag her several streets away until she could hold on no more and dropped to the ground, and the horse clattered away, a white cloud in the darkness.

Alorie curled in agony, her hands under her. Brock and Rowan were lost to her again. How had the Corruptor been able to reach her? She wiped useless tears away. Then she took a deep breath and staggered to her feet. Abandoned buildings yawned, and she darted into one of the open doorways, knowing that reken would be on her trail. Rowan had taught her well . . . they would follow her scent and her body heat until she confused them or outran them.

Howlings belled down the alley. She pressed herself to the wall and inched her way farther inside. A step gave way, and she fell, tumbling into a mouth of darkness.

She opened her eyes. She looked up at the night, and moonlight slivered down. Around her, gemstones glowed.

With a groan, she rolled over. Nothing broken, though her ankle felt as though it swelled inside her boot.

Alabaster walls gleamed at her, walls bordered with a fine powdering of dwarven gemstone. Alorie limped over to them and looked back the way she'd come. She was downstairs, under the street level. Then it struck her, even in the dimness, what sort of place she'd tumbled into.

She dropped to her knees. "Forgive me, All-Mother. I didn't mean to intrude."

Her whisper died out in the emptiness. She heard a drip, drip, and looked, and saw the moon reflected in a pool of dead water in the center of the temple. Alorie got to her feet a second time and held her hand out, touching the wall. She saw a faint picture there and leaned close.

Paintings on the temple walls, but not crudities as drawn by reken soldiers. No, this building was still inviolate, even from the fall of Trela'ar. She frowned to see in the twilight.

A white unicorn. She could see it repeated several times. Figures cavorted about it, dancing with it, enticing it, pleasing it, with wreathes of flowers and gifts in urns. Perfumes and oils, she supposed. Alorie traced the beast. It was not a pretty animal, but like the one she'd seen. Its anger and majesty could make the earth tremble. These youths did not have the beast captured, but rather seemed to dare it.

Her fingertips stopped as she encountered another drawing. The unicorn charged at one of the worshipers, horn down, a deadly lance. Alorie held her breath as she encountered the next.

But instead of showing a skewered boy, it showed him reaching up, boldly grasping the horn, that same weapon whose spiraled edges would make ribbons of his hands, and in the next mural, he vaulted in the air, tossed over the unicorn's head.

The last showed him riding the unicorn, the beast tamed for a moment.

Alorie's hand dropped away from the frieze as though burned. She'd never seen or heard of such a thing in her life. It charged her. Her thoughts fogged and memory tugged. What was it she should remember—and did not!

A stone dropped from above. She heard the rattle of armor and footsteps in the alley. The reken! They'd found her, or would, shortly.

Alorie bowed her head. Her downcast glance caught the edge of the pool. How deep was it? Nothing could be seen in its depths . . . nothing. She slipped to the edge of the sacred well and let herself down into the maw of the water.

It swallowed her whole. She clung to the edge of the tile by her fingertips, but the pool was slimed, and her grasp slipped. She held her breath and tried to listen through the muffled depth of the water.

The steps of the reken vibrated through the stone flooring to her. The water trembled as though affronted. Her ears rang and her lungs began to swell. She couldn't hold her breath much longer.

Her heart drummed inside her chest. She was going to have to breathe. Alorie pushed the feeling away. The steps faded. Her ears pounded. She clawed weakly at the edge, trying to pull herself up.

The water claimed her. She felt its soothing touch all about her, as though she were a naked babe, dipped in the waters for a blessing. She wiggled, fishlike, and opened her mouth, gasping. Even her closed eyes saw red. She had to breathe! Breathe, or let go forever.

The white unicorn brushed her thoughts.

It glowed in her head, a white light that pulled her from the water, pulled her from drowning, pulled her from the past.

As her head emerged from the water, she opened her eyes and saw the moon glaring down from the open ceiling. Alorie gasped and choked and dragged herself over the lip of the well.

Water poured from her clothes as she sloshed over

the temple flooring, washing away the dust of weeks. With a shiver, she climbed the broken stairway and walked out into the street.

The reken had gone.

Remembering Kithrand, she pursed her lips and gave a light whistle. A moment later, the white horse clattered down the alley. This time, she jumped for and made the stirrup and drew herself aboard. She sagged against the horse's neck. "Find Kithrand," she begged the creature. The horse threw its head up and neighed, and galloped down the street as though it knew what she asked of it.

Rowan heard the clamor. He flinched, having slept in a cramped hole in a wall, well hidden from any who might search for him, though he dreamed of the malison coming for him yet again. He rubbed his pinched neck and stretched.

Keeping a cautious distance, he roamed the alleyway for blocks. Nothing met his eye, then he kicked something, and picked it out of the gutter skirting the street. It warmed in his hand, and he knew it well. Brock's signet ring. Alorie had been here!

He ducked into an open doorway as two soldiers ran past, blades glittering in their claws.

"Get the girl! They've lost the Sergius girl! They want her cut off before she gets out of the city," one gasped to the other, and they split up, racing down the street.

Rowan smiled broadly as they went past him. He polished her ring absently, and it warmed again as he thought of her. He had to trust that Gavin and Kithrand and Pinch would take care of her now. He pocketed the ring and quietly scaled a broken wall and perched on a rooftop, marking the reken soldiers that searched the abandoned streets.

An orange blaze met him. He looked out, and saw Trela'on burning. That too made him smile, for he knew then where Gavin and Kithrand and Alorie would take the sword of Frenlaw to be repaired and wielded. Across the Straits, to the lower lands. He spread his Rover cloak about him and settled on the roof. In the morning, he would steal a fishing skiff.

Pinch and Jasper found her at the edge of town, the remains of a guard patrol scattered at their feet. Their swords were dark with tainted blood, and their donkeys brayed suspiciously as she loomed out of the night.

She smiled tightly. "We need to do this quietly."

"Never mind," Jasper said. "There's no one left to see us go." He took the rein from her hand and led her after him.

They reached the forge at dawn. Its glow lit up the skies brighter than the slanting sun, and Gavin stood at its edge, sweat-soaked, bare from the waist up. He gave a cry as they rode up, and thrust a blade into the air, a blade red-hot from the fires, a blade already set into the ancient hilt and pounded into a double edge. Even as they watched, he lowered it to the anvil and struck it yet again, sparks drifting into the sooty air, falling away.

The metal rang. With a shout of triumph, Gavin plunged it for the last time into a barrel of water, cooling its surface.

"The sword is finished!"

Chapter 22

"STAY WITH ME, milady," Rathincourt said.

"All right." Alorie looked out over the knoll, one of the few points of advantage over Dirtellak, which was to be a battlefield.

The regiments below were a colorful assortment of volunteers and mercenaries and lords' guards from all over the lands. Rathincourt had worked a miracle . . . four thousand men took the field. Her mare shifted under her and swished her tail as she settled comfortably in the saddle.

She wore a heavy, dark blue riding velvet, her hair was done back with net and pearls, and her worn hands were hidden inside soft gloves. The only reminder of the past few weeks' adventure was a battered pack, lashed to the back of her mare's saddle.

Lord Rathincourt wore full armor, but his helm was balanced on the saddle in front of him as he looked out over the fields and watched the army of the Seven True Races digging in. His full head of hair, as white as ever, fluffed on the morning breeze. He turned and smiled at Alorie, feeling her gaze on him. "I smell victory."

Alorie forced a nervous smile. "I wonder what Gavin smells."

Rathincourt laughed and slapped her knee. "Bullheart smells destiny. When he rides up on the crest beside us, a thousand voices will call his name."

"As well they should." Alorie stroked the black
mare. Gavin had cleaved a path through Trela'on that
would become legend . . . Gavin and the sword of
Frenlaw, with the rest of him at his back. That reputation preceded him to Dirtellak, and when they'd arrived, sore and worn, tired and dusty, Rathincourt awaited
them, knowing that the quest had been successful.

The victory lacked only Brock and Rowan. The dusky-
skinned mage was still lost or dead. And Rowan . . .
brave Rowan . . . she hadn't the slightest idea of his
fate, except that the Corruptor had spoken of him.
Before she could think sadly of Rowan, a chant rose on
the air.

"Gav-in, Gav-in, Gav-in!"

With a broad grin on his face, the dark-haired man
rode up and joined them, no helm on his head, the
sword unsheathed and resting hilt down on his armored
thigh. His mailcoat shimmered grandly in the sunlight.
As he looked down over the fields, the men scrambled
to their feet, saluting with their weapons and mailed
fists.

"Gav-in, Gav-in!"

His chest swelled as he took a deep breath and saluted back with the sword of Frenlaw. The chant gave
way to a mindless cheering, and Rathincourt laughed
heartily.

"This is your day, Gavin."

The big man nodded. "Not bad for a farm lad, eh?"
He twisted in the saddle. "Kithrand, Pinch! Come listen to this!"

Pinch's face twisted wryly as his donkey trotted up
and ducked away from the nip of Gavin's big bay
charger. "I like a humble man," the dwarf said. He
met Alorie's eyes and grinned.

They all shared Gavin's boyish joy in his role. Jasper
silently took his place at Alorie's side, prepared to do
her bidding. The Mutt looked down over the battlefield,
and he gave a wolfish smile.

"So this is where the Corruptor is to meet his fate."

"All-Mother willing. Then we must gather and wait . . . wait for the Despot to rise and try his hand. But that sorrow will also be our joy, for it signals the return of the High King," Rathincourt answered.

Jasper scratched the back of his ear with one tipped nail. "In our lifetime?"

"Perhaps."

"Good."

The chanting began again as Gavin lowered the sword. Then a cloud arose on the horizon, a great dun cloud, and his grin faded.

"Here they come."

A thunder boomed with the cloud, until Alorie separated the sound from reality, and knew it for drums, reken drums, keeping a pace for the soldiers. They rolled onward, an endless wave, and Rathincourt made a sound deep in his throat as they drew near, and Alorie knew what it was he feared.

They were outnumbered. The lord held out his hand. "Nearly five to one," he muttered.

"Good," Gavin replied. He took up the reins of his destrier firmly. "I don't want the men to be overconfident." With the sword firmly gripped in his hand, he kneed the horse off the knoll and down onto the battlefield.

Gavin wiped his forehead with the back of his sword hand. His destrier bucked under him, the horse's nostrils wide from the stench of blood and fire and reken stink. He dropped his hand wearily and flexed his back.

"They keep coming," he said to Tusk, the large-toothed littermate of Jasper who had fought to his side.

"Retreat now, Lord Gavin. The banners are down, the ranks broken."

"No." He looked out over the mangled fields, littered with torn bodies of all manner of men and beasts. Crimson blood ran with black. Malison hovered here and there at will, sucking a corpse dry. They'd broken the back of his defense. Nothing could stand against the

malison. The only thing that slowed them down was
the feeding, and now they meandered over the deathfield
at random.

He took a deep breath and ignored his own wounds,
feeling his blood trickle down his legs as he gripped the
bay stallion tightly. Like a slaughterhouse, it was. The
Tellak River would flow with sorrow on this night.

He gathered the reins again. "I have but one man to
kill, and when that is done, the rest will follow."

Tusk flashed him a dark look. "The Corruptor will
not come to you."

"That's right. That's why I'm going to him." Gavin
leaned low out of his saddle and plucked a bloodied
half-helm off a corpse. He studied the man's face in
sorrow a moment—he'd fought well. Then he placed
the helm on his head. "Follow me, if you will, Tusk."

Because of the kind of man he was, Gavin drew a
wake of men after him, any who could walk or ride
after him. He cut a swath through the ranks of reken
soldiers and headed inexorably toward the tightly de-
fended position where the Corruptor watched with his
lieutenants.

The sword swung in his hand. Unstoppable, he pressed
the bay stallion onward. The grass and mud churned
under the destrier's hooves, and behind him, the strag-
gling mass of men took up a cheer. He'd heard it
before, long ago, in happier times, he remembered
dimly, as a battle fever heated his blood and his pulse
drummed in his ears.

"Gav-in, Gav-in!"

The escort fell back, and he surged on alone, as
reken soldiers swallowed up on the regiment and the air
rang with battle. As his stallion crested the knoll, the
dark ranks about the Corruptor opened. He sat on a
chestnut stallion, alone.

The being waved a dark-gloved hand. "Let him come
to me."

Gavin sensed feral eyes hidden within the hood and
cloak. An odorous wind off the killing fields billowed

out the cloak, giving the being immense wings. The swordsman gripped his weapon tighter. He would not fail. He could not. The hilt of the sword of Frenlaw warmed in his palm. He remembered Alorie's chanting voice at Cornuth, and Viola's faint one as she prophesied from her death bier. No, he could not fail.

With both hands, he raised the sword and kicked his destrier into a charge, and the Corruptor laughed as he came.

At the last second, he raised his own sword to parry Gavin. The two blades met, with a belling that silenced the battle around them. The chestnut destrier gave under the weight as his master reeled back. Gavin drove his bay into them, and drew back for a second blow.

The sword of Frenlaw shimmered red and silver in the late-afternoon sun as its wielder swung it about his head and drove it to the sternum of the Corruptor. The rival blade glanced upward to meet it a second time.

No ringing of swords. Instead, with a horrible sound that made men weep, the sword of Frenlaw shattered. Metal splinters flew everywhere, piercing Gavin's face and torso. His eyes streamed with blood, but he saw long enough to see the blow that severed his head from his body, as the Corruptor laughed. His body toppled to the ground.

The being laughed again as he rode over the remains of his foe. "Now take the field for me, and secure it. And chase them down and kill whomever you can. I want no survivors and no prisoners . . except the dark-haired girl, if you can find her." He swept on down the knoll to a better vantage point to savor his victory.

A reken darted in long enough to tear the empty hilt from the slack fingers of its wielder. The beast rubbed the pretty carvings, tucked it inside its breastplate, and ran for its life, as a malison drifted by, drawn to the scent of fresh blood and the inestimable courage of the dead man.

"This way, Alorie. Quickly!"

Alorie paused, slowing her mare. Her damp face cooled in the wind. She'd seen Gavin go down before Jasper had grabbed her, under orders from Rathincourt to get her out of there.

"How could . . . I don't understand. How could he be dead?"

The Mutt paused, then took his own reins and whipped the mare savagely across the haunches. "Rathincourt will take care of the living. Now let's go, milady!"

The mare bolted, and Alorie bent over her neck, holding on tightly. A branch caught on her hair as they lunged into a sparse woods following the bank of the Tellak, and it ripped her net away. The silver-and-pearl ornament fell to the mud behind them, and Jasper's mount churned it under his hooves.

They forged past foot soldiers with faces pale and bloodied, who also ran through the woods. Jasper yelled at them, "Regroup upriver—it's your only chance," and they swept past before he could tell if any followed orders. It was a rout. All ran for their lives before the ranks of the corrupted who did more than kill.

She hadn't seen Pinch for most of the day, but Kithrand rode ranks with his elven brethren, and they alone had held off the malison and turned them back. No others had the courage to stand to them. She was alone again, save for valiant Jasper, who'd fought to open a pathway before them to the strand of woods. Now he desperately drove her before him.

A reken sprang from the tree above, snarling, and bore her to ground. She hit heavily, unable to breathe, tangled in her thick dress. As it stood over her, its breath thick and foul, a madness gleaming in its yellow eyes, Jasper laid a dirk in the beast's shoulders.

The soldier collapsed, Jasper's dagger in his back. Alorie pulled out from under it, fighting just to breathe.

"Are you all right?"

"Get the horses!" Cowards swarmed through the woods. They'd be at their mercy without their mounts.

Jasper nodded and swung away, running after the two creatures.

Alorie staggered to her feet. Mud and blood stained the royal blue of her outfit, and she looked at the reken a moment, unthinkingly. Then she saw the bulge in its armor.

"What have you looted?" she cried in anger and tore at the armor, ripping it away from the dead reken. Her hands black with its gore, she came away with a silvery object and stared at it in horror.

It was the guard from the sword of Frenlaw, still wet with Gavin's blood. She held it up to the sky and shouted in anger, "The gods owe me a few answers!"

Chapter 23

ROWAN COCKED his weary arm to swing his blade yet again, as a gore-and-ichor-covered figure popped from the deathfield in front of him. His boots slipped in the mud and slime of the trampled ground. He staggered back, just as the gnarled being snarled, "Take that, you misbegotten son of—"

Rowan ducked and caught the ax on his sword, and held it for a moment. He grinned. "Pinch! Is it you?"

The gnarled figure froze. The wide eyes blinked from the indistinguishable face. "Rowan! Can it be you, boy?"

Instead of decapitating each other, the two reached out and held each other and danced a moment among the bodies.

Pinch staggered back, gasping. "I didn't see you behind those reken leathers."

The Rover shrugged. "I scavenged what I could, following you down from Trela'on. Where's Alorie? Did Gavin and Kithrand get her out? I saw Rathincourt still mustering the retreat."

"It's no retreat. It's a brawl." Pinch beckoned to him. "Let's get out of here ourselves, before the damned malison come after us."

Rowan followed the gnarled man away from the battlefield, down to the slick banks of the Tellak, where the host had already crossed and recrossed, going south.

He knelt beside Pinch and washed his face, though the water was already fouled with mud and gore.

Pinch began to trudge down the river. The cavalry had already swept through, and what foot solders were left either still slugged it out, or retreated, returning to home and family, defeated.

Rowan put his hand on the dwarf's broad shoulder. "Alorie, my friend."

Pinch nodded his head wearily. "I heard you. Rathincourt sent her out, o' course, but I don't know if she made it or not. The reken are looking for her. The Corrupter wants her scalp, I've heard."

His hand tightened on his friend's shoulder. Pinch shrugged out from under his grip. "Easy, lad! It's not me that gave the order."

"But she was here?"

"And looking beautiful, too, next to Rathincourt."

"What about Gavin and Kithrand?"

"Gavin had the sword," Pinch said slowly, his throat tight with pain. "He went down, Rowan. Never had a chance. The damned sword of Frenlaw is still cursed, new blade or not. It shattered and the Corruptor cut him down. As for Kithrand . . ." The dwarf spat to one side. "I don't know what happened to him."

A sense of loss filled Rowan. He walked silently, unable to speak, for quite a while beside the dwarf. Then he remembered something out of the days past that he had tried to forget. "What happened to Viola, Pinch?"

The dwarf's voice grew tighter. "She killed herself on the beach below Cornuth . . . to prophesy the future for us, to tell us about the sword. We left her body burning in elf fire." Pinch cleared his throat and began to tell about the days gone while they were separated, and Rowan listened. His knuckles grew white as he clenched his sword tightly, for the dwarf made no bones of Kithrand's cowardice that had lost Rowan and then Alorie.

And when he was done, he turned a stricken face to

the Rover. "There's only th' two of us can help her
now. And what about you, boy? Where have you been?
I shoulda known you'd slit reken throats and get away."

"Not that easily." Rowan haltingly told Pinch bits
and pieces of what he could remember, but not about
the malison. He couldn't yet bear to tell anyone of the
malison. When he finished, Pinch halted on the riverbank.

"Our throats deserve a good mug of beer. Let's find
where Rathincourt is pitchin' his tents."

Rowan laughed at the dwarfish understatement. They
had at least a couple of days' march ahead of them.

Alorie paced inside the tent. Rathincourt sat at a
writing desk, scratching away on a hide map. He pretended to ignore her until she stopped at the table.

"We have gathered fully a thousand men here. And
sources tell me enemy casualties are high as well. They
outnumber us perhaps three to one now."

She clenched her fists. "I don't see how you can sit
there calmly and prate statistics at me."

Rathincourt ran his hand through his white hair. "Because, Lady Alorie, the battle may be lost, but we're
lucky enough to be alive. And because we're alive, the
fighting isn't finished. It won't be finished until we're
dead. The Corruptor hasn't enough troops to hold
Dirtellak, not with the numbers we still muster. No,
he's got to drive us down, harry us, until we've nothing
left. Then he can fall back to Dirtellak and dig in. And
there he can expect Aquitane to back him up."

"After what happened at Trela'on?"

"Aquitane has no choice, if he wants any lands at
all. No, he'll come crawling back to his commander."

"And what about us?"

"Hunted."

"We'll be hunted?"

"To the last man."

Alorie opened her hands. Rathincourt bolted to his
feet and put out a hand to steady her. He added gently,
"On the other hand, we might yet win. A good many

allies have yet to send their forces. I took what I could gather to Dirtellak. More are on the way.''

"It wasn't supposed to be this way.''

Rathincourt guided her to a stool and helped her sit down. "The sword of Frenlaw wasn't the answer.''

Her thoughts jolted, Alorie looked at the map before her. Her mind reeled, and she seemed to see days flashing in front of her eyes . . . days with Brock and Rowan. She rubbed her forehead. Before she could say anything, a piercing cry broke her silence, and a guard called in through the tent flaps, "Messenger coming in, sir.''

"Bring the bird right in.''

Rathincourt stood to receive the hawk, which flared angrily until he hooded it. Then he placed the hawk on a perch while he sliced the parchment off its leg. The lord smiled as he unrolled the missive.

"It's from Kithrand, for you. Good news. Rowan has been sighted, with Pinch, making his way south to join us here.''

She jumped to her feet, heart pounding. "Rowan!'' Her eyes flooded before she could stop her emotions. She grasped at the parchment and read the flowery script.

"Glad I am to send these tidings to the Lady Alorie, encamped with Lord Rathincourt, from your servant Kithrand.

"On this morrow, a crusty dwarf and a bold Rover were sighted, boating upriver to Rathincourt's encampment. From the descriptions given, could be none other than our own Rowan and Pinch. Take heart, my lady.''

Alorie's voice choked to a halt as she finished the scroll. Rathincourt gently handed her a delicate handkerchief, and she wiped her eyes. The knowledge that Rowan lived and sought her gave her a courage she'd been looking for. She cleared her throat and bunched the handkerchief in her fist, dropping the parchment on his writing desk. "No, we're not finished yet. Rathincourt, you said the sword of Frenlaw was obviously not the answer, though we went to Three Towers at Cornuth and read the prophecy. Well, the gods owe me a few answers.''

''And where would you go to speak with one?''

Alorie went to the door of the tent and looked out over the plains beyond. ''Brock told me once—or maybe it was Rowan, I can't quite remember—that he thought the unicorns were one of the secret races. And then, in Cornuth, when we needed help desperately to reach the city, a white unicorn came to battle the black. And again, in Trela'ar, when the Corruptor sought me, I found refuge in a temple, and on the wall . . . the unicorn.'' She shuddered and walked back to the desk. ''I haven't anywhere else to go.'' Her fingers tapped his map. ''Here, to the south, you have marked the Forest of the Unicorns.''

''That's legend!''

''Here!'' She stabbed. ''Here is Sobor, and Dirtellak and Sinobel. Are they legend?''

''No, but—Alorie, this is insanity. The Corruptor will hound you to death in that wilderness.''

''I will go, milord. Will you send me an escort, or will I go alone?''

Rathincourt's lips thinned and his jaw clenched.

Chapter 24

"MANY'S THE TIME I've eaten hawk," Pinch said lazily. He lay on his back, his head pillowed on crossed arms, and he watched the sky above the river. "For a bow and arrow now."

Rowan stopped poling a moment and looked at the dwarf. Then he craned his neck back and watched the creature encircling the blue sky above them. "Do a little work and we'll get to camp before the rations are gone."

"Done enough work. My stomach thinks my throat's been cut." Then Pinch looked at the hawk. "It's dropping lower."

He stopped poling and braced the flatboat so that the currents of the Tellak wouldn't carry them back. He watched too as the red-tailed bird flashed lower and lower across the sky.

Rowan blinked. Jesses! The hawk trailed jesses behind it. "That's a messenger!"

The dwarf sat up. "By the horn, you're right. Maybe Kithrand . . . could it be looking for us?"

"I don't know." Rowan vigorously aimed for the bank as the hawk whistled and glided around again.

Before the flatboat could nudge land, a black arrow pierced the sky. The bird fell with a single shriek, disappearing into the scrub woods.

"Damn! Reken arrow," Pinch said. "I marked where it likely went down." He helped Rowan beach the boat and then pointed. "That way. I'm right behind you."

Rowan pulled his sword and kept it ready, moving through the brush with as much stealth as his Rover training could muster. Yet the reken had heard something, for when they came upon it, it was standing over the hawk, ears pricked, searching the landscape, a scroll in its free hand and a longknife in the other.

He charged before the reken could go for his bow again. Pinch covered the ground from the flank, hurdling the shrub with all the might of his short body. Rowan hit the reken low. It snarled and clawed at him, tearing away his shirt at the throat.

Pinch got a knee on its head, and it lay wiggling under the two of them. A thread of blood gurgled out from its lips . . . and as Rowan rolled away, they saw the longknife twisted in its gut.

Rowan pinched the missive from its tightening fingers. "It's from Kithrand, all right. He says that they spotted us two days ago, and that Alorie has found an escort and left Rathincourt's army. She's headed south for the unicorn woods. It's a fool's mission, but Kithrand wants us to know, to catch up with her, if we can."

"The unicorn," repeated Pinch. "Why?"

A look misted Rowan's eyes, and then he frowned. "With Gavin dead and the sword failed and Brock lost . . . it may be the only thing we can do. She's gone in search of the secret races."

The reken surged under him, throwing him off, panting. It pulled the longknife from his stomach and raced from the glen. Pinch reached out and caught Rowan, stopping him from trailing.

"He'll not go far."

"Maybe."

The dwarf looked up to meet his eyes. "Alorie needs us. That's our place now."

"But the reken knows—"

"Likely a deserter, looking for hawk breakfast, just like us."

"Maybe," Rowan echoed. Then he hooked his thumbs in his belt and eyed the messenger bird with the reken arrow through its breast. "Then let's take our breakfast and leave. I want to catch up with Alorie if it's the last thing I do."

Pinch rubbed his ears superstitiously. "I'll not be a-hearing that. I'll build a fire if you pluck feathers."

Alorie halted her mare. The horse flicked her ears uncertainly as her rider eyed the purple mountains looming ahead. The warm air encouraged flies to buzz low, angrily, and the mare swished her tail.

Jasper and Tusk turned around on their mounts. They rode horses now, persuaded by speed to leave their sturdy donkeys tethered in Rathincourt's camp. The two Mutts waited for her.

"What is it, milady?"

Corey drew even, and she smiled at the Rover. Rathincourt had found a most impressive escort for her—Corey and Tien, the two Mutts, and a score of Rathincourt's personal guard. She couldn't move through the countryside inconspicuously if she had to, but she also couldn't move more safely.

"Where's Tien?"

"I have him backtracking us." Corey crossed his wrists easily and leaned over his mount. "I think they're after us already, Lady Alorie."

She sucked in her lip to chew on it, caught the movement, and tried to smile instead. "We've already faced them once. Can't be so bad the second time around."

Corey opened his mouth to say something, and hesitated.

"What is it?"

"Nothing."

He moved to edge his horse around hers. She tried to catch at him and missed. "No, tell me . . . what is it?"

"I'm a Rover, and I like clean soldiering. Hand-to-hand combat, things I know . . . not these malison and Ungravens." He shook his head and brushed back his hair with one hand. "I don't like it, milady."

"Ungravens? Has he sent the undead after us?"

"Looks like. Kills bloodied and then rent. Tien's found some ugly signs." Corey spit. "Rathincourt ought never to have let you go."

Alorie collected her reins again. "Maybe so, Corey, but I have a purpose. You can turn back here, if you wish. The map is clear enough."

"Map!" Corey laughed at her. "Rovers been through there, and there's nowhere in all these lands where unicorns be."

"I've seen them. And I'll go where legend says they are, because I've no other choice." Alorie kicked her mare and rode between the two Mutts, who had watched them argue.

She rode as though she had a hot poker up her spine, and indeed, she might have. Doubts chewed at her that she couldn't let the others see. If she was indeed foolish enough to find a unicorn, which would it be? Light or dark? Good or evil? And would it suffer her to get close to it? That last question she could not look in the face. As Viola had put it, she was no virgin girl child any longer. Her mission was doomed even before it had begun, but she had no other choice. Not for herself anymore, but for all the lands, because the sword she had brought them had failed.

In night camp, she woke. She hadn't awakened in the night for many, many weeks, but she woke this night. Alorie put her hand out and quenched the candle burning by her side in the tent, in order to see in the dark better. She heard a rustling past the canvas, and sat up. She slept fully clothed, and reached now for her pack and longknife.

The tip end of a dirk slipped through the canvas and began to slice down. Alorie watched, fascinated, pulling on her boots, as the intruder broke in.

The creature came through with a hiss even as Alorie stood up, screamed, and threw the longknife. It landed with a solid thunk. The beast fell back, clawing at the

tent. The canvas collapsed around them. Alorie grabbed
her weapon and pack and swung them both, tearing the
tent from around her as it threatened to pull her down
with her attacker.

Tien finished the Ungraven off with his sword, and
Alorie stood shuddering as the beast stuck a crimson
tongue out and died. The Rover was shirtless, with his
breeches half on.

"Are you all right?"

"Yes." She whirled around as the camp came to life.
"Get those damn horses! We're riding!"

"But milady—"

She looked at Corey. "It was I it came after. I won't
stay here and wait for them in the morning. Saddle
up."

"You'll ride the horses to death."

"Then I'll walk the rest of the way."

But Tien smiled approval on his yellow face, nodded,
and fled to do her bidding. Rathincourt's soldiers stood
in embarrassment, caught literally with their drawers
down. They shuffled around in their blankets, trying to
dress. She whirled on them as well. "And from here on
out, sleep with your pants on!"

Tien brought her mare, grinning. She climbed on.
"What are you smiling at?"

"I was thinking of the shy little creature Rowan
brought back from Sinobel."

Alorie blushed, then ducked her face as the Rover
laughed. "Just get me out of here," she said.

They rode at night from then on and camped in the
day. Yet stragglers got picked off, until less than a
half-dozen of Rathincourt's men remained, and the Mutts
and Tien and Corey.

Alorie's little mare staggered to a halt and put her
head down, wheezing horribly. She slid off the beast
and stroked her neck harshly. Other than laming, this
was the worst that could have happened . . . she'd

broken the mare's wind. Tien swung off next to her. He
drew his skinning knife.

"No. Unsaddle her and let her go. I'll ride one of the
extra horses."

"They'll find her, Alorie. She deserves a clean death."

"No! I can't stand to see anything else die. Maybe
she'll make it. Do as I say!"

The Rover shrugged and put his knife away. He
signaled for one of the packhorses to be brought up
from the rear.

The little mare put her soft muzzle in Alorie's hand.
She rubbed the skin gently. "Go," she whispered. "Go
find green grass and safe haven." She slapped the horse
fiercely, and it hobbled off in surprise.

The horses began to drop under them. Too tired to
graze when they camped, the beasts staggered to halts
and then dropped, sending their rider pitching over their
heads. Wolves and other things harried at them from the
woods, as if knowing it was only a matter of time until
a soldier would drop into their jaws. The dark unicorn
ranged behind them, and Corey killed another Ungraven
stalking their camp in the early morning.

Alorie kept her eyes to the southwest as they swung
around a tall mountain range, knowing that beyond it
they would reach the unicorns' range, if the map were
right. The air here nipped at them, fresh and clean. The
trees wore needles instead of leaves, and forest creatures stared at them as if they'd never seen any of the
Seven True Races before. Corey had to be wrong.
Rovers couldn't have come through this area . . . no
one could have.

She'd lost her second horse, and stood over it as it
thrashed on the ground, having stepped into a chuck-
hole and thrown her. Now it tried desperately to stand
up on a broken leg. Tusk reached her first and sat on
the horse's neck, talking to it quietly, easing the animal's thrashing, for it was only hurting itself worse.

Tien killed it before the beast could move. The blood

splashed both Mutt and Rover, and Alorie looked away. The other mounts stood, nostrils flared with suspicion at the death of their brother. and one of Rathincourt's guard swung down.

"Take my gelding, milady. I'll ride double."

She looked at the young man. How old could he be? she wondered as she took the reins. A horse ridden double would be pulled down that much faster by what trailed them. But she said nothing, and swung aboard the animal.

It was then the malison struck.

Like a bat-winged beast from the treetops, it screamed and curled down over them, dark stormcloud reaching out and curling around Tusk and Tien, drawn by the blood.

Alorie's horse reared, and she fought to curb it down. The Mutt howled, and the malison cracked his skull open like an egg and then reached for Tien. The Rover straightened from his crouch, his hand going to his belt, and pulled off a familiar-looking pouch.

With a curse, Tien threw its contents into the malison. The herbed powder scattered, and the beast screamed again, its shroud exploding from about it. Alorie caught a glimpse of elongated limbs and a reptilian face, and then the malison disappeared. A wraith of blackness crawled into the sky and left the forest.

"Brock's powder," Alorie whispered, as Tien picked himself off the ground. Jasper rode up and looked at his littermate's face, with sorrow in his large brown eyes.

Then he looked to the young soldier. "No need to ride double. Take my brother's horse."

The lad did as he was bidden.

Two days later, they made the end of the mountains, and a wide plain stretched ahead of them. Corey reined up. He looked at the blue sky, just dawning, white fluffed clouds crowning it. He took a deep breath.

"We'll be open targets out there."

A dark green woods loomed beyond the stretch. A thick, heavy, massive woods.

"But once inside, we'll be nearly impossible to track,"
Alorie answered him.

"If you can get inside."

"Why not?"

"If it's the unicorn realm, they'll not let us in, lady.
The secret races want nothing to do with us."

She sat a moment, dealing with her own fears and
uncertainties. Even if she could gain the woods, was
she good enough to treat with the beasts? And what of
the black beast pacing them once more?

Then Corey made a movement, as though he'd been
talking with himself. He looked back over the remnants
of the escort. "I'll go with you, milady. Let them guard
our backs."

Tien and Jasper and six of Rathincourt's men. They
looked back at her. Jasper put up a paw.

"This is what we came for. Let us do what we know
best."

The soldiers drew their swords. Sunlight rayed off
the blades.

"All right." Alorie nodded, and turned away quickly,
not wanting them to see the tears that filled her eyes. It
would be their last stand. Let it be a clean one, she
prayed to the All-Mother. She kicked her gelding in his
painfully thin ribs.

Corey paced her, his bare head to the wind. He held
his sword unsheathed, as if charging across the meadow
into the enemy's face. They left the others behind,
unseen in the tall prairie grass. The horses ran with the
last of their stamina and heart, cupped nostrils wine-red
and necks lathered white with foam.

Alorie's hair snapped in the wind, which tore the
tears away and dried her face. The race pounded in her
heart and her pulse. She knew if her horse went down at
the edge of the woods, she would go on, on foot. She
would crawl if she had to.

The forest reached out for them, immense, thick-
rooted trees that blocked out the sun, and gathered them
in. Sanctuary. Alorie felt soothed the moment they

ducked under the first spreading branches. Taken in. Yes. How could Corey not fail to notice it? She let out a glad cry, and turned to him—

—and received the whipping branch right across the eyes. She fell backward off the horse, grasping the leather, and the pack ripped off with her, but she landed with a hard thud that slammed the breath out of her.

Corey plunged his mount to a halt and ran back to her, his sword at ready, tip at her throat.

She fought for air. "Wh—what?"

"We'll wait here," the Rover said, "in the shade, just out of sight, for my friends to catch up with us."

The sword point wavered a moment, played with a lock of her hair, then shaved it from behind her ear. Corey grasped the soft dark trees. "A souvenir," he said, and tucked it into his swordbelt. "A Sergius for a Rover kingdom. Not a bad deal at all."

She looked at him. The sun glinted off his gray hair, and she lay back with a groan. The reken's iron-haired master, and the traitor within Stonedeep. Alorie closed her eyes briefly. A branch moved behind Corey, and she couldn't bear to see the friends he mentioned. To have come so far.

Then she opened her eyes. She wouldn't face her death meekly. Alorie stared at the impassive face. "I saved your life," she said, bringing to mind the night at the grate when the reken attacked.

"Indeed you did. Imagine my embarrassment, when I was trying to take yours as well as I could. Dead or alive, you're worth a kingdom to me."

Alorie stifled her cry as a man sprang from the brush and hit Corey between the shoulder blades. She flung herself to the side as the Rover went down, sword point first, solidly into the bruised grass where she had just been lying.

The second man stood up, panting. Her heart jumped. She struggled to get to her feet, unable to believe her eyes. Reken leather armor over faded black and silver, and that dark auburn hair that caught the sun so well.

"Rowan!"

The Rover gathered her up in a ferocious hug. He twirled her until she thought her ribs would break. He kissed her until neither of them could breathe, everywhere, her cheeks, lips, nose, ear, and then Rowan leaned back his head and shouted.

Alorie silenced him with another kiss, before asking, "How did you get here?"

"Kithrand sent a hawk to us, telling me your plans. We took a shortcut. We rode the Tellak into the mountains, and then a whitewater stream down. Remember? You taught me how on the Frostflower. We have to move quickly. The Corruptor has the better part of an army on your heels."

"An army? I thought it a tracking party, at most."

"No, an army. And thanks to Kithrand's feisty hawks, we've got Rathincourt moving at his heels."

Pinch hobbled up from the underbrush. "Hist, younguns! We've enemies at the rear."

Alorie broke from Rowan's embrace and caught up the dwarf. He sputtered and coughed, his nose at her chest, and extricated himself. "Are you both daft? Get on your way!"

A shadow broke through the forest's edge, and the three of them froze. With a toss of his head, the black unicorn moved closer. He shook his head and pawed the ground and bared his fangs. Corruption ate into his flesh, and the bony planes of his skull sharpened his image. The air grew rank.

Pinch pulled his ax out of his belt. "You two run for it. I've business to settle here."

"No, Pinch—" Alorie caught at his arm, but Rowan dragged her away. She heard the familiar cry of hunting reken.

Rowan led her into the deep of the woods. The branches folded thickly behind them, but the drums and barks and howls never slowed. They ran until she staggered, out of breath. He stopped at a knoll and looked out over the thick woods. He pointed.

"There's a glen down there, well hidden. Make for it, Alorie."

"Where are you going?"

"I'm going back. Pinch and I—we'll keep them off your trail. Run for it."

"No." She shook her head stubbornly. "I won't go without you."

He caught her shoulders. "No time to argue. We're here, milady—here! You knew it in your heart, and you were right! Look about you. Haven't you seen it—the sign? We saw it after we came out of Sinobel. The sign of the unicorn. The trees marked. The ground marked. Are you blind?"

And he swung her around and pointed off the knoll, toward the way they had just come, to saplings, peeled bare, and prints in the moist ground. She gasped as she saw what he showed her.

"Somewhere in here, you just might find what you're looking for," the Rover said, and gave her a long, lingering kiss.

Alorie blinked at him. "I thought I'd found what I was looking for."

He grinned. "I'll be back for you!" He jumped from the knoll and ran back through the forest, disappearing with Rover grace, and his own customary boldness.

She stood a moment, then discovered she still carried her pack. She turned and made her way down the knoll toward the hidden glen.

Chapter 25

THE FOREST stopped her. She paused, unable to force her way through branch and bramble any longer. Alorie knew the glen lay behind the last border, but she stopped, defeated, and laughed mentally at those who said that the forest wasn't alive. It had taken her in thus far and cradled her, and now blocked her from her final goal.

A white rock marked the border. It was pure and clean, its top sheared off, and jutted from the mosses and ferns as though it marked an altar. Alorie dropped her pack at the foot of it.

A tiny streamlet ran by its far side. She knelt on hands and knees to drink at it, and saw the sign that rabbit and deer and squirrel had done likewise, probably that morning. As she looked up, a canopy of leaves hid the sky from her. Noon? Possibly later. She and Corey had ridden hard to make the forest, and much had happened since then.

Alorie backed away from the brook and sat down, one hand on the rock. She hadn't prayed since becoming a woman, almost certainly not since leaving Sinobel, though she remembered her feelings of awe at the abandoned temple in Trela'ar. She opened her pack, and the empty hilt of Frenlaw tumbled out, bedded on the white material given to her at Jasper's village.

She stripped her gloves off and caressed the material. She'd saved it, thinking of a day perhaps when she and Rowan—

A twig cracked.

Alorie froze. Something moved in the glen beyond. A whicker sounded, an imperious whicker, demanding attention.

She closed her eyes tightly. Was it dark or was it light? She wouldn't, couldn't know . . . until she went to meet it.

And once having faced it, would she measure up? Alorie stood and found her knees shaking.

The whicker came again, louder, with a snort and stamp cutting it off. She looked to the shrubbery and tried to see through it, but the forest wouldn't let her. Alorie stepped back. "What do I do now?" she whispered, and only the stillness answered her.

She stripped. She washed in the brook, scrubbing off days and days of trail sweat and dirt—and fear. Then she took the white fabric and tore off lengths. First she bound her breasts, then girded her loins. Enough fabric remained that she tucked in a small white skirt about her hips. She left her feet bare.

Using her longknife, she cut off a thong from the pack and tied back her long hair. It hung down nearly to her waist. In her mind's eye, as she worked, she took on the aspect of the youths she'd seen on the friezes in the abandoned temple of Trela'ar. White or dark, good or evil, she would meet the unicorn. The gods owed her answers.

She knelt by the white rock and prayed. She gave her mind to the litany of her hopes and fears and sifted through them. If she was to be judged, and found wanting, she wanted to know why. When she lifted her chin, she added fiercely to herself that she would never ask for forgiveness for loving Rowan. Never would she give that up!

A third trumpeting, and this time Alorie moved forward from the rock to answer it.

The brush parted easily before her, and she stepped from the cool darkness of the forest into a sun-dappled meadow, and the smell of sweet grasses surrounded her.

He stood in the shadows opposite her. The sunlight dazzled her eyes, and Alorie realized she couldn't tell the color of the beast. He thrust his muzzle toward her, eying her.

She stepped out toward the center of the glen, trying to ignore the sudden sweat on the palms of her hand. She saw the horn with the light glancing off it, a brilliant spear toward the blue of the sky. Even if he was white, would she be able to face the beast?

A vision wavered before her . . . faces . . . her grandfather's and father's deaths . . . Tusk . . . Pinch . . . Gavin . . . Bryant . . . Dalla . . . Viola . . . a line of death and sacrifice strung behind her, all the way back to Sinobel. All for her. Alorie shook her head. No. Not for her. For the Seven True Races. Always for what she stood for.

Chin up, she faced the beast. "You called for me, I answered. Show yourself."

The unicorn pawed the ground, tearing up grasses, and moved into the open. His snow-white body bedazzled her in the full sunlight. She threw up a hand to protect her eyes, but the animal gave her no grace, for he lowered his horn and charged.

Instinctively, she somersaulted to the side and landed on her feet, as the ground trembled beneath his pounding hooves. The unicorn slid to a stop, half reared, and charged again. His horn shone molten. Alorie gathered herself, and the beast missed her again. He slowed to a trot and circled then, with arched head, snorting.

She sensed his pride in her. She raised her arms into the air and danced toward him. He pranced toward her then and reared, and she glided in under his striking hooves in a pattern of light and dance.

Not physical perfection, no. She saw the scars on his neck and withers, welts that had healed, from fights with other stallions and wolves and other rivals. No . . .

the unicorn reached for and drew out of her a perfection of spirit . . . of love and courage and hope . . . and refined it. She gave him whatever he asked of her, bruising the sweet grasses under her bare feet until at last she stopped, winded.

The unicorn whickered, coaxing her on.

Alorie laughed for the joy of it. She answered with her own dare, running lightly across the meadow and springing at his back, an attempt to conquer him, if only for a moment. The stallion dodged aside and teased her on again. The two of them touched and sprang apart and touched again, until the unicorn paused.

She stood again at the center of the meadow, hands outstretched. He seemed to appraise her, then lowered his head and charged, the horn a deadly lance aimed right at her bare midriff.

Alorie knew then what she had to do, the final movement lacking in this dance to please the unicorn. She waited. The ground thundered under his hooves and he trumpeted, noble anger ringing the air.

Alorie kept her hands up. In the last moment before he pierced her, she moved slightly, reached up, and grasped the horn.

Pain lashed through her palms. She gasped in agony and almost let go, but the momentum of the vault took her. She threw her heels up and over as the unicorn tossed his head. She flew through the air, letting go of the horn, and tumbled, and landed on her feet, on his broad snowy back.

The stallion drifted to a halt. Alorie sat down and then slid to the ground, her palms staining his hide crimson where she touched.

The beast snorted. Then, with a sad expression in his amber eyes, he kneeled to her. She reached out to him, suddenly appalled that she had tamed his fury.

With a quavering movement, the stallion nodded to her. She hesitated, uncertain of what he wanted, then held her palms out to him. The unicorn touched his gleaming horn to her hands. Lightning ran through her.

Her heart fluttered and pulse quickened with the magic
of his touch. Before her eyes, the cuts sealed and then
disappeared. Then the stallion returned to all four hooves
and moved to her side, and walked with her to the edge
of the forest.

Alorie's eyes opened wide. She saw the forest border
had receded, and the white rock now lay within the
boundaries of the glen, her clothes and pack piled next
to it, with the empty guard of Frenlaw shining in the
sun.

The unicorn moved to the rock and struck his horn
with one movement. The horn rang out and belled, and
she thought she heard the forest shake and quiver at the
noise, and a chill wind touched the back of her neck,
and then the moment fled. The horn fell from the
stallion.

She looked at the massive spiraled horn lying across
the altar. The unicorn put his forehead down to her, and
she trembled as she saw the hole in his brow, ichor
leaking from it.

"Put the horn into the guard," the beast told her. His
voice was chimelike, and far away.

Alorie, hands shaking, did so. The guard captured it
perfectly, and she stood with the weapon in hand, as
long as a great sword, but light.

The unicorn touched her shoulder with his soft, lightly
feathered muzzle. "Like most weapons, this one is
truly double-edged. Only you can know if you will
heal—or slay."

"But—" Alorie began, and the beast withdrew.

His outlines shimmered. She blinked, to see the dark
touch of the forest beyond the glen shadowing through
him. He lost substance and ceased to be of her world
and time, growing more and more transparent.

He diminished rapidly. The magic of the glen went
with him, as he turned and trotted away from her, neck
arched and hooves striking the ground with a muted
fire. His tail bannered behind him, a proud stallion of

his kind, as he grew thinner and thinner. Then he disappeared into the trees as though he'd never been.

Alorie swallowed. She held the unicorn sword at arm's length, frightened by it, and what it had cost. Then, faintly on the wind, she heard the sound of war horns and drums. Rathincourt would meet with Aquitane this day.

She dressed. Then she ran back through the forest to the crest of the knoll, searching, praying for a sign of Rowan. Nothing met her eyes. She followed the tiny breaks in twigs that he had made, the path he intended to follow back to her, and she found them at the forest's edge, a pile of reken around their forms, and with the black beast dead beyond.

Then she saw Rowan stir, as she ran up behind him. He turned slightly, his hands busy with Pinch and his face was dampened with tears.

The dwarf saw her too, and smiled tightly. "Skewered," he muttered. "Like a good lunch. But I took my toll of him, milady."

The dark unicorn would never strike again, she saw; the ferocious head and neck had been ax-cleaved from his withers. For a short man, the dwarf had done a big man's work.

Alorie moved past Rowan, the sword in her hand. Pinch's eyes widened as she lowered the horn toward him, to the gaping hole in his side that leaked away blood and soul.

She touched him gently, with a lump in her throat that tried to stifle the words she wanted to say to him. "It's—it's going to be all right."

The dwarf gasped and gargled and tossed his head, and Rowan held him even more tightly.

Then the wound sealed itself. Color came back into the gnarled man's pale face, first a light pink, then a darker flush, and his dim eyes brightened.

"By all the gods," he whispered. " 'Tis a true unicorn."

*   *   *

The three of them walked from the woods, skirting the bodies of reken and foul trails of malison, and Corey's form, and the horns on the wind sounded clarion, and the drums thundered back angrily.

Alorie raised the unicorn sword. "I'm coming," she answered, and the sun shone at her back as she went to meet the challenge.

About the Author

R. A. V. SALSITZ was born in Phoenix, Arizona, and raised mainly in Southern California, with time out for stints in Alaska, Oregon, and Colorado.

Encouraged from an early age to write, she majored in journalism in high school and college. Although Ms. Salsitz has yet to drive a truck carrying nitro, work experience has been varied—from electronics to furniture to computer industries—until she settled down to work full-time at a word processor.

Married, the author matches wits daily with a fantastic spouse and four lively children, of various ages, heights, and sexes. Hobbies and interests include traveling, tennis, horses, computers, and writing.

Although this is her second full-length adult fantasy, it is the eighteenth published book to date.